THE RESURRECTIONS

THE RESURRECTIONS

A Novel

By Simon Louvish

Four Walls Eight Windows, New York

Three lines from "Burnt Norton," *Four Quartets,*
by T. S. Eliot, used by kind permission of Faber and Faber

© 1994 Simon Louvish

Published in the United States by:
Four Walls Eight Windows
39 West 14th Street, room 503
New York, N.Y., 10011

First printing September 1994.

Library of Congress Cataloging-in-Publication Data:
Louvish, Simon.
p.   cm.
ISBN: 1-56858-014-2
I. Louvish, Simon. Resurrections from the dustbin of history.
II. Title.
PR6062.0785R47   1994
823'.914—dc20   94-10509
                                                   CIP

Printed in the United States

10 9 8 7 6 5 4 3 2 1

Footfalls echo in the memory
Down the passage we did not take
Towards the door we never opened . . .

– T. S. Eliot, *Burnt Norton*

All other quotations in this book are from texts
not published in our time stream.

Part I
Mobilisation
November 1967–January 1968

Extract from *Terror Campaign 1961*, by Rachel Levy

Montgomery, Alabama, November 1: The Greyhound Bus Station lounge. Already conquered territory: from wall to wall, the great white banner cries its message –

KEEP AMERICA WHITE AND ARYAN
RUDOLPH HITLER FOR PRESIDENT

Over the ticket counter portraits of the four American Party grandees glare at the travelling public: Rudy the Candidate; Gerald K. Smith the hopeful Veep; Senator Adolf Hitler père of Illinois; Wallace, the Cotton State's favourite son. So close to power now, with the election fourteen days away . . . Here, in the cyclone's eye, it's so easy to believe in the reality of the onrushing nightmare.

I have three hours to wait for the New Orleans bus, which should ferry me off, I hope and pray, to comparative safety, south, oddly enough, while the shock troops of the Aryan Vengeance careen north with their sawnoff shotguns and their thick knotted ropes. Rachel Levy, will you be alive to see the end of the '61 Campaign trail, or will you just be another strange fruit on the lynching tree, a final ripening of solidarity with the poor and the oppressed?

All about me on the plastic lounge seats are draped the carless poor whites of Alabama: ravaged youths, hair plastered to their foreheads with sweat, which oozes down their knotted necks and the hairs of their bare thick arms; a quartet of Air Force ensigns in toy-neat blue; two old men with tanned leather hides, snoring under wide-brimmed hats; a couple of overdressed shabby-genteel ladies, red lipstick a gashed wound in taut gleaming faces. Along the walls a small knot of subdued black travellers, standing: three young men in casual white shirts, a family of five, pa in black suit and tie and soft hat, mother in her Sunday best, two small boys wriggling in collars starched for the trip, a silent pigtailed girl whose eyes roam, bewildered, over the waiting room, drawn despite herself to the two plainclothed Klansmen at the entrance with their swastika armbands and yellow-cross badge on their lapels. Their arms folded in easy dominance, guarding the captive land. Oh lord, is this the future face for us all? Where will it end? How did it all begin?

Ernesto
Moscow, November 7, 1967

Trotsky is dead. To me, these words will always be synonymous with cold, the biting, bitter penetrating cold, as I stand shivering in the throng, the cortege slowly passing between us, the people, and them, the inheritors, arms stiff in salute on the podium of the renamed Lenin-Trotsky Mausoleum. The shoulders of eight tough Kronstadt Marines bear the red draped coffin's weight. The funeral dirge echoing across Red Square, the Kremlin spires obscured by the snow swirling to cap the silent thousands with a white patina.

What will these people think, when they finally confront the embalmed, shrunken carcase on the displayed bier? Filing past, will they marvel at the dichotomy of power and mortality: Is this he? this mummied wisp, with skin like pharaonic parchment, almost disappeared into his own crumbling bones, was this our ruler for forty-four years?

I remember clearly the last of our only three meetings: the dacha by the Neva, May '64. I had just come from the Argentine fiasco, no brave success there to report. The gentle giant Sklyansky, his deputy-cum-heir, ushered me into the Presence. It was not, alas, the flashing fire of our earlier forums. At eighty-five his limbs had finally betrayed him, condemning him to the wheelchair. His hands, taloned and bent by arthritis. The famous head, however, still as leonine as ever, the shock of white hair, the snow-white goatee and moustaches, the eagle eyes, unnaturally enlarged by his immensely thick eyeglasses, retaining their full power. They pinned you down like a butterfly, boring into your own as you wriggled on the stake, the undimmed mind extracting the most critical data, discarding the mere lumber. He had lost none of his harsh directness, neither, addressing me in Spanish – how the man loved to demonstrate his polyglot fluency!

'A right ballsup in Argentina and no mistake.' His voice, too, alas, was fading, rasping like a rusty file. 'You are still marred by

Latin sentimentalism. True, old Peron is an immaculate arsehole, a corporal with delusions of grandeur. But the petit-bourgeois phase is still valid for that country. Peron is still a tool to be used to blaze the way for workers' power. But you are like a lovesick child, ever the incurable romantic. Personal distaste leads you into leftist adventurism. Subjective quibbles take over even when history's iron is still heating up in the fire. So, the proletariat splits, Peron falls, and the Junta returns to power. Fundamental errors lead to a crushing defeat. If we can't learn from history, who can? Ilyich and I would have been jackal bait if we had gone the same way.' He caught himself. 'Pardon an old man's ravings.' The great head lolled a little, as if the body could not bear its burden, then snapped up again, the hand raised: 'Africa, comrade! That is the agenda now. The Gold Coast, Kenya, Abyssinia! The Colonial Empires are on their last legs. If the true revolutionaries don't seize the time now we all deserve to be on the scrap heap of history. I can tell you,' the head dipped towards me, 'I have people around me who wouldn't move if Marx himself, or Christ, or Moses, thrust a stick up their arse! Abyssinia! I yell at them till I'm blue in the face – the Italian link is the most rotten in the colonial chain! Mussolini is tired, half dead, bedridden, all around him corruption seethes like the Borgias . . . Abyssinia, God damn it! But does anyone listen? No, they just nod and cheer sycophantically and whisper in corners as if we too were the Medicis, tut tut tut, the Boss is going senile, the old yid has gone off his head . . .'

The grand rabblerouser is dead now, the endlessly haranguing voice stilled. Grimly the Soviet Guard of Honour march past in funereal step. I raise my eyes, reluctantly, to the dumpy greatcoated men standing like tiny chunky dolls behind the snow, on the reviewing stand. Those dour, humourless men with their cadaver souls and punctilious obsession with empty ritual, a world removed from their dead leader's fire and brimstone. Trotsky straddled the world, the twentieth century's Bonaparte (despite his own distaste for the comparison). For better or worse, there would be none like him. The jowly bureaucrats on the ramparts may have come to praise Caesar but none the less to bury him very, very deep. I am suddenly struck with a deep sense of personal loss, which Trotsky himself would have scoffed at (more Latin sentimentalism!) . . . And something else, an insight difficult to define . . . That there are crux moments in history, which blend with the sense of a turning-point of one's own mission . . . An inheritance? An individual burden? A heresy, untouched by the collective will? Are you, Ernesto Che Guevara, fit to carry this load? Old friend, I'll do what I have to, to press on with that lifelong struggle . . . The self dies, the body may be embalmed or rot – the necessity continues. Goodbye, old comrade, wherever you are now, I'm sure you will, like myself, be stirring up trouble for the powers that be . . .

Joseph Gable
Carpentersville, Illinois, November 8

Visited Adolf for the Saturday bridge game, not without a linger-
ing reluctance, I must say. After more than forty years, Adolf's
company does wear a little thin. A jumped-up man in a crumpled
suit, I recall my first impression. Then, the second look, the
reflection . . . Was I wrong, all those years ago, to cast Adolf as
the receptacle for all our hopes and longings? Would I not have
been better suited myself to lead our tiny exile group through all
these traumatic years? Saturday frustrations again, the regular tics
and twinges of old age's might-have-beens. If . . . if . . . if . . . if the
fatherland had not fallen to the communist vermin four decades
ago . . . if we had remained behind, to fight it through . . . if my
grandmother had had wheels, she would be an automobile.

Shown through the new electronic gates. Frieda, the maid,
takes my hat and coat at the door. Respectability and routine.
From the hallway I can already hear Adolf haranguing Hermann,
holding forth, as I knew he would, on Trotsky's death in Moscow.
Frieda announces me, as always, by my old-world name and title:
'Doctor Goebbels, *meine herren*.' Adolf, seated as usual in his fine
morocco armchair, his suit as ill-fitting as ever, acknowledges my
entrance with the usual half-insolent flick of the eyes, without
faltering in his tirade. At seventy-eight, he has not lost the knack
of talking his audience into the ground.

'That Jew,' he expatiates, underlining the obvious, 'should have
demonstrated to all that the Talmudic plan has long entered its
decisive phase. The apparent withdrawal of Yiddish cadres from
the German Communist leadership did not fool me for one
minute. Mark my words, the Kremlin will now similarly pass
into so called non-Jewish hands. There may even be a pathetic
purge. It is this act precisely that signals the true danger. While
functioning in the public eye the Bronstein-Luxemburg clique
had to work perspicaciously and in stealth but I have no doubt
that now, behind the scenes, the world-conspiracy shifts gears and
prepares for the kill. Germany, Germany should have been the

8

engine of the destruction of the Talmudic menace. Failing that we must not waver in our faith in the arousal of America's Aryan elements. Youth must be forged and purified in the fire to face the sacrifices to come. Under no circumstances must we pause in the work for one moment . . .'

Hermann has fallen asleep again. Who can blame him? Of course, he has been slipping for some time. His obesity is by now an affront to mankind, as he waddles from bottle to bottle like a giant red doughball. On drugs again, too, by the look of him, experimenting with his loathsome chemical compounds. Look at him slobbering on the divan. How he has lasted to the age of seventy-four is a complete mystery. Only four years older than myself and already a foot and a half in the grave. A truly pathetic example of the lack of fresh air, physical and mental exercise and natural sexuality.

Adolf's Annchen glides softly into the room with coffee and cakes on a trolley. Ignoring the storm clouds, passing round the cups and saucers, sailing as ever on her calm seas, as if unbuffeted by the typhoons that have raged in her man's life. Force of circumstance (and my cajoling) may have led him to take refuge in her father's adopted land, so long ago, but, as the decades passed, and she bore him his two sons, watching his passions incinerate one and alienate the other, one wonders, which of them is living in the other's world? True, she tamed his old bohemian mannerisms, or at least damped them down, bringing her shrewd knowledge of America and the Americans to the service of our cause, but has she really Americanised Adolf? I think rather, she has been subsumed in his world. A believer, yes, Adolf attracted such types in droves. It was watching her almost slavelike devotion that confirmed my belief that even here, in this alien country, it was Adolf who should be the one groomed . . . Yes, Annchen epitomises the mass that must be reached, inspired, made pregnant and set on the path . . .

The bridge game begins badly, as usual, Adolf in his worst ranting mood. 'The two faced rottenness of the Jew-York Times . . . They mutter meekly of the tyrant Trotsky but bemoan his passing, terrified of the weak men following the strong . . . Sulzbergerism cannot hide its Bolshevik horns, the circumcised hammer and sickle! So-called President Rockefeller sends a message of condolence to the Soviet Government! The mask of Rothchild-feller too is slipping. Hermann, you know you cannot lead from your own hand since the last trick was from the dummy . . .'

Verbal drivel, the same old cracks I wrote for him long ago. Do we have to go through this every week? More and more I am becoming convinced Adolf's relevance to the current phase of the Plan must be held at the absolute minimum. His oratoric talent has turned in on itself. He is becoming the worst sort of windbag. Luckily he soon grows too hoarse to carry on and the last half of the game is conducted peacefully, with nothing but a sporadic 'bid three diamonds', 'two no trumps', or 'pass', to break the soothing weekend ambience . . .

Rachel
New York, November 19

Sitting in my apartment on West 83rd with two empty suitcases before me and the flotsman of ten years all around. How to get as much of this into these as possible. Or dump the lot. Set forth across the Atlantic with a toothbrush, the pills and sanitary requisites and one week's underwear and redarned socks. Leave the old life behind. Start the new clean, if not cleaned out . . .

Bring on the wastebin, now: The morning's mint-fresh rejection letter, latest of the mounting pile – 'Dear Miss Levy, we have read your offer "Terror Campaign 1961" and it does have some new insights into what is after all an old story but not enough, we think, to justify its publication. There have been numerous books about the Hitler Campaign and we do not feel the market can bear another at this stage. Yours sincerely . . . blah blah blah.'

Don't rock the boat, girl, in this era of Rockefeller 'stabilisation', none of them old negative vibes! Ghosts of the past? No thank you. Keep the skeletons locked in the closet. In fact there have only been three books, as far as I can remember, but . . . tear it up, girl, into the bin it goes.

Preserve, acceptance note from London Film Academy, which will be pleased to see both Rachel Levy and her cheque lined up for the coming January term. Signed, Patrick Kinross, Principal. *Gottseidank!* An escape route at last! Exchange the betrayals of the written word for the hopes of the celluloid image. Learn something new, instead of chewing a stale old cud . . .

Halloween masks and paper hats, where did those come from? Into the wastebin they go. Old *Newsweek*s and faded *Time* covers: President Joe McCarthy, the UnAmerican Hearings, circa 1954 . . . Senators Nixon and Hitler père behind old Joe, the all-party glee club, before it all fell apart . . . 1953 – the old warrior Chu Teh and the 'Fall of China' . . . and the fallout of '52 – the 'Atomic Menace' issues, the sickly weeds of the Los Angeles Bomb. Your List of Atomic Diseases, What to Look Out for in your West Coast Friends. Eyewitness reports of the L.A. Holocaust and our own

11

Tokyo revenge. Sick, sick, sick! Memories you wouldn't want to carry in your baggage, if you dare leave them out . . .

Whaddaya know – the old man himself, Leon Trotsky, Man Of The Year 1956. His fifth 'Renewed Revolution'. An impressive Topolsky head. My father would have certainly mourned his passing. 'If we had our own Bronstein,' he used to say, 'he'd have soon put all the Nixons, Smiths, Hitlers in one bag and pitched the lot in the East River. He could never abide a double-dealer, even in his own camp! That son of a bitch Stalin, for example – to the wall, one volley, and goodbye Charlie!'

My Pa. And what have we here? Truly ancient leaflets in Yiddish, scan over the once familiar Hebrew script: 'Workers and Intellectuals of South Manhattan Unite!' Forgotten prehistories – Papa, trudging in a February blizzard to attend, like the most devout believer, the I.W.W. Saturday afternoon debates, all the old saws grinding away: Permanent versus Renewed Revolution, Syndicalism, the Mass Strike, the merits of Rosa versus Leon, did Luxemburg sell out? Was Liebknecht a Revisionist? Over the chess tables of Washington Square Papa and his cronies would range wild over world affairs, castigating Wall Street, the decaying British Empire, German Soviet Restructuring, the German-Russian cold war. Papa, true to his Silesian origins, was a staunch Luxemburgite, and his admiration of Trotsky was tinged by doubts as to the rigour of Industrial Terror. Mom had no truck with any of this, as she glared at him through the stretched out pages of *Forwaerts*, galled over the uneaten supper: 'Trotsky, Protsky! first he starves the poor Russians, then he gets to work on my husband. Just a rag doll, Nachman Levy!' The puppet dance of the blasted expectations of both, laid to rest now, bless their souls, as I rushed out, on my own, God, so stereotyped revolt –

More Hebrew now, in the 'Holy Tongue' itself – Kibbutz Ashpatot's stencilled newsletter, Palestine, 1963: Shattering success of the '62 fig harvest, Arab infiltrator from the Nazareth Canton killed at the security fence, League of Nations (i.e. British) patrol finds arms slick in neighbouring Kibbutz Matta, Zvika the librarian sues for divorce. A fitting candidate for the wastebin. My God! The search for Jewish roots ending in the overwhelming smell of radishes and the sweaty embrace of Shraga, unhappily married kibbutz treasurer . . . Some people are not born for a return to the soil and religio-ethnic pride, even in the heat of the struggle still ongoing for a Jewish State (chimera or not, not this sacrificial lamb . . .) No, it's a different quest for me . . .

Lost chapters, volumes of my life lie scattered, upturned on the carpet. A stack of letters from Marvin Blumenfeld, Jesus Christ! Save us, Lord, from First Loves. The mattress at Aunt Katie's. Why did I preserve all these old words? An aspiring Proust, with no memory. But the reading brings back no enlightenment, just a sort of nauseous flu. Embarassment at these adolescent gushings. Enough, down the hatch with you too.

Boxes of knick knacks, horrible candles from Jerusalem, fake Aztec relics from Mexico City (when did I go there? ah, yes . . .), jingling bells from who knows where – discard, discard, discard . . . Keep the old *Time*s and *Newsweek*s though – history, that dies hard . . . Bundles of more letters, old typewriter ribbons, abandoned notes for half a dozen novels, art catalogues, tubes of rock-hard gouache, moulted paint brushes, pictures of the dead Stars – Bogart, Gable, Bette Davis, Stanwyck, the grisly hall of bombed fame . . . Boldly divide: This pile out, this to storage with
Sarah Nichols in the Bronx. The vital books and records already sent on by boat – Parker, Mingus, Happy Turner, Steinbeck, Mark Twain, Alice Rathbone whom McCarthy killed . . . some of my life will nevertheless follow me. And a copy too, one can't avoid it, of the *Terror* manuscript. Perhaps over in Europe . . . pigs might fly . . . But the old adage – you can't leave yourself behind . . .

The apartment buzzer, Sarah Nicols at the door, the van ready, parked as close as she can. The laconic drawl of my friend at the doorphone. Come on up. Time to move, Rachel, time to go. All the goodbyes said that had to be said, all the telephone calls made that had to be made, all the addresses taken that had to be taken. Anything left then, to keep me here? Let's go, let's go . . .

Alex
Athens, December 5

Slumped mournfully over a third ouzo, with Christos, at Nikos's Taverna, eleven o'clock at night. Cold, rainy and depressing outside. I can see, if I look up, my own bald patch gleaming in the mirror in the light of Nikos's candles. Twenty-four and falling apart already! Christos's self-rolled cigarette has burned down right to his Zapata moustache, poised to fall over his permanent stubble. In the nick of time, as usual, just as the hairs are about to catch fire, he grinds the stub out in the ashtray and speaks for both of us:

'My friend, at our age we should stop masturbating. Either we stay here and act, and go to jail, or we leave now and use our time and our life for at least some purpose out there.'

An inescapable choice. Apart from apathy and paralysis, there could be no other. It was now exactly one month since the Good Lord – according to the great panjandrum, Archbishop Chrysostomos – had granted the Greek people his two synchronous gifts: the death of the Antichrist, Trotsky, and the Divinely Inspired Junta of General Spandidakis.

I remember that night vividly. November 7. Awakening to a loud rumble shaking the entire house. Slipping into the living room to find my father, as if a taut spring was holding his wispy frame, standing in his dressing-gown at the window. Outside, the tanks thundered, a dozen British Centurions, churning the asphalt of Solonos Street. Two of them turned, tracks screeching, down Masalias towards the University. The rest continuing in the direction of Syntagma and Parliament.

When the tanks had passed the streets were silent as a graveyard. The old clock on the mantlepiece tick tocked towards four. My mother was up, boiling water for coffee in the kitchen. My father slumped in his armchair. I took out the Lebanese arak and poured one for him, one for me. Turning on the radio to hear the medley of Italian marching tunes. How like the guardians and paragons of our 'National Honour' to turn to Mussolini's geriatric fascism for emotional support. I thought of that seminal summer day, June something, 1958, the old bastard's 'Reconciliation Visit' – my first 'political' act, at the tender age of twelve, when I was poured, along with busloads of other squalling brats, en masse on to Syntagma Square, to cheer for the visiting Duce. I remember how the great Rolls Bentley purred along in the wake of the white-sleeved military police motorcyclists. In the open back seat, the nice white-haired gent who was our Nation's Saviour of the day, Tsolacoglou, and beside him, the famous, portly guest: a puffy, wrinkled old face with piggy eyes darting right and left, the head bobbing up and down as if stuck on a blob of jelly pinned with rows of medals and ribbons, under that black velvet hat, with its emblazoned silver eagle . . . The schoolchildren, each holding their two little flags of both nations, waving them and jumping up and down, crying: 'Zito Ellas! Zito Duce!' at the tops of their voices. Yours truly, Alexi Panoulis, adding his voice to the rest . . .

'Put that crap off!' my father yelled. I turned the marches down, explaining, 'There should be some announcement soon.'

'I don't need to hear it.' My father poured himself another three fingers of arak. 'I've heard it all before. Metaxas, Tsolacouglou, Koundoumis. Three saviours for a doomed country. And your Lambrakis, your communist anarchists, you think you can break the circle with speeches and demonstrations! Democracy, Liberty, kick out the King! You think they don't hear you also? You live in your fantasies while the Army makes its plans, moves its troops and tanks. These people don't play by your rules. Into the cells and pliers in the balls for good measure. Ach, the naivety of it all! Dreaming anarchists on one side and fascist louts on the other! Why have I stayed here so long?'

I turned the sound up, nevertheless, for the announcer's voice. What we had all expected:

' . . . Tonight, at three-thirty a.m., the Greek Armed Forces, in order to forestall the imminent danger of a communist takeover of our beloved homeland, acted in response to the growing conditions of anarchy and disorder. His Majesty the King has approved Extraordinary Powers for the Chief of the Royal Staff General Spandidakis, and declared a State of Emergency. A strict curfew will be imposed while the enemies of the people are dealt with with the full rigour of the Nation's implacable will. Once again, as in Ancient Greece, all laws must be set aside to carry out the one supreme law, the law to save our own country. Long Live Christian Greece! Long Live the King! Long Live the Armed Forces!'

'Warn your friends,' said my father. 'Phone Christos. Keep all your bloody heads down.' With a despairing look, he went and shut himself in the bedroom.

I woke Christos, I found out later, in bed with the lissome Elena, the Bakuninist chick with the long dark hair and the soulful brown eyes. In post-coital bliss, he had missed the orgasmic point of the coup. Christos's father is a retired policeman. A religious devotee of the Law. His mother is an invalid, so there remains contact, despite the old traumas of Bolshevik literature found under the teenager's bed. Father threatens son with his service revolver. Son denounces father. A Greek tragicomedy. Now this would just turn the screw. We gathered the next day – First Day of the New Greece (another New Greece!), at Spiros the Bakuninist beachboy's apartment, the sign on the door saying PROLETARIAN KINO already chiselled off in the night. An abrupt stop to the plans to produce Jeremiad documentary films to warn the populace about the danger of what has already been done. A familiar process to follow: the arrests, the disbanding of all political parties, censorship of the press, books, theatre, films, 'communist' music (Theodorakis) banned, loud singing in public to be outlawed, along with the 'disorderly' breaking of plates . . .

For safety's sake, our entire group moved, with our equipment, the Bolex camera, the editing bench, the film stock, to Elena's flat deep in suburbia. In the chic heights of Kolokynthou, where no unpleasantness intrudes to disturb the Attican bourgeoisie, we dumped our bookloads of Trotsky, Serge, Sosnovsky, Bakunin, Marcuse et al on the Axminster carpets, laying low while the miasma of the New Order settled over the land . . . The Junta does not ask for enthusiasm. No, it has learned from experience. Just keep your heads down, children, while we cut out the tumours of subversion. Hear, see, speak no evil. No shrieks from concealed torture cells . . .

Nikos's Taverna is about to close. Christos nibbles at his

loukoumia. We both know the decision we have made is a retreat, to fight another day. The two British visas granted after the acceptance letters coming from the London Film Academy. The fees, offered and paid by my father, to keep us both out of trouble. We can learn our trade, and be better communicators of our cause, when we return. Yes, what a fucking retreat.

The rain has stopped, we leave the taverna and walk in the empty street, the lamplight gleaming yellow on the peeling walls and potholes of Odos Filis. How long before we see these familiar signs again? To sit in summer in Aristotelous Street, watching the old waiter manoeuvering back and forth across the main road, weaving his tray of drinks past honking buses, cursing taxi drivers? To saunter about Syntagma at dusk, ogling the braless American girls? Or lie on the stony Piraeus beach? I remember the first time I went with Christos to this beach, after our Libertarian Meeting – arriving to find the aircraft carriers of the British Navy steaming in to port, our apotropos! The King Edward The Eighth, the Lord Halifax. He pointed past the apathetic sunbathers accusingly: 'The arms of the hydra! It's that enemy's lair we have to enter – that creature that we have to behead!' And here we are, ironically, years later, setting out to shelter in the armpit of the beast . . .

Michael
London, January 10

Saturday afternoon at Rabbi and Rebetsen Lamb of 35 Golders Green Crescent. Their weekly après-*shul* tea. The guests twitter and flitter over the chopped liver sandwiches. Skullcapped, blue-suited adolescents, sporting their Bar Mitzvah tiepins, sit bolt upright gazing across the room at their female counterparts, demure under the adult gaze. The flattest whitebait couldn't wriggle through the generation gap here.

Michael Pinsker, né of Federal Palestine, Jerusalem Canton, present and incorrect as usual. Noblesse oblige, I must visit my diaspora family at least once, en route to the London Film Academy and proper diversity. Once is quite enough.

'Zionism is a failure!' cries Doctor Moss. 'It's plain as a pikestaff by now!'

Becky Lamb, the Rabbi's mousy wife, anxiously watches the china teacup precariously balanced on the lanky quack's knee, as he vibrates like a coffee grinder, black hair falling in his eyes, poking egg and tomato excitedly at his host. She trills apologetically at me. I'm the emissary from the frontline, the bearer of the crucial message: How Goes the Union? the Cause of Jewish Statehood. Pardon me while I hiccup. The consummation, so devoutly to be wished, of two thousand years of Hope, sixty of direct struggle . . . I can feel, particularly here, the British Jew's ambivalence and torn loyalties: After all, despite Dominion status, it's still British troops and tanks clamping the lid down on both Arabs and Jews in the disputed land.

'Don't take any notice of Mossy,' Mordechai Lamb reassures me, wagging his suave goatee. 'He was always a bit of a bolshie.'

'No, no, no!' the good Doctor leans forward, the teacup tottering, Becky Lamb flinching, 'I won't let you get away with that, Mottel. Look at the facts, the facts, stop dreaming delirious dreams! Since Herzl you've been predicting disaster and cataclysm, some sort of mass pogrom, the goyim slavering for Jewish blood down Whitehall, and everyone should ponce off to Palestine and what, for all the shrying, we got? Nothing. Nix. Rubbish.'

'Nothing? You call the lynching of Jews in Florida nothing?' the Rabbi, losing his cool, endangering every teacup with his fluttering hands, 'when the Hitler party almost hit the jackpot, that was just a caress?'

'Hitler was just another American fruitcake,' scoffs Moss, 'they breed like rabbits over there. He just rode on the coat-tails of southern nigger-haters. Pure hysteria, he never had a chance . . .'

'I beg to differ with you . . .' The Rabbi wags his finger. 'But why cross the Atlantic anyhow? Your memory is *oysgemotert* on our own antisemites? And Mosley's Jewish Repatriation Scheme? If his were not a minority government we'd all be on the boats by now, getting a little fresh sea air. The Zionist warning still holds water, more than ever today! Jews are inherently unsafe in the diaspora! What about Poland? Rumania? And don't think Germany and Russia, your great paragons, are immune! The founders of the Soviet states may have been Jews but that's all over now. I tell you, there's more antisemitism in Soviet Russia and, yes, in Soviet Germany today than even in the United States!'

'Rubbish!' Moss's teacup still survives.

'A Jewish State *must* be set up in Palestine!' A fat man named Rosenzweig, I think, spits out a gob of chopped liver on to Becky Lamb's rug. 'Somewhere Jews must live of right, not sufferance!'

'And what about the Arabs?' shrills Moss. 'They'll just fade away? The Civil Wars have shown they'll also fight for their land. What do you expect them to do?'

'The *yishuv* brings prosperity to all,' says another congregationist, 'why should they make trouble? We have a visitor here from the horse's mouth, why don't we ask him?'

Oi! No thank you, brothers. This is what I came to Albion to avoid. Shall I tell them, these upright *landsleit* of Golders Green Crescent, all gungho for the Cause, shall I tell them how it really looked to me, as I flew out of Lydda Airport by B.O.A.C.? Should I uncover for these brave souls the part played by my friends and I in the Heroic Struggle?

Well, Rabbi, two nights before I left, we celebrated Sylvester,

19

the pagan New Year, in suitable Hebrew fashion, five tots of whisky each, followed by heavy puking in the toilet. Next day, January 1, splitting hangover, mother's admonition, during packing: 'You're a grown man now.' Meaning, You're still a helpless baby, you can't even zip your fly. My father merely mumbles, 'Don't forget us.' The Cause, of course. I mumble indecisively back.

Last night in the Holy Land: Wandering with gang, Yossi, Gideon, Amiel, to the Eden Cinema, showing BANZAI!, colour epic of the Holocaust of Hollywood. Authentic doubles bring to life the vanished golden age, the martyred stars: Gable, Cooper, Bogart, Garbo, all zapped to nuclear ash by Mishima, the Nipponese kamikaze pilot, in 1952. Elbow our way to the ticket window, fight for the tickets, totter in, crunch sunflower seeds through the Gaumont-Movietone Newsreel: Funeral of Trotsky in Moscow, snow-iced tears on muzhik cheeks. Visiting revolutionaries pay last respects – Egypt's Nasser, Gold Coast's Nkrumah, the Latin Pimpernel Guevara, exiled wretched of the earth. We pummel each other on the seats. What do we care for politics? If it was our own Dayan or Begin on the screen, we'd care not much more, and jeer at the pompous patriots who would clap in the theatre. No politics! Enough is enough. It's laughs and a good time we're after . . .

The mushroom cloud engulfs Los Angeles in ElstreeScope and we stumble out into the cold Jerusalem air. People slinking home quietly, the falafel shops on the corner of King George shut, the British soldiers are about tonight, bundled in their flak jackets. The Irgun, as is its wont, shot a Sergeant in Mamilla Square just the other day, commemorating Hannukah – remember the Maccabbees, and all that rot . . .

The world's policemen! At Ben Yehuda Street two large Tommies bar our way. 'See yer card, Jock.' We winkle out our battered i.d.s, ungloved fingers freezing. The Scotty looks at our faded horror snaps, flicks an eye, hands 'em back, moves on with languid colleague. My friend Gideon seethes with fury. 'International Peacekeeping Force!' he fumes. 'Of course it's international,' Yossi recycles the old quip, 'there are different nations in it – England, Scotland, Ulster, Wales.' Gideon has clear Irgunist tendencies. He fancies himself gobbling campfire potatoes in the Galilee hills, slithering with a Lee Enfield through layers of mud in illegal training jaunts. Or better still, infiltrating like Menachem Begin in a bowler hat and false moustache through the tight borders of 'Free' Europe, with a money belt tied round his kishkas. Teasing him, Yossi, Amiel and I pipe up with the amended version of the Irgun anthem:

> 'Upon the barricades we shall meet, we shall meet,
> At a quarter to six, at the Cafe Cassit . . .'

I can't believe this! Rabbi Lamb would protest. A Jewish youth, brought up amid the tribulations of the Homeland, repudiating the National Cause? What of your parents' sacrifices, leaving the fleshpots of Great Britain to embrace the uncertainty of Federal Palestine, living through the horrors of the Cantonal Civil Wars? The thousands of dead . . . the pogroms of Bucharest, Warsaw? Is this the future we face?

Don't misunderstand me, Rebbe. It's not that I'd betray the Cause. I'd lift no finger to help the Oppressor, the wielder of the British truncheon and boot. But I can't share your rosy vision. The reality of Palestine is different, for me: Clenched fists, contorted faces, two fanaticisms set to stomp each other into the ground. Some of us are not taken with the hemmed-in, besieged statelets the two chauvinisms, Arab and Jewish, have made of the original cantons. I can't take refuge in dreams, Rabbi, after two years as an assistant to a newsreel camera team, rushing to see the sights of inter-communal war, the riots, the retaliations, the tit-for-tat killings. A plague on both their houses! Blood and fire, glory, Israel, Falastin, not my cup of blood, good sirs. The Cinema, that is my Nation: the golden age, Chaplin, Laurel & Hardy, Keaton, like them, I seek but to amuse! Make people laugh, divert them from wars, Armageddons! The London Film Academy, brothers, that's the end of my rainbow, my escape from Manifest Destiny!

So Good Yonteff, Rabbi Lamb, the chopped liver was delicious. I'm sure I'll come again, I'm not sure when . . . But just don't speak to me of History! My ears are blocked up, touch of flu, man, it's a cold, damp day . . .

Part II

Initiation

April–July 1968

Extract from Terror Campaign, 1961, by Rachel Levy

Miami Beach, September 5: It may have been Joseph Gable's sly humour which led him to choose the Holiday Inn as the venue for the American Party Convention. That being the choice, all the sunkissed trippers, boozed jewellery salesmen, suntan lotion executives and incumbent mafiosi (or those of them not attending as delegates), were shuffled away, any protest met with a little artistic persuasion in the shape of a Klan mask bogeyed outside their window, or a Star of David splashed in pig vomit over their bathroom tiles. Red, white and blue-striped swastikas draped from the tenth storey down, billowing in the sea breeze . . .

As I enter the lobby my heart's doing a fandango in my kishkas. 'Don't do it!' Sarah Nichols had said, 'they'll see Jew in your eyes and hear Jew the minute you open your mouth. They'll plaster you all over the walls and beat the remains with nightsticks.' 'Never fear,' I answered brashly, 'I'll be a sweet young American thing from New Jersey. Restricted golf clubs and no pluribus unum. I'll wear my best infatuated grin of Aryan adoration. My hair will be straightened, I shall wear one of those Jane Russell brassieres and be Miss Fife-and-Drum Majorette of nineteen-sixty-one.' But I'm no longer so sure, standing alone in the very nub of Hitlerland with square-jawed crewcut crackpots in flowered shirts and swastika campaign badges. (That nose, Rachel, pull in that nose!) The lobby dominated by a twenty-foot-high portrait of the Candidate – 'Major' Rudolph the red-nosed Hitler with his set grin and his wide vacant stare, neck tightly enclosed in dress uniform, the Congressional Medal of Honour, incurred in the Pacific War, just flush with the lower frame of the picture. Flanked by two smaller, more modest blow ups of G.K.L. Smith, the Vice-Presidential Candidate, and white-haired Adolf, the Party's Founding Father . . .

In the event, access is relatively painless. A young southern belle at the reception desk flashes me two rows of faultless teeth, caressing a pure white phone. 'Doctor Gable? A Miss Sheila Anderson, from the Tenafly *Courier*, by appointment with the

Senator. Yes, surely. Please go up, Miss Anderson, tenth floor, elevator B.' She hands me a swastika ribbon. 'They'll be waiting for you. Have a good day.'

An unlikely prospect. But the person awaiting me at floor number ten is another blonde goddess (are they making them in chemical baths somewhere?), who leads me up the red-carpeted corridor towards the Candidate's sanctum.

Rudy Hitler, face to face, not thirty feet tall on a hoarding or ranting on television to a legion of fans shrieking for the blood of the impure, turns out nothing special: a dapper all-American kid, every pound the Modest War Hero, with football shoulders out of place in a stiff shirt and tie, as if aching to get back into pads and helmet. The only outstanding feature is the Glare, Papa Adolf's inheritance, stabbing right at me, like a zombied mackerel, but compelling. A hynotist's weapon, disquieting over that neanderthal moose jaw.

The Watchdog is with him. Sunk in a brown leather armchair, immaculately manicured fingertips held together in front of that acquiline nose with a kind of unsettling daintiness. His face looks lifted, though pockmarks still show faintly in the carefully tended skin. His hair a distinguished grey-white shot with streaks of black, as if dyed by an interior decorator: Joseph Gable, formerly Goebbels, the brain of the Hitler campaigns. He gives me my second bad moment, gimlet eyes boring in after my racial descent. But theory either does not hold, or he decides to let me by. Rudy, on the other hand, ignores my nose to fixate on my uplifted chest, as planned. Boys will be boys.

'I have seen the Tenafly *Courier*,' Gable says, his accent suavely modulated to suppress the teutonics, 'as a supposedly patriotic magazine it is consistently misjudged and misinformed.'

'We're a straight down the line Republican paper.' (Thank God I made sure to cover my back, anticipating the suspicion.) 'We consider ourselves to be pro-American, running the gamut of views in the Party. We support the President, when he's right.'

'We've supported a lot of President Nixon's actions,' Rudy chips in, bright and chirpy, 'he's stopped the Reds in Cuba, just as we urged him, but why was Castro allowed to get so far? Only a blind man, or woman, can't see the termites eating the G.O.P. from inside. And only a fool, pardon the straight talking, mam, can ignore the real truth about the power brokers at the core – the Rockefellers, Goldwassers and all. Nixon might want to be pro-American, but he is tied hand and foot by the Jews.'

The Interview:

Q: Senator Hitler, to what do you ascribe the meteoric rise of the American Party since 1958?

A: We are the Party in the right place at the right time. We have answers where everybody else has questions. We see ourselves as carrying on the work of our finest President, Joe McCarthy, a great American, betrayed by his own Party. He held us together after the Pacific War and didn't shirk from putting the blame where it was due. We all knew the Germans had given the Japs the Atomic Bomb. How could an Asian race develop nooclear technology? McCarthy showed how President Wallace had conspired to conceal that fact, because Henry Wallace was a card-carrying member of the Communist Party. Our own President! And you ask whether the country needs a clean sweep? The American people know this cleansing is necessary, if we are going to survive as a nation. The Republican Party has tied Nixon's hands in this. The Democrats have not repudiated their Communist past and present, from Rosenfelt-Roosevelt to Addelhead Stevenshein. Those solid, Aryan, working Americans who were tricked into voting Democrat have at last woken up. They see New York social workers marching hand in hand with nigras to provoke unrest and Communism. They can hear the cooing messages of Stevenshein to Moscow, under the guise of, what do they call it – a 'thaw' between the great powers! And the people do not forget Los Angeles – one hundred and fifty thousand dead, another half a million scarred for life due to government treason. A hundred and fifty thousand victims of Bolshevism's slanteyed puppets! And you want us to shake the murderer's hand? The American people want to make a firm stand, to prepare for the next sneak attack, and our two big Parties go on bickering and playing the plootocratic game, the game of divide and rule. You mentioned our meteoric rise. That's not the rise of a political Party, but of the American people, united under a new leadership! We stand for an America

27

that does not lick its enemies' boots . . . an America proud of its Aryan inheritance, proud to be Christian and White! The other Parties may be the past of this nation, that's true. But we are its future. That's why we're going to win this election.

Miami Beach, September 8: The Convention! Packed crowds! Flowery shirts over vast Bermuda shorts! Havanas in every slobbering gob! Multitudes slip on sweat-covered floors . . . Hundreds of portraits of Rudy and Gerry bobbing frantically about. Southern belles with red-white-and-blue swastika sashes and top hats cheerleading, releasing multi-coloured swastika balloons to fill the Holiday Inn's Grand Ballroom. 'Roo-dee! Roo-dee!' The bloated southern circus, an obscene harlequinade, America with her brains blown out, the waggon let loose and gathering speed into the pit. Bizarre effigies of Negroes and Jewish politicians bobbing and weaving in the craze. Journalists from east and west gaze stunned at the proceedings, the sheer scale and ferocity of the challenge thrown out to the two-party system . . .

The crowd goes completely crazy as Rudy mounts the rostrum. Two thousands right arms stiffen in the Roman salute. Cheerleaders faint with the emotion and are dragged off by stewards lest they get stomped to death in the ecstasy. Then Rudy speaks. A rapt silence. The amazing discipline of the lead. This is how it used to be, I'm told, at Papa Adolf's get-togethers in Illinois, the Chicago Crusades of the mid-forties, before Los Angeles and McCarthy . . . Adolf was a runt of a man who packed a mighty bellow, but he could never quite shuck off that German accent that set him apart from the mass. Rudy, in contrast, is a hulk and an indifferent speaker, but an authentic American cry. The faithful lap it up like nectar. The future belongs to us! At thirty-five he would make the youngest President ever – and after this, who can call that a rabid fantasy . . . ?

A standing ovation. Cheers. Firecrackers at the back of the hall. And then the master stroke: with a gesture, Rudy calls for silence, drops his voice now, close up to the microphone, begins to croon about the Bomb. The Bolsheviks, the Nips, the Jews, the Commie Wallace . . . a hush of frigid rage in the Ballroom. The sea of placards parts, and down the center of the Hall, the

American Party's Sacramento Congressman is wheeled up to the podium. His spine bent, half his face burned away, but, as Rudy acclaims, his True American Spirit is totally unbroken – one of the few surviving film stars of pre-Bomb Hollywood – Congressman Reagan rises slowly, from his wheelchair, left hand gripping whitely at its aluminium arms. Weakly but determinedly he waves his right stump at the rally. The crowd watches, breathless, as he finally totters, unsupported. 'This!' cries Rudy, 'this is America! Wounded in battle but unbowed! We *can* stand! We *can* make our country whole again!'

Uproar! A hurricane of applause! Another thousand swastika balloons surge upwards! They know, they know they are riding the wave!

Today, Miami Beach. Tomorrow, the White House? And, the cold morning after – ?

Ernesto
80 miles from Debar, Abyssinia, April 1968

A miserable wattle hut, rotted twigs bound with festering rags, the roof of caked dung, the floor the hard rock ground. Roaches scurry among the inhabitants' dismally few belongings: some rags of clothing, a few rusted cooking utensils, a couple of Italian pots, a broken clock, a torn straw mattress. Seven people live here: mother, father, five children, all gaunt, with aged-looking, wrinkled faces. All are ill, of one malady or several. Not one has healthy eyes. The children already bear the telltale distended belly of malnutrition. Flies settle everywhere. They will not bother to scatter far when slapped, simply move aside in a horrible communal mass to resettle their infested kingdom.

I, too, am their subject. The only escape is at night, when I can squat, at the hut's entrance, my rifle strapped to my back, the rolled cigarette burning down to my lips. Remembering the luxury of cigars! As the family behind me scrape into their maws the last of the captured Italian K-rations, then settling down to the 'normality' of sleep with their plethora of sighs and hisses.

What can they dream, these isolated people, eking out their daily struggle for existence in the furthest clefts of the dying Italian Empire? For myself, I am home again, in my own way, home among the lost and the forgotten. Argentina, Cuba, the Gold Coast, Libya or Italian East Africa, it is the same. The One Enemy, and the battlefield enclosing the earth . . .

All the riffraff, the fallen, the dispossessed, the shirtless, the pantless, the shoeless. The barren and the expendable. Those full of hate, those full of despair, those drained of both hate and despair. Dwellers of *favelas* where hopelessness runs like a wide open sewer. The *bohios* of endless unrequited labour, the *barracones* of latinfundist's slaves. The crop pickers of Central America who wander barefoot over asphalt and gravel, stone and briar, on their odyssey from one pittance to another. Squatters, evicted by United Fruit or Union Miniere, scratching a living outside the fence, collecting the garbage thrown from the van of capitalism's brave progress. The kraals of indentured South African workers, the bare tukuls of the Ethiopian peasant. Everywhere – the malnourished, the sufferers from trachoma, malaria, worms. Everywhere – the dead, dead of starvation, dead of misery and the fading of hope, dead of the exploiter's whip and the Coloniser's bullets and shells –

I hear the wind's crack over the sleep of slaves,
a thousand ancient beings,
scarred by storms, smoothed by scarlet streams . . .

1946, in Argentina: The students and workers in the streets of Cordoba, fighting the false idol Peron . . . Red blood from cracked heads and pierced stomachs imprinting the pavements like a surrealist street-artist's sketch, while up the road in the Presidential Palace the siren Evita still wooed the *descamisados* . . . In the world outside, the Yankee preoccupied with his Pacific Wars, as he and his Asiatic rival cut wide swathes through China, Indonesia, the Philippines, battling for their lucrative markets, until the vultures swooped home to roost in the bombed-out ruins of Los Angeles and Tokyo . . . Would the terrible lessons be learnt? China gains her freedom under Chu·Teh . . . The Japanese withdraw from the world Imperialist stakes . . . But Yankee greed – no, that still knows no bounds . . .

1954 – Guatemala City: Facing the mercenaries of Castillo Armas. Arbenz, the nationalist reformer, called on the people too late. There we were, lit up by our youthful hopes, a few old rifles, two mortars, a clutch of grenades, against the tanks and planes of Monopoly . . . Children running in the streets clutching carbines they cannot load. Peasants and workers barricading the streets with their bodies. Again, the red stains . . . An old man spreadeagled in the dust, while chickens peck their way around him . . . In the jailyards, the fusillades echo . . . The sleek North American executives, their patrimony reclaimed, purr in their limousines down 'purified' trails . . . And again, the sorry path of exile – Mexico, 1955, at last – Fidel and Raul. The three sticks of dynamite to be bound together . . . The sparks, to light a flame which would burn, for a time . . . But of those three I am here, alone . . .

A crunch of sandalled feet from my left. A cigarette end briefly

31

glows from the next *tukul* and is then extinguished. Quick eyes gleam in the dark beside me. A curious man, this exile like myself, but wielder of a quite different weapon . . . An Italian, of the Socialist Resistance, he has trekked six hundred miles with his cameraman and camera to rendezvous with us on the escarpment. I had heard his name before, but seen none of his work. Pier Paolo Pasolini. Eight years ago, he outraged the Duce's censors by presenting on the screen a caricature of the great leader as an insane rapist. Like so many of his colleagues, exile was the only option, other than jail or rotting on a far island. Free expression, to Fascism, is not the decadent playground of the Imperialist nations' arts, but a threat as lethal as grenades . . . We had met, Pier Paolo and I, in Argentina, in the aftermath of yet another Peron Coup, and then again, in Berlin, at the Party Congress, where the seeds of his present project were sown . . . 'A new form of document,' he had suggested, 'of a culture we Italians have, in our stupidity and arrogance, tried to defeat but is defeating us, or, we can rather say, saving us from our darker side . . .'

We sit and discuss the tactical situation; neither of us sleeps well at night. Soon the food we took from Il Duce's 3rd East African Rifles will be consumed and our small column will have to leave the shelter of this impoverished village, to play the waiting game elsewhere. In a thirty-year war, there are inevitable lulls. I may fret, but I cannot ignore the rooted knowledge of the Ethiopian strategists. As long as the Italians keep their troops in their barracks in the major towns the Committee of Equals, the Dergue, which runs the Revolution, prefers to consolidate its political hold on the country rather than goad the enemy into retaliation raids. They are not in a hurry, confident as they are of victory. 'Like the desert and the mountains,' says the old lion Walda Sion, 'we have been here a long time.' But what is uncertain even after victory is the Dergue's control of what follows. Feudalism and the old Emperor Selassie, ensconced with his caviar in Claridges, London, might well rear their ugly mane . . . I have learned to live with patience, but never to like it, considering the magnitude of the task ahead, the forces which would yet have to be ruptured even after the breaking of the stranglehold of Mussolini's Italy – Britain, France, the United

States, and all this with a Socialist world wary and weary of conflict, with both Germany and Russia walking a tightrope of evasion and appeasement . . .

We sit, the film maker and I, long into the night, under the canopy of stars, two strangers on a mountaintop plain in East Africa, waiting for the new day to dawn . . .

Joseph Gable
Chicago, April

. . . Buried Hermann this morning in the Volkisch cemetery. Tears rolled down Adolf's cheeks. My eyes were as dry as a Rabbi's on Sunday. Hermann could have lasted longer if he had realised one lived in one's body and ought not use it as an experimental carcase. Viewed in the mortuary his fat arms were pockmarked with needle pricks. What a wasteful and loathsome degeneracy!

Watching Adolf stagger like a stricken dachsund down the cemetery path on Annchen's arm I was seized with a pang of anxiety. Will he hold out under the strain? Or have that quack Mengele's 'longevity' treatments actually set him miserably back? That creep's influence on Adolf must be broken. His presence among us still, alas, necessary, as a symbol of the old guard. Maudlin reflections on mortality: how few of us still left – Amman and Esser in Atlanta, Neubauer wallowing in West Palm Beach, Feder still breathing but capable of little else in Seattle. Adolf, Robert and myself in Illinois. And can we keep Freddy firmly away from Dixiecrat materialism, the dead clasp of Smith, Wallace, Wayne? No repeat of 1961 can be tolerated. This time, with deadly accuracy, one must home in on the right target. With both America and Europe in a fool's paradise, lulled by a false, emasculating stability. The crucial era is the one that is now upon us, we must not shirk History's personal commands . . .

(THE TIMES, APRIL 15, 1968, OBITUARY
Mr Hermann Goering, also known as Göring, once commander of the legendary Richthofen Squadron in the Great War, died yesterday in Chicago at the age of 74.

Mr Goering, a popular air ace in the German Imperial Air Force during the 1914–1918 War, joined the right-wing National Socialist German Workers' Party (NSDAP) in 1920. With the collapse of German democracy in 1923 Mr Goering, together with Party chief Adolf Hitler, was forced to flee to the Austrian

Republic. After disagreements with the newly proclaimed dictatorship of Engelbert Dolfuss, Mr Goering, together with Messrs Röhm, Goebbels and others, followed their Party chief Mr Hitler to the United States in 1925. In 1926 Messrs Goering, Röhm and Hitler participated in the Polish Civil War but were expelled by the victorious Nationalist government of Marshall Pilsudski. After some months in Italy, Mr Goering returned to the United States where he became a U.S. citizen in 1934. He played a prominent part in the so-called 'German Clique' of Illinois and in Mr Hitler's Senatorial campaigns of 1946 and 1952. In Mr Hitler's American Party of 1958–62 he played an administrative role in the organisation of the Party's internal security. Mr Goering never aspired to or held elective office and was a well-loved figure in the German community of Chicago. He leaves a wife, three children and eight grandchildren.)

Rachel
London, Spring

London, hub of the Empire and of a strange, heady freedom. Strange, coming from a country shaken into an impossible rigidity by a war past to one still fighting wars around the globe but basking in an unexpected slackness . . . Dominion over palm and pine, o'er lesser breeds without the law, but an odd disorder in the heart, a sense of loosening to some, collapse to others, of old bonds and ties. The old historian of the British Empire, Winston Churchill, once wrote that Britain and the United States were two nations divided by a common language, and I can see what he means. There is an inertia here, exemplified by the solid buildings and monuments nailing the city to the ground, the ubiquitous old wise monkey look on picture postcards of the ageing King Edward VIII . . .

That entropy already apparent on the liner coming over, the aptly named *Ramsay Macdonald*, as it seemed a little unsure, in mid-Ocean, which way it wanted to turn. Friends suggested I should try the new fast transatlantic air crossing, but finances and faith in the suspension of the laws of gravity's lacking. The passengers were mostly British tourists returning from the excitement across the pond. Tuckered out by their exertions, they played shuffleboard on deck or weakly rattled the doors of their cells. Recalling the old films of ocean liners with luxurious cabins, stewards and room service, rather than these mass produced cabinettes, four to a cupboard, with silver-wrapped dispensed meals . . . The brave, if crowded new world . . .

The England that I carried with me in image was, I suppose, dying before I was born: the England of grassy knolls, green fields, dinky churches, an unfrenzied quiet confidence, Winnie the Pooh ambling in the woods or Rat, Toad and Mole drifting lazily down the Thames in a boat. Pipe smoke chugging from the willows. Pigeons in Trafalgar Square. But there is barely room for pigeons in the square this summer: no sir! Making my way out of Victoria Station towards my hosts' address in Finsbury Park my

36

taxi's brought up short against a police diversion up Whitehall. A roaring crowd, those bobby helmets bobbing on nervous horses, leaflets strewn across the road. The Whitehall buildings gashed by bold graffiti, old and new: FREE GAMAL ABDUL NASSER! TROTSKY IS ALIVE! VICTORY TO GHANA PEOPLE'S ALLIANCE! BRING THE TROOPS HOME!

My taxi driver is voluble: 'Send 'em all to Germany an' Russia. Let's see aar they like it there. It's a bleedin' disgrace Miss, pardon my French. I 'ad to fight for King an' Country. Three years in bleedin' Kenya, with the savages cuttin' up any white man they could find. Free the colonies! Don't know where their own freedom comes from, these stupid kids. Don't know what war is. You've 'ad your share, in America. But these bums – the fat of the land . . . don't deserve an Empire, these animals . . . They should never have let 'em off the draft . . .'

Paradise scarred. The television screen reveals the day's skirmishes as I settle down with my hosts, Derek and Dianne, both students at the London School of Economics, the new bastion of the anti-colonial drive. Policemen's batons flail in their cavalry charges as wooden posts and banners go down. The crowd's roar taunting authority: 'Georgie, Georgie, hey hey hey, how many kids have you killed today?' The lockjawed P.M. Brown slurs softly: '. . . maintain calm . . . British common sense . . . repellent hooliganism . . . negligible minority fallen prey to anarchist ideas . . . wholly repugnant to the majority of the British people . . .' Familiar psalms and incantations, yes . . .

'The Chinese curse,' Dianne says to me, 'may you live in interesting times . . .' But reassurance is at hand – the King, and Queen Martha, attend the Chelsea Flower Show. The King's doctor is interviewed about the Sovereign's health. Robin Day concludes: 'Long may he reign.' The week's casualties from the East African Theatre, it takes me some time to realise they mean battleground. Next of kin have been informed. Julius Nyerere's appeal against his death sentence is to be heard in two days' time.

But I have another life to lead. The London Film Academy, a musky warehouse deep in the heart of Covent Garden, cockles and mussels, the bustle of the fruit and veg market, articulated lorries jacknifed round narrow alleyways, crates of exotic fruit from all corners of the Empire trundled round the busy malls, and in the building, two hundred rampaging egos ricocheting off the dark walls, budding Eisensteins or Pabsts or Cecil B. de Milles. Posters of the classic lost stars livening the English gloom: Garbo as she was in *Queen Christina*, Clark Gable in *Okinawa*, Bogey in *Algiers*, as well as colourful splashes of the British cinema's more recent hits (mostly directed by Italian exiles): Fellini's gargantuan *Los Angeles*, Antonioni's odd *Sunset*.

The two studios, the cutting rooms, lecture halls and cinema echoed and pulsated to the dreams of the age. The Principal, one Patrick Kinross, a large florid-faced and side-whiskered old gentleman, like Mister Pickwick come alive, presided, with his German wife Matilda ('the velvet fist in the iron glove'), and his crew of 'resting' local technicians, the slightly older cream of Denham and Elstree, over a battleground of competing cliques: most prominent, inevitably, the 'Hollybrooders' – striving to reconstruct, in short cameos, that old destroyed glory, before Flight Lieutenant Mishima, of the Imperial Air Force, glimpsed the target point of the Hollywood Bowl in his sights and, commending his soul to his ancestors, divebombed to nuclear superstardom. (See Michael Powell's strange epic *Banzai!*, which so enraged my countrymen . . .) Time stopped for these nostalgia freaks on February 4, 1952. Anything after that is just decline. So here too, as in Boston and Portland and New Hollywood, the student studios sprout ornate boudoirs. Mexican bars and haciendas, filled with costumes and props from the cellars of Old Times Incorporated, the pages of *Spotlight* scoured for those coveted lookalikes of the martyred Bogart, Grant, Bette Davis, Joan Crawford, Jimmy Cagney or Gary Cooper. The strong whiff of necrophilia, from which I thought I had escaped . . .

No. There's always this tyranny of the past, as well as that of false futures . . . But who am I to know? I have committed my own quota of sins in this regard: marching up Columbus Avenue calling for the International of World Workers, as well as the Impeachment of Richard Nixon (not a hope in hell there . . .) But this is a new breeding ground of political dissent: the declining Empire, rotting at the core, with new shoots growing on its margins – clique number two: the Politicals, climbing up and down the stairs of the Film Academy carrying old breech-loading rifles, ammunition belts and sachets of Max Factor blood to reconstruct the last stand of Fidel Castro in the streets of Havana. Forgotten mazurkas of the Polish Civil War echoing from the sound-recording rooms. Rosa Luxemburg and Trotsky, rehearsing their historic clash at the Seventh Comintern (1925), clomping about beetlebrowed, darting baleful glances at the adventurist riffraff in the coffee bar. The whiff of grapeshot from the London streets and campuses invading even this den of mirages, as little huddles over rusted film can lids splodged with cigarette butts and congealed sandwiches earnestly recycle the war, and two Greek students with eight o'clock shadow battle to convince a tall, gangling dark-haired colonial who seems to be a co-ethnic of mine (do we smell each other out?!) of the virtues of commitment and Theory:

'You are always putting down people who try to change things. Your attitude is like that suburban stockbroker who says, "The whole world can go to hell as long as I get my cup of tea." '

'I've nothing against people trying to change things . . . I just don't see the point of all this jargon . . .'

'You can take theory as a holy gospel. That's for sure nonsense. But you have to see the reality behind the analysis, the content, not the form. You look at the shell and reject it. Maybe you are just too lazy to look any deeper . . .'

'I've seen enough shells I can tell you. I've filmed enough dead bodies to know . . .'

'What you were doing in Palestine was simply to be a tool of authority. What control did you have as a newsreel cameraman of the material you shot? Nothing. Of course, is your own choice. You can sell your life to the highest bidder, or you can try to decide yourself what is right and what is wrong . . .'

The loud Mediterranean tones. Clashing certainties. High moral plateaus and low tolerances. What have I done to deserve this? Is there no way out of this frenzy? O.K., Rachel, just settle down, fraternize, just drift, again, with the wind . . .

Michael

The girl sat down beside me and said, 'I see you have the paranoid's watch strap.' Obviously spotting the leather watch cover special to our embattled Palestine, a legacy, I think, of Great War soldiers, used to keep away the muck and bullets. The time is always concealed, to give that frisson of discovery as you snap the cover back . . .

Later she said to me, 'I saw you sitting there in the coffee bar with that air of suspicion I remember from Palestinian Jews: you know, that fear of the gentile world mixed with disappointment that it's not fulfilling its pogromist image. The Zionist schizophrenia.'

I looked terrible, she revealed, which was not new to me. I had a ring around the collar and I hadn't shaved for three days. And she thought I was a Zionist, talk of auspicious starts. I had no chance. I could see she was attracted to Christos. He hadn't shaved for five days, and had Saturn rings round his collar, but a true oppressed *goyisch* firebrand. The Greeks had been trying since our first day here to convert me to the Cause – yet another Cause, they line up in threes, just waiting till you let your guard down – foisting on me books I had to read, not only Papa Marx but the German sage Marcuse, the usual Trotsky, Rosa, Sosnovsky, Mandel and other retailers of eleven-ton words. The 'Third Worldists' – Nkrumah, Kenyatta, Senghor, Nasser, all the anti-colonial dither. Preaching to me about joint Arab-Jewish Struggle against the British in Palestine. I told them they were naive. They think nationalism and progress go hand in hand. A *shoine metsiyeh*. They want me to march, shout, participate . . .

Ah! But where are these golden-haired *shiksas* they promised me in the homeland? Tales of the New Permissiveness said to be rife in the world out there: sex, drugs and collapse of social mores, the tempting spices in the sauce of Abroad. But the white cliffs of Dover loomed icy in a bitter January morning, behind the choppy grey sea, and the purgatory of the shabby bed-sitting rooms in Kilburn, landlords and landladies gnarled by decades of sexual restraint, the grey anonymity of those endless suburbs, the darkness at noon, the rusting Ascot gas burners, the shilling in the meter, lumpy cold beds. Aaaccchhh! Where are these warm gentile cunts?? Wrapped in padded capes and navy surplus greatcoats, they thrust past like the prows of dreadnoughts, bearing Warning Keep Off signs.

Come the Revolution!? Commiserating, as acquaintance ripens, with Rachel (up to the point which seems always out of hand) across the Thames along the southern embankment towards the National Film Theatre. (The Thirties in Soviet Germany: Fritz Lang's *November*, Murnau's *Wir Sind Spartakusten*, Pabst's *Liebknecht In Autumn*, Brecht's *Berlin Kommune.*) And Rachel softly explaining, 'I can't afford to be involved, really, with more Jewish angst. I had my bellyful in the kibbutz, enough said . . . Why can't you just realise you're now elsewhere, that you can make a fresh start? Just look around you. All sorts of things are happening. There are new ideas in the air.'

Ideas?! That's ten a penny. Give me flesh on flesh any time. Greek Alex is a prime example of the decay too much thinking can cause. Wandering the streets of the city looking for second-hand truth in such unlikely places as Tooting Bec and Muswell Hill, and then consuming the musky fruits in the ravaged and peeling hole he and Christos inhabit in Westbourne park, a sort of doss house presided over by a limping Irish landlady, Mrs Dunwoody. The sign on her door says 'No Coloureds', a distasteful but legal caveat, demonstrating that, though she had sunk far, she wanted to point out she had not yet hit bottom. Sheltering helplessly behind this shame the two Greeks share their cigarette papers and Old Holborn and waffle on about the Struggle: 'London – it's the world's clearing house.' (Thus Alex.) 'Understand the dialectic of England and you can see how the Empire is maintained. Watch how they jealously guard to themselves the freedoms they deny to others. Whatever pitiful crumbs of those freedom fall to us, we can use them, without guilt, to help, in our own modest way, the screwed, the oppressed, the silenced. To use the Knowledge you can gain here to turn the whole cart over.'

With torn underwear? And two mussed shirts? Ah, but the mind, the mind! Christos taps his kop with his finger. I am sure now that he is stupping Rachel, though where this takes place I cannot say. Certainly not here, in this rathole, with Mrs Dunwoody's complement of impoverished Greek and Albanian students, not to speak of the doubled-up Scots fluteplayers on a downward drift. Their melancholy lilt carrying on into the small hours putting off the hottest trot. No, it must be Finsbury Park, where Rachel's L.S.E. hosts bless these snatched moments of coital bliss in the revolutionary van . . . This is not getting me anywhere . . . as I trudge on my long walks away from the balm of the National Film Theatre's late shows (Pasolini's *Joseph Smith*, Fellini's *Manhattan*), nudging away, but nevertheless not quite able to cut the umbilical cord to the Homeland, the mad brawls of my so called patrimony as reported in the surreptitiously procured *Jewish Chronicle*:

TERRORIST BOMB AT MA'ALEH HAHAMISHA

FEDERAL GOV'T REFUSES BEGIN RETURN: THE STRUGGLE CONTINUES, IRGUN CHIEF SAYS IN ROME

EMPTY THREATS FROM NAZARETH: George Habash, newly elected Arab Council Head, re-affirms Arab claim to all of Palestine

God help us . . . it's clear to me that none of this amounts to a hill of beans in the long, dreary saga of Man's Essential Loneliness in the Universe, dragging up from the Embankment round the closed Covent Garden stalls, up Tottenham Court Road and the Royal Festival Tower, skirting Princess Elizabeth Park, up Saint John's Wood, Swiss Cottage and the Finchley Road, the unutilised Pinsker penis rustling in Marks and Spencer underwear, wondering when it might next make contact . . . The long dark night of the groin . . . Through lighted windows, one can perceive these archetypal English families, settled round their colour tellies, watching *What's My Line* or *Huggie Buggie*, or zapping themselves to sleep with *Hugh Gaitskell's World of Politics* (garn!), comfortably mired in the Edwardian Age . . . Naah! That's surely not for me.

Well, then. If you can't beat 'em, join 'em. Where are all the broken hymens, comrades? Bring on the next demo, brothers!!

Alex

Shallowness. That's always the first problem in trying to motivate change. The wish to see nothing but the surface. Just the top tenth of the iceberg. And how can one expect otherwise? For fifty years since the Great War no great event has managed to break this neat hierarchical 'stability' . . . Britons Never Shall Be Slaves. So say all the pundits, the chaps in the know, from *The Times* to the *Telegraph*, the *Daily Expresses, Sketches, Mails*, the *Sunday Pictorial* and the *Illustrated London News*. No crisis, just the usual pinpricks of subversion in the colonies – the New Commonwealth to you, squire! The natives would cool down sharp, if it weren't for those damn Bolsheviks . . . And people consume the pap of the press and the blithe bromides of the Royal Broadcasting Corporation and its insidious twin, the Commonwealth Service. Their children devour the jingoistic comics like *Eagle, Lion, Condor* et al, extolling the White Man's Burden and even carrying the Colonial ideal into outer space . . . Lulled to sleep by a language of lies. 'The smooth transition of Empire to Commonwealth', 'autonomous governments and dominions', 'the training of new native elites'. The rest is Red Propaganda, disseminated from Moscow and Berlin. Nkrumah, Nyerere, Nasser, Kenyatta, all Soviet stooges. How could it be otherwise?

And still, under the calm assurances of P.M. George Brown (after all, who could accuse a Labour government of actually stepping up repression?), the growing unease: The increasing voices against universal conscription, the flow of coffins shipped in from Asia and Africa that can't be totally swept off the T.V. screen, the increasing boldness of the student movement. I can hear it in the streets, on the tubes and buses, ordinary men and women of the lower middle classes, the backbone of British Patriotism, mumbling in new tones, 'Don't blame the kids who don't want to get killed in the jungle . . . 'tisn't like the Great War now, is it? Leave the niggers to sort out their own problems, that's what I say.' Quite so.

So Christos and I become involved. As ingathered flotsam

of the Empire's outposts we can hardly ignore the gathering storm. And from the washing-up sinks of the Acropolis Taverna in Camden Town (five nights a week), the spectacles through which we gazed at our own England were not so rosy tinted . . . Out of the nexus of our own Greek exile groups, the shaky anti-Junta coalitions of Trotskyite, Luxemburgite and Anarchist groups, leafleting at the gates of tube stations, attending meetings in dingy halls, we branch out into the wider spheres of The Movement: Marching up and down Whitehall, calling for France Out of Indochina, Italy Out of East Africa, Britain Out of Ireland, Portugal Out of Southern Africa, Belgium Out of the Congo, the U.S. Out of everywhere else . . . The number of our enemies is quite breathtaking! Attending lectures on the Eastern Europe Dictatorships, Ulmanisite repression in Lithuania, the resurgent Anarchists in Russia, the German Marcusian Dissidents . . . The slogans becoming, at times, so jumbled we feel we're being swept on an inexorable tide, a natural force over which we, nor any individual, had any power or control. Was this what both Trotsky and Rosa had written about – the sudden acceleration of history that precedes genuine revolutionary change? The upheaval that 'bursts the integuments asunder'? Are these the times we're living through?

Tensions rising, in a sticky English summer. May 1968. Christos and I finally convinced our term colleagues, Rachel and Michael, to devote our Film Academy exercise to the student rebellion. Humping our camera, tripod and sound equipment down the back of the market, we run the gauntlet of the police picket of Houghton Street to arrive at the battleground. Merging with the crowd of students and supporters just outside the main entrance, egged on from a soapbox by a wild-eyed Asian youth with a black moustache and a great mane of black hair. Slogans proclaiming SUPPORT THE L.S.E. OCCUPATION; NO SURRENDER! BRITISH HANDS OFF THE WORLD! and a caricature of P.M. Brown as a midget wrestler wielding a flamethrower against a black child. Inside, the corridors are filled to capacity with prone and moving shapes, students bedding down under mounds of blankets, rolled carpets, wrapped in gaudy banners. Poster-sized photographs on the walls of the heroes of the anti-colonial struggle – Ben Bella, Nkrumah, Nasser, Kenyatta, the martyred Fidel Castro. Makeshift flags of the liberation movements. The Russell Hall, renamed Jomo Kenyatta Hall, packed to the rafters with a motley, seething crowd: many students still in suits and ties, if dishevelled, others denimed and fashionably tattered, some still clinging sheets over their heads from the overnight occupation, some bare to the waist, sporting captured policemen's helmets, others in Arab-style *kufiyas* and African robes. Girls draped in towels, some with curlers in their hair, sit in the aisles with notebooks and pads. A number of grizzled elderly men and haggard women, off the streets in their worn clothes and reek of spirits, have taken advantage of this police-free enclave to abandon the besieged Embankment. On the podium speakers come and go, booming through capricious microphones. Clenched fists waving to applause. A hush descends as a bent, wispy figure clambers up to the stage, assisted on either side. He brushes his helpers away. Then overwhelming applause as the crowd realises who has slipped through the cordon to address them: reduced in size by old age, but the dark, aquiline face still as stark as ever, the boldness of implacable resistance – Jawaharlal Nehru, father of Indian Socialism, pushed out by the British when they handed 'independent' India to Subhas Chandra Bose . . . A living legend, he straightens up behind the microphone to convey his greetings to the new generation. 'The struggle goes on . . .' his quavering voice reverberates through the hall, 'the people will win, in the end . . .'

I struggle with Christos to thread the film in the magazine for Michael to shoot the scene in time, but inexperience lets us down – by the time we're ready, the man has walked back down the stairs, the magic moment linking the past, present and future is gone, the stage in front of us is bare . . .

Joseph Gable
Warsaw, June 10

Poland! One of the contagion's major sources! A center for the pollution of the world. If there is anywhere the Elders of Zion meet regularly it must be somewhere in this twisted rat's nest, this decadent antheap where they feel most at home. Black silk coats, dark brown asiatic headgear, beards straggling from coarse features – here they are, symbolising the reign of Chaos, the abyss forever yawning beneath our feet . . .

They are a more pugnacious breed here than even the black-garbed roaches of Jew York: as I descended the steps of Warsaw Central Station a hooknosed hawker thrust a Hebraic news-sheet in my face, addressing me in their vile jargon, that purloined mockery of the German tongue. To be mistaken for one of Them?! I was at the same time flattered and outraged. The old campaigner in me was amused to be so grossly misread, proof of the success of my cover, my ability to blend in with the crowd. But then revulsion overtook me as I elbowed the bug aside, tripping him on the wide steps. At the Hotel Koč I surprised myself by washing my hands so thoroughly I thought the skin would peel off. Such a gesture would be more typical of Adolf or of that mutt Streicher than myself. I must reject such emotionalism entirely. Hate and revulsion fuel the blood and produce insight, but the Planner must stand coldly, rationally, above himself, above the others who are mired in their compulsions.

Still, it is unsettling to see Nationalist Poland so overrun. One tenth of the population Jewish! Over three million maggots feeding on the rotten carcase of Slav sentimentalism! For let us not forget, it was the 'patriot' Pilsudski who 'emancipated' them after Independence . . . Nothing more clearly illustrates the rank stupidity and bankruptcy of the Sanacja and the Polish Estate in general.

June 15, Warsaw-Cracow by train:
. . . Stepanowski in the seat opposite. Uniform immaculate,

buttons polished. The Poles deify the superficial. It is a wonder they survived the Civil War with their cloud-cuckooland mentality. Cavalry was only phased out of their front-line posture in 1965! What a bunch of mutts.

Stepanowski's briefing on the domestic situation has revealed what I predicted: a dreadful mess. Never was there a so-called 'Government of Authority' with less control over events. Secessionism in the Kresy. Nationalism in Galicia. Volkisch revival in East Prussia. Anarchy elsewhere ('parliamentary democracy'). Good. The fruit seems truly ripe on the tree. Ten years of Pilsudski, twenty of Koč, and a decade of bumbling piss-artists are enough to befuddle any nation, let alone the Poles who start off with a mental disadvantage. The 'Little Colonel' Adam Koč! God how I despised that prick! A sucker-up to any pompadoured aristocrat who dangled some defunct or forged family tree before his eyes. His only claim to fame: the development of a new method of ruling by shutting himself in the bathroom whenever any crisis broke till it was resolved by his advisors. The 'Gourmet Leader'! Imagine the nation's commandant donning an apron to stew up a goulash in the Presidential kitchen! A true mirror of Polish childishness and irresponsibility.

The Polish State should never have existed in the first place. It was cobbled together merely to thrash Germany for her defeat in the Great War. And now the Polish flag flies, while Germany's lies trampled in the dust and muck of Bolshevism. Ironies of a cruel fate, which only those of iron will and patient dedication can reverse. Poland is useful now, as a tool, a weapon in the hand of reforged providence . . .

June 18, Oswiecim:
. . . An unprepossessing barracks of the Polish Third Army, outside a nondescript, ugly small town, set amid desolate marshes relieved here and there by wispy chestnut trees. Major Skorzeny has chosen this venue well. Out of sight, out of mind of the Polish High Command. Here we can sit and formulate strategy with little fear of infiltration and disturbance. Subject to Skorzeny's security . . .

As we arrived from Cracow, a personal messenger from Colonel Chmielnitski in Rome: the Duce, it appears, is fading fast.

Excellent news indeed! We have had false alarms before, but C.
assures me this time it is 'extremely likely' to be the real thing.
If this is so there'll be no doubt my trip here was timed by fate!
The bell now tolls for Benito Mussolini, History's Clown! About
time! At 85, he has strutted the stage far too long. Chmielnitski
wants me to consider an early trip to Rome, to join him at the
Rocca delle Caminate. To be in at the kill! Why not? (Adolf would
have gone like a shot; he always wanted to dance on Mussolini's
grave, not that he is much able to lift one leg after another these
days, even to piss . . .) Chmielnitski and the Wolf Corps, the
Duce's own praetorian guard, will be in the cyclone's eye . . .
Discuss with my command here a total extraction of all personnel
to this barracks. My personal leadership, at this delicate moment,
will be of paramount importance. With Mussolini going, Britain
and France embroiled around the globe, Moscow still infighting
over Trotsky's corpse, and the Berlin Luxists slumped over their
sauerbröten, Poland should be clay in the potter's hand . . .

As I write I feel the wings of History beating over me! I gaze
out the window of my simple soldier's quarters, west towards the
Polish-German frontier, transecting the Wisla River. The mist
hides the first signs of the border fortifications. Whenever I visit
this place I ponder the irony of being so near, yet so far, from
the Fatherland! How ironic that it was the Luxemburgists who
pushed the border east from Gleiwitz back in 1926 . . . In time
this portion of Silesia, too, will be regained for a Revived, Volkisch
Germany, purified of the Red Scum and of International Jewry.
Then this place, this insignificant pimple town of Oswiecim, will
find its place in the scrolls of History – it too, will return to the
Volk, and regain its true, German name of Auschwitz.

Ernesto
Lalibela, Abyssinia

Mid-June in the Ethiopian Highlands. The rains set in. Clouds appear to settle permanently on the mountain, disgorging a relentless downpour. The sky a steel grey. Safe weather for hiding and waiting, if for nothing else. I am here with Pier Paolo, his cameraman Ettore, and thirty guerrillas, in the shadow of the rock-hewn churches, once termed one of the world's seven wonders. Italian napalm scoured and blackened their millennial façades in 1946, but the guerrillas still come here to hide, oddly congruous with the gaunt priests who worship and guard the ancient site.

In the hollowed-out interior of Abba Libanos, by candlelight, Pier Paolo spends hours with his Marconi Recorder taking sound tapes of a shrunken old monk, translated by a local teacher whose Italian is in itself a subversion of the Empire: tales of the anti-fascist struggle merging with old battles fought hundreds and thousands of years before, going back to the Hebraic connection. From Solomon and Sheba to Zara Yakub, Teodoros and Ras Makonnen. In the evenings we sit together and talk through the twists and turns of our own strange fate. The Italian is thorough, he wants to recapture my own life and soul on his machine. He has a fascination with power, its capacity of alienation. Being Italian, he distrusts all hierarchies and authority, and worships a sort of instinctual spontaneity that I have found to be dangerous. He coaxes out of me reports of my meetings with Trotsky, with Thaelman and the daunting Ruth Fischer, elder stateswoman of the German Party. He agrees with me that Brandt is a welcome infusion of new blood into a bureaucratised movement, and tries to draw me out further than I would like about Heydrich, the appalling Minister of State Security. But I can buy him off with tales of Trotsky, the Old Lion never fails to fascinate . . . The time he whisked me off, duckhunting, of all things, at his vacation dacha on the Neva. He commented on my taking five birds to his three: 'Of course, you've had more experience, potting homo sapiens.' He told me tales he thought were highly amusing, about ex-Minister Kruschev, for example, who had a lake dammed so he could shoot more wildfowl like decoys at a fair. 'A faker like that. Always cutting corners. Of course, we had to put him up against the wall. Shoot enough people in authority, comrade, and you will not have to shoot the common man.'

He had that special affinity for me. 'Our hope,' he said, 'is in the younger revolutionaries of Asia, Africa, Latin America. We and the Germans have hardened arteries, if the Imperialists didn't hold us back by nuclear blackmail we'd find some other excuse to stand down. You, Ernesto Guevara, are on the agenda of history. I am already in its archive. Poor old Leon Bronstein, potting ducks off a boat. Soon I'll be wetting my pants in daylight while my good *tovarischi* measure my coffin. Why didn't he go early, like Lenin, they all whisper, behind my back. Marx had piles all his life. Rosa smoked herself to death and let the marionettes take over the theatre. We are all ridiculously mortal. Our only purpose is to be tools of History, used, and then thrown in the dustbin. Remember this, and you may die unbetrayed by yourself, the only betrayal that really matters . . .'

That was 1960, and only five months before the tragedy that engulfed Cuba . . . The miscalculation, the real betrayal that Trotsky was warning me about, but I, in the flush of revolutionary fervour, failed to come to grips with in time . . .

The pain, the pain of loss, the pain of grief, of the horrors witnessed, of the horrors experienced . . . There are some wounds that never heal . . . The poet Neruda, as always, articulates, speaking of another place, another time:

The broken smiles, the hearts gashed by fire . . .
The butcher's apron darkened in the sun . . .

July 12, 1960. The night the U.S. landing craft disgorged their troops upon the Playa de Giron and simultaneously marched from Guantanamo. Catching us transfixed by our hot wind of rhetoric, the 'certainty' of the Soviet aid which did not come, from either Russia or Germany.

And Fidel, Fidel who died in my arms . . . His clothes burned to shreds by a phosphorus bomb which had killed three of the men standing with us at the window of the Moncada, a submachine

50

gun in each hand, festooned with ammunition belts . . . His last words, as he leaned out to fire: 'The bastards! the bastards! the bastards!' The litany of rage, as the burst took him in the forehead, spinning him into my grasp . . . No, even in this, too, we were trapped by this Latinesque compassion . . . We knew the cities could not be held in a fullscale invasion, with the bombs of the B-57s raining death on Havana, Santiago, Santa Clara, Holguin, Camaguey . . . But with the people, peasants, workers, men, women, children, fighting the paratroopers hand to hand in the streets with everything they had, with machetes, spanners, crowbars, partisan cocktails, axes, picks, how could we sneak out to leave them to their grisly fate? We could not leave the people that legacy, that Fidel, Raul, Armando, Che, had run from the burning ship like rats. We could only leave them the example of our own deaths, our blood watering the roots of a long-lived resistance, of an ultimate rebirth . . . But in this too, an unwilled betrayal . . .

'So you survived,' says Pier Paolo. 'Is it an act of cowardice to live?'

To that I have no answer. That was an outcome I had not planned. I walked, for a long time, among corpses, a shadow in the burning city, ragged fighters springing up from nowhere, casting red-hot, jammed guns aside and snatching others from the dead. I read later, in a newspaper article, that I led the last remnants of the Fortress in a suicidal battle charge. I have no memory whatsoever of that. I do recall commandeering an abandoned Yankee tank, with a group of men I'd never seen before, and punching out into the countryside, continuing by foot through the burning night, eventually finding Osvaldo, organising once again in the mountains . . the Sierra Maestra, second time . . . the invader pressing us back relentlessly . . . bombs and noxious chemicals withering the forests, scorching the valleys . . . Men died in their thousands. I lived, untouched, till the flying shrapnel piece that caught me, and the nightmare stretcher journey, the decision to evacuate me taken against my will . . . the shame, repeated . . . the delirum, the burnt out face of Fidel, glowing in the Moncada's rubble . . . helicoptered out, at the orders of the guerrilla command, to the Dominican Republic, then to Caracas, then, in a German hospital plane – to Europe, and the cold days . . .

Neruda, once again:

> Do not look for me in this house,
> I am a stranger.
> There is no kiss of clear water,
> no cool breeze.
> Do not ask for my name,
> I have none.
> You may seek me in the pale wounds of the moon . . .

The wizened Ethiopian monk squats, watching me quizzically. What ancient wounds is he contemplating? Can one truly imagine the pain? Pier Paolo's machine has reached the end of its magnetic spool. It revolves softly, in the moonlight. We sit, silently, by the old stone churches, waiting, with the patience of the scarred.

Joseph Gable
Rocca delle Caminate, Romagna, Italy, July 20

At last! Mussolini on his deathbed! A truly pathetic sight. A wobbling mound of jelly beneath the silk sheets, wheezing like a beached whale. I cannot see his eyes – eyes, nose and mouth vanished in the flesh like currant sunk in a lump of dough. Even Hermann, as a fully fledged corpse, was more prepossessing than this. Doctor Shacht, perspiring over the cadaver soon to be, deserves the booby prize of the decade for keeping this decayed blancmange alive until this day. Extreme longevity is certainly not worth this excrescent fate. Cunt Ciano, the bald vulture, trembles on the edge of a bedside chair, mewling hypocritically into his lace pocket handkerchief. Bottai, Castellani and assorted servants and family survivors flutter in the background of the immense bedchamber like chickens waiting for the butcher's knife, while Wolf Corps guards and Ciano's OVRAs warily watch each other from their positions round the walls. Snuffles, moans and croaks befoul the air like so many baboons' farts. The Duce cannot even die without his passing being a *commedia dell'arte*. Under the façade of Leader, General, Emperor and Sage he was just another fat Italian spaghetti-swilling slob. And so he takes no glory with him to the grave, and leaves behind the full foul measure of his gross incontinence.

Tension is palpable throughout the corridors of the Castle. Closeted all evening with Chmielnicki and his most trusted aides, Piasec and Mannheim, we have reanalysed the Wolf Corps' true position. My decision to hurry here has been fully vindicated. The inner core (Chmielnicki, Rakosy, Stulpnagel), have been considering the immediate assassination of Ciano as soon as the Duce croaks. I have convinced C. of the strategic blunder such a course would be. We all know Duce, aping the Caesars, tied the Wolf Corps as praetorian guard to him alone by isolating them from any other power. As a mixed bag of German, Austrian, Polish and Hungarians they would be lost in post-Duce Italy. On the other hand Ciano, while controlling his secret police, the OVRA, cannot liquidate the Wolf Corps overnight. Bearing in mind the Plan and Camp Auschwitz, the following should be our policy: the Wolf Corps to declare its loyalty to Cunt Ciano as Duce's heir. This will confuse the enemy and buy time, so it can withdraw intact, as it must, or face defeat in the face of OVRA's numbers, and become confused and weakened with the Cunt's regime. Ciano, for sure, will give in to Liberal pressures that will ensure his undoing. Fascism cannot compromise. It must stand firm or perish.

Chmielnicki sees immediately this is the right course. This man is no fool. With his granite looks and snow-white hair, like a Prussian of the old school, he appears a formidable ally. Perhaps too formidable? A risk one has to take. God save me from more milksops, from more compulsive, sexually decayed Dixiecrats. The worldwide phase is now upon us, and we need finely forged tools . . .

July 13, 03:00:
My telephone rings. C's voice announces: Shacht has pronounced the Duce dead. Oh, blissful moment! To have lived to see this day! Goodbye, past era! Welcome – the birth pangs of a brave, new world!!

Part III
Baptism of Fire
October 1968–May 1969

Extract from *Terror Campaign 1961*, by Rachel Levy

October 1961: America, lost in the wilderness . . . what are these pangs, injured patriotism? Rachel, beware! And yet it is as if a beloved friend, feckless and infuriating but very close, lies gasping and retching in the terminal ward. After a dozen straight-faced interviews with lunatics, fanatics and assorted scoundrels it's a relief to water at the home of Dick and Rosie Smith of Dothan, Alabama. The Smiths are practically all that remains of the Democratic Party in Dothan, just about the sole dissenters from the mass stampede to Hitler. Certainly not the way to endear oneself to the good burghers of Dothan: every Sunday Dick has to saunter out with bucket and paint to cover over the week's quota of swastikas, crosses and epithets such as 'nigger cocksuckers', 'jew assfuckers go home' and 'red slime back to Washington'.(!!)

'It's going to be all right,' Dick reiterates, against all the odds, 'there's no way a Third Party ticket can make it. This madness will stop right here.' He trots out his political manuals and almanacs, reassuring himself in the inexorability of Election statistics:

'Millard Fillmore, 1856; La Follette, 1921; Huey Long, 1935; Thurmond, 1948 . . . none of them made it. You can't beat the system. This is a storm that will pass, and we'll be here to pick up the pieces when the people wake up . . .'

You better believe it. If you are that strange, practically extinct animal, a Southern liberal Democrat, an Adlai Stevenson man in the heartland of Rudy Hitler . . . No wildlife conservation here! This is gun country – Niggers, Jews and raccoons watch out!

The television is in the Smiths' cosy living room (bookshelves of Faulkner, Steinbeck, Walt Whitman, Thoreau, de Toqueville, Dewey, Emerson, Palmer, the well in the oasis . . .), purveying, between Coors Beer and ring-around-the-collar, the latest campaign grand guignol: the FBI are worried about the disappearance of eight operatives in Louisiana. Eternal Cronkite speaks. Hoover is, it seems, livid. Is the South becoming an independent fiefdom, shades of the Confederacy? Democratic Party Headquarters burned to the ground in six towns simultaneously. A Sheriff Lynch (I don't believe it!) in Birmingham is interviewed. A Communist conspiracy, he says, a provocation to stir up trouble. Communists, in Birmingham? Even Republicans are run out of that town on rails . . . Three black men said to be members of the Reverend King's Freedom Alliance hanged in Mississippi. A Democratic Candidate tarred and feathered in Decatur. The Confederate Flag and the Swastika flying side by side in Yazoo City. Fresh horrors for old. Last week it was burning homes in Tuskegee, and the trainload of Atlanta's Jews shipping north out of the tornado's path . . .

'They'll take the Deep South,' says Dick Smith, 'and maybe Virginia, the Carolinas, Tennessee . . . But they'll be nowhere where it counts, in the industrial states . . .'

'What about Texas and California?' Rosie puts in. 'Those are huge blocks of votes . . .'

'They won't make it there. All they'll do is help massacre Stevenson. It's gonna be Nixon, four more years.'

'God help us!'

'The lesser evil, honey . . .'

The Lesser Evil appears on the TV screen, urging calm. A speech that is all that's needed to make people really panic. Fistfights reported in the House. Hysteria on Capitol Hill. The North is throwing up its arms in horror, while in the South the Klan and American Party Storm Troopers roam unchecked. Over it all the ghost of Tail-Gunner Joe McCarthy shrieks with dead mocking laughter. We fools, who thought there could be nothing worse than those five years of Clown Rule. The terrible trauma of the Pacific War and its climax, the devastated West Coast, the recriminations, the search for scapegoats, spies and traitors, the Washington Show Trials, the execution of Alger Hiss . . . How relieved we were when Vice-President Nixon took over on Joe's boozy demise. (Until Cuba . . .) McCarthy's madness seemed to have been curbed by his own Party. But Hitler's? The old saw of Yeats's poem: Things fall apart, and what rough beast, etcetera . . . ? The Exalted Cyclops, the King Kleagles of the Klan, the need to hide their faces gone, throw their hoods back, basking in the glow of the fires, the Invisible Empire made visible in all its dread brutality. In gutted Tuskegee, reclaimed for the White

Race, the elder Senator Hitler harangues the Party faithful in their brown uniforms and Sam Browne belts. Small but erect, the snow-white cowslick brushed to one side, his sharp words drowned in the rising cheer of Victory Approaching . . . In New Hollywood, built on the ruins of the old, his puppet son speaks to fifty thousand in the New Hollywood Bowl. And facing that mass? the Dick and Rosie Smiths, the decimated Civil Rightists to be, the sainted courage of a Martin Luther King . . .

Reeds in a hurricane. But didn't a Chinese General once say: the reed bends but does not break? After the loosing of the madmen, the voice of that all too human courage would not go amiss. 'An interview with the Reverend King?' Dick says, aghast. 'You'll blow your cover wide open. The man is under siege, in Montgomery, that's Wallace Country, Goddamit!'

But can I tear myself away from the fear? Can I go back into that den? Calm the chattering of my teeth, smooth my goosepimples, take my guts in both hands and plunge back into the fire? Is such an act of faith possible?

Calvinetti, Giuseppe, Major
Semien Province, Abyssinia, October 1968

The landscape could almost be that of another planet. Blue rocky buttes thrust into the sky, lava slabs cut into mountainsides like layers of a sombre cake, great gorges and ravines dropping into inky valleys. Here and there, on a plateau, a hint of thin grass, cut short by a great drop into yet another chasm. Not a sign of life from the air. If I were my younger, religious self, I would have said: God is alone with His Creation. But appearances can be misleading.

Of course, it is not silent. The howl and clatter of the chopper's blades carrying us deeper into the heartland . . . though I walk through the valley of the shadow of death, I will fear evil, because I have carried evil into this valley on so many routine missions . . .

Are You On The Right Path? I remember those letters, printed high on crumbling posters of the nineteen-forties, my childhood . . . Thrift, Sacrifice, Steadfastness could defeat both the Depression and the Greeks. Thus saith the Duce, glaring from every wall and parapet, from every billboard and pissoir. How I used to fear those staring eyes, those thick jowls, the bald crown, the blubbery lips. Ironic, that to defeat that fear, I signed up for the Duce's Army. Another urchin trying to hide his poverty of mind behind a neatly pressed uniform. Lucky that my father, a secret reader of Gramsci, would have cut my balls off if I'd donned the Fascist black. Khaki was dark enough for him . . .

Honour. Duty. Faith. Pregnant words, aborted by life's reality. I remember the time I returned from my first Colonial tour: I reached Milano Centrale at six thirty in the morning. A dour autumn day. Drizzling rain. The city seemed clad in mourning. I had not slept on the train. I had not slept on the transport plane from Tripoli. None of the returning soldiers had. They had tried to perform the role of homecoming warriors, exchanging gruesome nigger jokes, boasting of the scores they would rack up with the girls, puffing adolescently on Ras cigarettes. Their laughter was more of hysteria than joy. They were almost all nineteen or twenty years old. I was twenty-one. I had never slept with a girl I had not paid. I had not slept with a white girl. Few of us had. Our innocence had been gouged out with bayonets.

I took a streetcar to Santa Sofia and walked from there. I could somehow not bring myself to go straight home. To have my mother's tears over the butcher's uniform. At the corner of Ariberto and Crespi I turned into the church. I was long past my religious phase, then. I just sat in the back of the church, watching the sacristan prepare his act, as the devout, mostly middle-aged women, began trickling in. I looked up at the man on the cross. From a distance, in the warp of my fatigue, and the cold grey shadows, his features seemed to be Abyssinian. I was suddenly seized with an inexplicable terror and ran out, across the two avenues into the Parco Solari, where I stood, in a daze, letting the rain drench me through.

The same terror that returns to me now, as I hurtle, like a loose cannonball, over the primal Semien Range. The old terror of meeting the Accuser. The fear of Judgment – not of priests, not of judges, not even of my father, dead not long after in a quiet despair while the vast bloated spider still crawled in its web at the Palazzo Venezia . . .

Seeking penance. Penance, for our cowardice in acting too late. The cowardice, that let us be used, year after year, tour after tour, squeezed to the last drop in the service of a barbaric cause . . .

'Ras Dashen!' The pilot points ahead. There it lies, a ridge of rock with one escarpment higher than the rest, Abyssinia's Everest. The last place you would hope to find a human way out of this misery. The helicopter veers east, losing height, skimming the peaks. 'There!' Captain Spinetti, till now silent behind me, points. A rocky cleft in the mountainside. I consult my map briefly, tapping the pilot, who, with the maniacal grin of chopperboys, hurls the machine towards the gap.

Entering, between the peaks, a bleak valley, widening into a plateau strewn with volcanic rocks. Signs of life here: Mules grazing on sparse grass, peasant tukuls dotted here and there, the telltale glint of metal in the rockface. Anti-aircraft guns. If we were not expected guests, we realise, we would never have made it through the gorge.

The plateau more open. Nothing hidden now. Five barrack

huts down below, surrounded by a large number of tukuls, a virtual village, with gun emplacements, trenches and a barricaded fence. In the enclosure's center a long flagpole flies the black-white-red tricolour.

We fire a flare. A flare answers. Dozens of figures pour out from the rocks, many in khaki battledress, as many others in the white distinctive highland shammas. The pilot, 'Mad' Vincente, sets the chopper down gently just outside the fence. The three of us, Spinetti, Vincente and I, disembark, struck by the eerie silence that falls as the rotors come to rest. Ebony faces stare at us impassively, surrounding us like rats in a trap. The eyes wide and unblinking, whites flecked with yellow. Eyes I cannot read. Sounds fade in now to replace the chopper's thunder – the faint shuffle of feet, the quick guttural calls to comrades still hidden in the rocks, the clatter of rifles dragged across stone. From the tukuls, the sudden wail of a child. The sound of two hundred breaths, rising and falling. The flap flap of shammas in the wind.

A disturbance in the ranks. Several figures emerge from one of the huts, the guerrillas let them through. Six Ethiopian men and two women, engulfed in battledress with black berets, all except one: the foremost, clad in a faded shamma robe. His hair a white stubble, his face pitted as the lava rock around him. He is the only one of them not wearing dark glasses. He has no need to. He is blind, the gleaming empty whites defying the burning sun. The last time I saw this face, I recall wryly, was on a wanted poster on a Gondar office wall. Here he is, the ironically named Mebrahtu Walda Sion – Light, Son of Zion – field commander of the Ethiopian Resistance.

Shall I fall at your feet, old man? Father, forgive me, for I have sinned? I have slaughtered your children, scattered your flocks, burned your houses and fields, desecrated your holy places, laid waste your country, ground your people in the dust. I know you well. You are, without a doubt, the face on my cross, the terror of my autumn days . . .

'Major Giuseppe Calvinetti, I presume?' Speaking perfect Italian, with dry humour. Walda Sion is no mountain sorcerer, but a graduate of Oxford University (First in Economics), a Trotskyist Marxist of the old school. 'Come.'

He leads us into the largest hut, set out with a bare table and a dozen rickety chairs like those of a provincial restaurant, with a lone man rising towards us as we enter. This one, an unexpected sight, if familiar – another poster face come to life. The famous shoulder-length hair, now streaked grey, the fringe beard and moustache grey too, the face lined, scarred and gaunt under the tan. A rough-hewn, nervous glitter as he appraises us like sides of beef. The large cigar, true to the image, clamped in his mouth, as if specially produced to impress us. A long-sleeved nondescript khaki shirt draped loose over baggy pants. The day for living legends. Doctor Guevara I presume?

We sit, awkwardly facing each other. An orderly brings a carafe of water, and grimy, chipped glasses. What do mortal enemies say to each other, after thirty years of carnage? What has the coloniser to say to the colonised after decades of repression? Sorry, comrades, it was all a ghastly mistake, let's just shake hands and no hard feelings? The eight Ethiopians gaze at us impassively. We three fiddle with our flight jackets. The incongruity of a historic moment.

The blind man breaks the silence.

'Good, Major. We requested this meeting as a gesture of your commitment. Let us now waste no time treading around the issue like cats looking for a place to shit. You represent what you call the Armed Forces Action group founded in nineteen sixty-one by Brigadier-General Amendola, at that time as a reformist group merely demanding the rationalisation of colonial policy, an appeal to the Duce's "finer instincts". So fine that three months later General Amendola was found in a ditch, battered to death with iron poles.

'Next we find your movement in sixty-three. Colonels Andreotti, Spezzo, Tiano. The Duce is taking too long to die. The pay is lousy. The Colonial Administration is corrupt and the wars are being lost. Never the less, the Army, as is its wont, continues to do its job, the nature of which you know as well as I.

'Then the Duce dies. Ciano takes over. Power games. The Duce's Wolf Corps fades away, who knows where. OVRA controls the State. But OVRA is infiltrated by American and British Intellience. They have their own ideas for Ethiopia and Somaliland. They have a puppet king, Haile Selassie. The Lion of Judah, to be re-enthroned under a British-Italian condominium.

Feudalism is to replace Colonialism. An innovation in social progress, no? But the rebellious natives will have none of it. Those savages continue fighting their selfish war for dignity, humanity, socialism. The Italian Army goes on bleeding, and now for what? Their officers know they are beaten. Confined to the central towns, the countryside lost. The Italian Empire is going down the drain, and Italy with it, starved of money, her economy ruined. Just the same as the poor Belgians and Portuguese. Doomed to a second-rate existence.

'Disillusioned with the war and with Fascism, the Army is riddled with subversive cells: Christian Democrats, Social Democrats, Socialists, Communists, Anarchists. As a fighting force it has one remaining card: air power. The capacity to bomb and strafe and kill as many niggers far from base as its fuel allows. But alas, there are twenty million of the blackamoors to be dealt with, organised, war wise, niggers who can now scent victory.

'So, Major Calvinetti, we are not in a position of give and take here. Our people have given everything for far too long. Now we are interested in taking. We know we can win. But we also know it will yet be bloody. There is only one offer you can make that can interest us, and that can save lives on both sides.

'Surgery at the heart, Major. A coup d'etat in Rome, followed by the immediate ceding of independence for Ethiopia, Somaliland and Libya. Rid yourselves and us of this putrid gangrene of Fascism.'

Silence falls around the table. I gaze at my hands, then at my two colleagues, then back across the table at the blind man, and the ember eyes of Guevara.

'Yes,' I reply, 'I can tell you that we have reached the same conclusion.'

Chmielnicki, Ignacy, Colonel
Oswiecim, Poland, October 12

I watch the old man climb up the steps of the outpost with wry admiration. The flesh may be weak and limping, but the spirit? Will I be as spry and vigorous, as full of schemes and stratagems, at the age of seventy-one? But combat soldiers can hardly count on getting so far down the line. Joseph Gable might outlast me yet, and knowing him, dance on my grave. Or at least climb over my tombstone to his further destiny . . .

I follow him to the top, standing by him as he gazes, raincoat flapping in the wind, through his Zeiss binoculars (manufactured in Red Dusseldorf) past the triple fences, watchtowers and barbed wire of the border, at No-Mans-Land, blurred in the fog: the jagged treestumps, lumps of twisted, rusted metal of armoured trucks and tanks littering the flat reed-grown marshes hiding the River Wisla. A dead landscape, frozen in time at the end of the Polish Civil War. 1926, a burning memory, the end of the first hopes of Soviet Germany's collapse . . . I know what the old man sees through his lenses: looming, in the furthest distance, like gothic dark castles, the barbed watchtowers of the Enemy.

To him it is Gog and Magog. The War of the Sons of Light with the Sons of Darkness. What lies out there to him is a pure evil, a plague which has thrown the German people into a comatose state, hypnotised them into obedience to an alien creed. A sleeping beauty, waiting for Prince Joseph and Adolf to wake her with their kiss.

Romanticism. Not for me. I am a weapon, choosing to be wielded by the right hands. I like to draw the parallel with my historical namesake, Bogdan, who led the peasantry in 1648 to burn the chateaux of the noblemen, the priests and the Jews. Like him, I am a class traitor, a turned member of the small gentry. I too, dabbled in my rebellion, my 'Officers' Plot', my own attempts to burn the *szlachta* to the ground (attempted overthrow of Adam Koč, 1946 – a young man's hot-blooded fancy, and from that setback, to Rome . . .). The Duce understood this symptom, this contempt for bourgeois decay. 'Only strangers can be trusted completely,' he said, appointing me his Guard Commander. Good, if bloody years: strangling counter-revolution in its cradle, by knife, garotte, or just bare hands. Simpler choices, those days . . .

The old man climbs down from his lookout, gathering his coat against the bitter wind. I follow. He snaps a look at his wristwatch.

'About time, is it not?'

I gesture for the jeep to draw up. His limp, despite so many American operations, still gives him that lopsided look, which, I recall, repelled me when I first saw him, at the Rocca delle Caminate. At that time he appeared simply as the American Senator Hitler's messenger to the Duce's Anti-Communist Alliance (1954?). But when we talked, I realised here was an intellect head and shoulders above the mob. A man with a vision far more compelling than Mussolini's corner store . . . But that was long ago . . . The fiasco of 1961 cost us years of stagnation. And perhaps I was at fault as well. Perhaps I was wrong in the only condition I set for our alliance – that I would keep the Duce alive. A deal's a deal. There must be honour, somewhere. But now the waiting game is done . . .

Gable is sunk in thought in the jeep as I drive him towards the barrack huts of Camp Auschwitz proper. As we come up to the gate he turns to me sharply.

'Keep an eye on Skorzeny. The man has putschist tendencies. At the first sign of impending trouble – kill him.'

He strides in briskly to the admin block, taking his place at the head of the table without even a nod to the officers already seated around it. Skorzeny, Rakosy, Stulpnagel, Piasec, Stepanowski, Istevan, Slawek, Poniatowski, Tykhonov, Grant. Six Wolf Corps, four Polish insiders. Seeds of conflict, which Skorzeny might try to exploit. But I can handle palace intrigues . . . I give my attention to our Commander as he delivers his briefing in that low, seductive voice, reviewing the balance of forces, assessing the aftermath of Mussolini, evaluating the conflicts to come:

'. . . this base becoming fully operational . . . Phase Siegfried to commence forthwith . . . units under Poniatowski and Tykhonov to operate in the Eastern Kresy, units under Piasec and Slawek in Galicia . . . a nice constant simmer, if you please, gentlemen, we are performing delicate surgery here, not butchery . . . Stepanowski to maintain contacts with Warsawski in the High Command . . . Colonel Chmielnicki to have sole authority over co-ordination and internal security . . . He speaks for me and is answerable to me alone.'

Stony faces. No personal cards revealed. Security and trust are antithetical. This is a game of multiple chess in which only Gable sees all the boards. Skorzeny wears his usual mask of amused innocence. Gable delivers his peroration:

'Comrades, we who are gathered here today are not a company bound by outworn obligations to kings, parliaments or constitutions. Nor are we soldiers of fortune seduced by adventure or gold. We are a band of brothers, loyal to a higher ideal, to our heritage as the vessels of Destiny. It is our actions which will determine History, and decide whether the low or the excellent will inherit the earth. Against the false "enlightenment" of the Enemy, we are the truly Enlightened. In the heat of battle, in the frustration of waiting and inactivity, when we are tempted to bicker over selfish material interests, let us all remember The Goal. Comrades, I ask you to rise for one moment of silence in order to honour those of our brothers who have given their lives for the Cause since the founding of our glorious Party in the year 1919.'

All rise to their feet, standing to attention in the light of bare lightbulbs. The low hum of the camp generator can be heard from outside, along with sporadic shots from the shooting range, the rattling of windowpanes in the wind, the faint creaking of the hut's woodwork, the far whistle of the Oswiecim train coming into the adjacent town's railway station. Then the toast:

'Sieg!'

'Heil!'

Eleven arms rise stiffly in salute.

In the morning I drive Joseph Gable out the camp gate. The Polish guard not even bothering to salute. This is, after all, just a forgotten border garrison, innocuously processing routine. All quiet on the Silesian Front, that is all that Warsaw needs to hear. We rattle down the obligatory Pilsudskiego into the town, past the rows of cheerless three-storey Polish houses, their rooftiles grimy with the chemical plant's smoke. The Civil War put a stop decades ago to plans to make Oswiecim an industrial center. Now it is stagnant, no past, no present, no future. The railway station a provincial stop, a gravelled square flanked by dilapidated chestnut trees. A faded sign proclaiming 'Oswiecim, No Spitting, No Littering.' Apart from Joseph Gable only an elderly couple and a fat shawled woman with a silent child on her lap are waiting for the Cracow train. The ancient locomotive puffs laboriously into the station. Gable offers me his hand in a firm handshake, our eyes lock briefly in mutual knowledge. 'I will call for you when the time comes,' he says. Then, bearing his small battered suitcase he steps stiffly aboard, ignoring the old station porter's helping hand. I stand watching for a while as the train huffs out of the station, bearing Joseph Gable on the first lap of his journey home, back across the world, to America . . .

Dear Adolf,

What is happening here in Poland is *important*. I am not neglecting the home front, as you suggest. But we are riding a very different horse now than the one which threw us in '61. All we need to do is *keep our nerve*! Let us not let old animosities and mistrusts foil us now, when we have entered the decisive phase.

Italy remains unchanged, but it is the calm before the storm. Watch this space! As for Chmielnicki, I am quite satisfied his mother's Aryan genes are dominant over his father's weak Polish blood. When gold is struck, only a fool rejects it. I wish you were not so obsessed on this score.

I am glad you stopped taking Mengele's concoctions. That man's a quack. I told you that long ago. You could have spared yourself much pain and discomfort. But you *will* go your own way. Just hold on, for all our sakes. Your example is much needed now. For the moment, a mere twelve acres of a dingy Polish barracks are our only tract of Liberated Soil. But not for long! We will move onwards and upwards. Give my love to Annchen.

Yours,
Joseph

RBC One News
London, March 5

Logo: the Crown and Union Jack.

Announcer: 'This is the Nine O'Clock News, read by Richard Baker. Good evening. Revolution in Italy. We have the first newsfilm from Rome.

'Here in Great Britain, Prime Minister Maudling calls the cabinet to an emergency meeting at Chequers. The King has cancelled his appearance at the Royal Horse Show. A spokesman for Buckingham Palace says there is no cause for alarm at the state of His Majesty's health. The Princesses Martha, Margaret and Elizabeth are at his side in Sandringham.

'Expeditionary Forces casualty figures, released today, show a slight increase on last week's figures, though the number of seriously injured has fallen. This reflects, the War Office says, the new offensives in the West African and South East Asian Theatres.

'It has been reported from Berlin that the Soviet dissident Professor Herbert Marcuse has been arrested and charged with "corrupting the German Soviet Republic's Youth".

'In the United States, further allegations have been made by the leading candidate for the Democratic nomination for the Presidency, Senator Joseph P. Kennedy, Junior, against his rival Democratic aspirant, Senator Frederick Hitler of Arkansas, about Senator Hitler's alleged loyalties to his extremist father's defunct American Party.

'But first, the crisis in Italy. It was confirmed this morning that, eight months after the death of Benito Mussolini, the government of Count Galeazzo Ciano has been toppled by a coup d'etat carried out by a group of Army Officers. No details have yet emerged about the identity of the Officers, but it is understood they represent groups in the Army, Navy and Air Force calling themselves the Armed Forces Council of National Liberation. A statement read out on Roman Imperial Television only an hour ago said the Council had proclaimed the abolition of Fascism and promised a later statement naming a Provisional Junta to prepare for the first democratic elections in Italy for over forty years . . .'

Rachel
London, Spring

The world turned upside down. The insurrection, suddenly, is real, the clichéd round of marches in the street, turmoil in colleges, mass demonstrations, protests, has suddenly taken on a new air of actual danger and potential. A sort of mad enthusiasm seems to have taken over, as people whose furthest aspirations were of a Gramscian martyrdom were suddenly measuring the contours of Downing Street. If it could be done there, after fifty years of Fascism, then why not here? France? Spain? Portugal? Anywhere?

The Italian students at the London Film Academy, a group of fifteen Politicals, have barricaded themselves in Principal Kinross's office, protesting against new British government measures to register and control their numbers in Britain. Kinross is bringing them packed lunches from the nearby pub, passing them, his plump apple cheeks puffed, through the sliding windows of his reception lobby and retiring to relax with Tartan bitter. His wife, Matilda, the Iron Glove, stormed away home to North London, unreconciled to his laxness. He chuckles into his beer.

'God save us from dull times.'

I'm not sure I could join him in that. Uncertainty is not what I 'crossed the pond' for, God knows. Enough of Papa Levy marching off to war, ending up at the chess tables of Washington Square. The real thing, for us, acted out not in fantasy but in the crushing legacy of Los Angeles and Tokyo. Already the jingoistic press here, *The Times,* the *Telegraph* et al, are recycling Second World War paranoia. The Italian Revolution as an aggression by Soviet Germany and Russia. The fears of nuclear war between the Blocs. The elections which replaced George Brown with Reginald Maudling seemed an irrelevant farce in our radical universe, but the atmosphere has subtly changed. No longer the shrinkage of Empire at the end of the rainbow. The spirit of Cecil Rhodes rides again! God gave England a task, which She Shall Not Shirk: the alliterations of War Minister Powell.

'Well, I'm intrigued at least.' Kinross raised his tepid mug. 'I'd like to see the next reel. As long as they don't shit on the files, like at the L.S.E. That will make my wife terribly cross.'

Christos and Alex, blinking around the pub table, Alex nervous, Christos methodically rolling his Old Holborn tobacco. Michael, looking fed up as usual, though his libido should have been calmed down lately. He met a girl on the Bakerloo Line, who recognised his Palestinian watch cover, and introduced herself, sweeping him off to bed and breakfast. Sarah, a plump activist from North London College, who sculpted, painted and marched for World Revolution. 'I can't escape from the madness of the times,' he told me woefully. 'What happened to the spirit of Laurel and Hardy?'

It's manifest in him, as he totters after the fallen star of a dead respectability. Looking for a quiet life in Babel. Escaping the frying pan into the fire. Alex, meanwhile, is trying to sound out Kinross on his most ambitious film project:

'We shouldn't allow this opportunity to pass by. I know it's irregular, but these are irregular times. We should pull the Academy out of its parochial concerns.'

He wants us to go to Italy, to film the Revolution, as it unfolds on the streets, in the squares, the fallen Bastilles and meeting halls, utilising the Film Academy's equipment.

'But how can I insure it, darlings?' Kinross's thick, almost white, eyebrows flutter, his cheeks even redder than usual, his lips puckering, longing to be seduced. Behind that Pickwickian façade, we discovered, lies a Puck, for whom anything would go, had he not been tied down to earth by the pragmatic hand of Matilda. Roaming the corridors and studios of the Film Academy with his emberous cigar, like a double-faced emissary of chaos, the figure of Sunday in that Chestertonian fancy, the Policeman and Anarchist rolled into one.

'If I allow you to go everyone will be at it. I'll have more film crews abroad than the R.B.C. Students bouncing about in America, Hong Kong, Australia, Borneo . . .'

'Palestine,' said Michael, 'don't forget Palestine.'

'I've forgotten it already,' Kinross said.

We are living in a strange warp of the imagination, where dreams can be willed and sculpted in reality. A strange Saint

Vitus's dance seems to afflict the real world, making it an odd mirror of our desires. As if the Italian events were willed into being by our own yelling and dancing in the streets, in Trafalgar Square, down Whitehall and the Strand. The rebellion that at root's not about politics but about the act of creation . . . BE PRACTICAL, DREAM THE IMPOSSIBLE, one sly graffiti cries at the foot of the half-blind stone admiral, crowned with pigeon shit. What can we will into reality next? The Fall of the Empire? Colonial Independence? Democratisation of the Soviet German bureaucracy? Freedom breaking out every which where?

The apparent fading of the feeling of helplessness. I can scan my old manuscript: The Terror Campaign, the deep South, 1961 . . . the paralysing fear in Montgomery, Alabama . . . the burning crosses of the Klan, at junctions, the swastika displayed everywhere . . . the terrified walk, into the trap . . . reaching the phalanx of white police faces, uniforms, in front of the burned-out home of the Reverend King . . . the ambulances taking out the still remains, tied in canvas bags, on stretchers, wheeled lumps of charred hopes, to the morgue . . .

'There's nothin' for you here, Madam. Jest go back where you belong.'

Not an easy order. The flight through an unhinged land . . . the open truckloads of dishevelled, inflamed rednecks brandishing their shotguns and torches . . . apocalypse horses, galloping free, shadows in the night of broad daylight . . . my attempt to drive an anonymous black teenager free of the mobs, the stalled car that had to be abandoned . . . I never knew his name. I never knew his future. He left me at the entrance of that Greyhound Bus Station, the Party goons at the exit, the question mark gap between escape and trap . . . And trying to set it all down . . .

Dear Miss Levy,

Journalism and current affairs are by their nature ephemeral. Publishers might well consider 'classical' pieces of reportage by some well-known figure. But, alas, the market won't bear what is simply yesterday's bad news, however well written or observed, recycled by an unknown. I'm sorry if this sounds offensive, but sometimes you have to be blunt to be kind. If you could write fiction about the period, with a strong cast of invented characters, it would be a different ballgame. This agency, unfortunately, would not be geared to handle such a work, but I am sure there would be someone out there who would be willing to represent your work.

Sorry if I seem to be unhelpful, your sincerely,

Blah

Fiction. Yesterday's bad news. Do I blame them for wanting to forget? But the past doesn't slide off so easily. It'll creep up unawares. The London *Times* lists for me the candidates for November's Presidential race: President Rockefeller is a shoe-in again for the Republicans. The Democrats, dead and waiting since Henry Wallace in '53, face a free-for-all: Hubert Humphrey, Minnesota. John Connally, Texas. Jesse Griggs (who he?), Michigan. Joseph P. Kennedy Jr. Massachusets. George McGovern, North Carolina. Frederick Hitler, Arkansas.

The Other Son also rises. Is there more here than meets the eye? I would like to just live my life, please. I'd like to not care what the newspapers say. I'd like to find my own little corner where I can work my own thoughts out, sifting the avalanche of impositions, expectations. Determining my own fate, Goddamit! Is that too much to ask?

Michael

In, out, in, out! Thrusting the night away on creaky bedsprings. Living the cliché. A physical balm. The necessity fulfilled. And for Sarah? The same, perhaps, and a mission, to win another soul for the Cause. Always the Cause, always something bigger than ourselves, Michael! Like Greta Garbo, in *Algiers*, looking into Bogart's eyes. But he, having left the Foreign Legion, is less enamoured than the Parisian Mata Hari with the French Colonial task . . . *I shtick my neck out for nobody!* Even her tears fail to move him. But she dies, before they can part . . . Sarah is no Greta Garbo, being more like a human dumpling, cuddly and willing to be devoured, but committed – ah, to the toes! She is prepared to die for the Gold Coast, for Kenya, for Cyprus, for Palestine, for anything but England – which is at least one plus. 'But chéri! why die for anyone? Isn't there a long enough queue?' 'You don't believe in anything, Michael. But you know you can't sustain that.' You can't sit on the fence. It's either or. Imperialism or Liberation. Freedom or death. Beans or peas.

'I want to sculpt you. Your head.' Well, rather that than taxidermy. She lives in a shambles in Golders Green, still a little, or rather a large corner of Poland in England's green and dour land, with entire swathes of shops named only in Polish and Yiddish, with the occasional cyrillic Russian. The recent attempted coup in Poland is discussed as if it happened next door, affecting everyone's relations. The great fifties migrations from Rumania are manifest in a whole streetful (Wentworth Road, locally known as Ganefstrasse) of Rumanian Groceries and Grills. We would go to the best one, Mendel's, after an early evening fuck and reminisce about the Unholy Land, using his kebabs as madeleines. Sarah, like Rachel, was seduced to spend some months on the soil, until the early rising and brutish puffing of the requisite kibbutz male sent her back across the sea.

'I don't see any contradiction between Zionism and Arab

75

nationalism,' she said, 'they both have a common enemy. If the British withdrew there would be popular pressure for a unitary state.'

'These pickles are fantastic.' She doesn't want to hear my reactionary response, that if the British withdrew everyone, losing the common hate figure, would tear each other to shreds. Jews against Arabs, Jews against Jews, Arabs against Arabs. Togetherness is not our strong point. The Civil Wars of '44 and '55, the Irgun putsch of '45, the assassination of Jewish Council Chiefs Ben Gurion and Golda Myerson by the Irgun in 1948, the betrayal of Begin by the Haganah to the British, and that's only our own internal hates – the other side has done itself just as proud . . . Oceans of blood under broken bridges . . . Nevertheless – the golden images that can't quite be swatted away: Jerusalem at dusk, the sunset on the red roofs, the dusty trails up brown hillsides, the creaking carts of old junk merchants, the etched solidity of the stone walls, and the sounds: the religious crier's ramshorn tooting in the Sabbath from his bicycle, the jingling of the gasolene man's bell, the raucous rumble of markets, even the alien cry of the muezzin wafting over the rooftops. Their loss leaves something to be desired. Quite what, it's difficult to say . . .

In, out, in, out . . . this at least is not imagination . . . The real thing, in a Golders Green flatlet, with strange paintings of human-headed animals, and an incipient bust of Michael Pinsker, looking like a stale bagel with warts. The brave new world. It all becomes a bit clinging. The creation of me in someone else's image. Again. Solidarity meetings, with the unsolid. Mounds of leaflets, bunched fists, stamping feet. Secret conclaves in which hashish cigarettes pass round, magic embers to cauterize our cut umbilical cords with the way things used to be. All generations until now trod in the furrow. Now we're breaking free, floating over the globe. Principal Kinross, ever the soft touch, grants Alex and Christos their heart's desire: the Film Academy's equipment, to be released to us to film the Revolution in Italy, if we can pay our own way . . . God save! Alex and Christos disappear for a week into Tavernaland, the backrooms of Camden Town Athenaeums. Exiles donating their dishwashing proceeds. Party sugardaddies coughing up manna. Today Italy, tomorrow the Hellenic homeland. And après?

'Will you come, Michael? Will you do the camera?'

A working class hero is something to be, sings the Liverpool balladeer, Hannam. But what do I know from heroes, workers or classes? Just wind me up and set me free . . .

Alex
Milan, April 7

8:30 a.m. The Calais train pulls in to Milano Centrale, spewing out its load of weary, expectant, apprehensive travellers. Huge suitcases held together by string manoeuvered through narrow carriageways. Choruses of alarm, denunciation, despair. Porters rush forward with squeaking metal-wheeled trolleys, nasally announcing their services. Peasant women in grey tattered shawls run crying their loved ones' names while sons and husbands draped over open windows crane their necks to seek them out. Loudspeakers blaring in a loud and almost tearful tone instructions no one can quite make out.

The Mediterranean cantata.

We feel at home, Christos and I, though I can't say the same for Michael and Rachel, who appear disoriented . . . The surging crowd of peasants, workers, city folk, bourgeois from the First Class battling through, soldiers with rifles slung across their backs, red or white carnations in their top buttonhole, children bouncing like rubber balls, women and men hauling cases, teachests, trunks, kitbags, baskets and misshapen bundles.

A red banner, lettered in gold, has been slung across the entrance to the platforms:

UNITY. LIBERTY. PROGRESS. ARMED FORCES AND PEOPLE, FORWARD TOGETHER.

Decorated with bunting, under each loudspeaker on the station's posts, portraits, two and three feet wide, of favourites long unseen, unmentioned, unthought of in the Duce's Italy: Karl Marx, Lenin, Trotsky, Rosa Luxemburg, Gramsci, Turati, Matteoti, Malatesta and lesser-known local martyrs. At the top of each post, the red flag and the national tricolour bound together. On every side, over every available pillar or wall, a dadaesque collage of posters and inscriptions blazes across the great arched hall. A dazzling graphic forest of clenched fists, red flags, hammers, sickles, purple arrows, red-green zigzags, more portraits of political idols dead or alive, initials of the parties which have sprung up since March 5 like mushrooms after the rain: PSI, PCI, PP-DC, MLSP, MOP, PdPO, PdPO-M/L-T, ARiv, PA, PATr, and more and more and more. The Revolution may be barely five weeks old, the promised elections at least five months away, but the political circus is on the road . . . Even the ceiling, far above, has not been left out, a veritable sistine chapel of new saints: Marx, Engels, Gramsci and all, gazing down with a hundred painted eyes. And already, over everything, the grafitti slogans:

NO TO BOURGEOIS POWER!
FREE ETHIOPIA – ALL TROOPS OUT!
EXPROPRIATE THE MAFIA! SMASH THE PRISONS!
EXILE THE POPE!
EXHUME THE DUCE: A FAIR TRIAL FOR THE CORPSE!

Only here and there an unsmothered glimpse of 'normalcy' – the tip of a deodorant ad, a railway timetable peeping through a ripped fist, a surviving notice of the Lost and Found Department . . . We stagger with our heavy silvery camera boxes through the concourse, brushing past the porter calling out 'Revolutionary service! Double speed! Treble tips!', down the sweeping flight of station stairs, to be swept up by a battered yellow taxi under the great grey street arches. The cab is garlanded with blood-red roses woven through its roof rack, festooned boldly with hammers and sickles and 'Partito Comunista Italiana' scrawled demonstrably if obstructively half across the windscreen. We load our boxes in the boot and are jerked off at maniacal speed into the morning traffic.

'Via Malpighi,' I tell the driver. 'You got it,' he says, pressing down the accelerator as if it were the Duce's balls. Dangling from his mirror, instead of the expected mini-teddy bear or Virgin icon, is a double vignette of Lenin-Trotsky, in gaudy Mediterranean colour, bright-eyed and rosy-cheeked, swaying with the cab's progress. The driver, burly, bald-patched, with five o'clock shadow rushing down his bull neck, rambles on at me, as the sole obvious Italian speaker of the group, waving his hands, the cab hurtling like an unhelmed dodgem through pitted and cobbled underpasses, between arches, over tramlines:

'Liberty! The sweetest word in any language! Italy is like a newborn child! A resurrected carcase! Fascism was a beast that we finally slaughtered. But some of the dogs are still prowling about. Yesterday they caught two OVRAs in a block in Cimabue. The animals shot and killed a child before they were taken, a small boy, not this high, ten years old. Animals! Drown them in a borehole of shit, that's what I say! Mutilation is too good for them . . .'

Does he protest too much, or is this the true Italy beneath the fascist skin? Last month there were three million registered members of the Fascist Party. Where are they all today? Have they also garlanded their cars with roses, their windshields with the PCI?

We are heading for the address given me by Luigi Aldini, ex-editor of the London exile news-sheet *Italia Libera*. Via Malpighi, a short, narrow street of tall dour buildings long fallen into disrepair. The taxi driver lets us out at number 37, the most decrepit-looking block in the alley. He gives us the clenched fist as he drives off, crying 'Viva la liberta!' in a cloud of dusty righteousness.

The only entrance to number 37 seems to be a tiny eatery with 'Ristorante' in simple fading letters over a pale grimy window shedding torn adverts for Renzo Cola and Milanese Oil. Inside, several men with tanned and wrinkled faces, in simple grey jackets and scuffed trousers, sit over a game of backgammon. A stringy waiter clears away the remains of breakfast, snapping checkered tablecloths off the tables with routine flicks of the wrist. A smell of coffee wafts from a kitchen beyond an open doorway. Freshly tacked posters on the peeling walls depict a red flag held in a muscular hand, over the initials PdPO.

'Is Luigi Aldini here?'

A muffled bellow answers me from within the kitchen, and his massive bulk slams through it, discarding a slab of bread and jam to smother me in the Aldini bear hug, the golliwog head of hair and jet-black beard, which he always used to explain thus: 'In my youth I went to a fascist barber, a member of the Party Militia who performed all his duties in uniform. The walls of his barbershop had seven photographs of the Duce, the retouched version showing him with a thin fuzz of hair. My barber had adopted this hairstyle, and passed it on to all his customers. "Hair shelters parasites!" he would say, as if hordes of Bolsheviks were invading our scalps. Little did he know the invasion was internal . . . but since then, maximum growth was de rigueur . . .'

We are soon seated, all five of us, round one of the rickety tables, with steaming cappuccinos and baskets of bread before us, the backgammon players continuing their game as if nothing has disturbed their ritual. Luigi holding forth enthusiastically:

'You've come at the right time. The situation is escalating. The pace is so fast you need seven eyes, three heads and thirty arms to keep up with it. I myself haven't slept for five days, or is it five weeks? I am not quite sure which decade I am in . . . there are people around living in 1905, or 1917, or '23 – some are even reliving Garibaldi . . . I'll show you your rooms, and then off to the action. I know you want to sleep, but there's nothing like being thrown in, how do you say, at the deep end . . .'

Leading us through a back door in the kitchen, into a stone courtyard overlooked by a labyrinth of twisted staircases, snaking washing lines, women with bare fat forearms leaning over rusty railings, the squalling of children, the syrupy wail of morning radio shows. We spiral sweatily with our burden of camera boxes up to the fourth floor, tottering along a stone corridor to an iron prison-like door, opened by an immense key with a lusty creak, revealing three small rooms, peeling whitewash partly concealed by threadbare blankets and yet more vivid political posters. 'Imperialism Out of Africa', lush reds, greens, yellows, guns flourished by black and brown hands, chains snapped below bearded familiars . . . 'My brother's nest,' Luigi explains, 'he is away in Firenze. A little on the poor side, but, as you can see, very ethnic . . .'

Make yourselves, as far as possible, at home, comrades. The springboard of *your* revolution . . . Luigi clatters off down the stairs, bawling Italian answers to the Italian queries cackled at him by the curious women: More of your red pals, Luigi? Well, the more the merrier . . . anything's better than that dead old fart, blast his memory! gobs of spit shower down from the railings, spattering on the cracked courtyard stones. Raucous cries of support following the prodigal son, the hairy messenger of a new dispensation . . .

**Joseph Gable
Carpentersville, Illinois, April 8**

'Italy, you say Italy has gone red, Joseph?'

'Not quite yet, Adolf, but soon, hopefully.'

'The twilight era . . . the murky dusk before the night . . . the Insiders never sleep . . . the Rothschildfellers . . . Elders of Zion . . . the Illuminati . . . and we, we are just the husks of the fighting men of old . . . Odin . . . Thor . . . Siegfried . . . our blood poisoned by the world plague . . .'

He is becoming more and more prone to this. 'Don't let the melancholia take over, Adolf. It's probably just that goddamned flu. At your age you can't afford to give in to fatalism. What's that you have there? More of Mengele's patents? Flush them down the toilet, for God's sake. Cheer up old friend. Don't you remember the Plan? This all fits in admirably. This is not a defeat, it's a necessary step towards victory . . .'

'And Mussolini? That fat blob? Have they strung him up by the heels . . .?'

'You know he died last year, Adolf.'

'Assassinated? Garroted?'

'In bed, surrounded by his snivelling sycophants.'

'The swine!'

'Don't excite yourself, Adolf. Annchen, prepare some of that herbal tea I brought you. If Mengele tries to approach you again set the dogs on him. Here, Adolf, relax, wipe your mouth on this . . .'

'Freddy! Have you spoken to Freddy? I need to see my son, my only remaining son . . .'

'Freddy is fine. He has his own task to carry out. Remember, we agreed on the separation. He has to distance himself from us, especially from you. Until the proper time.'

'Proper time . . .' I can't stop his dribbling, he has gone off on his usual tangent. 'You're fighting all the wrong battles, Joseph . . . the real enemy is within . . . the demons, at night . . . they mock me . . . they stretch out the fingers of the plague from the other side . . . the black skullcap of doom . . .'

I have to leave him to Annchen now. The whole scene is too heavy. Mengele's concoctions have finally tipped him over. How soon before the inevitable cannot be avoided? But I have to keep him alive, as long as possible. I must not let personal revulsion take over. We still need our living symbol, our heart, as long as fate allows it to tick over. But the head . . . it is clear consultations are out of the question now. There can be no challenge any longer. Amman, Esser, Ley, and Freddy too, can't gainsay that. At last, I am in total control . . .

Miami Beach, April 9:
A certain frisson, back at the Holiday Inn. Freddy pacing about my room, his brow furrowed, his mouth set in that disgruntled cherub look that takes me back to his childhood. No nostalgia please. The Gideon Bible by my bed was open, when I took the suite, at Psalm 74: 'O God, why hast thou cast us off for ever? Why doth thine anger smoke against the sheep of thy pasture?' Those ancient Israelites had a passionate rigour, destroyed by thousands of years of mongrelisation. The Germans, it only took one generation. On the television, by a strange stroke of chance, the local Bavarian Club cavorting, lederhosen, feathered caps and beer steins, in a local show, 'Ein Prosit'. Freddy growls at me to turn it off. I oblige him, watching him wear down the carpet. He has his father Adolf's coiled spring tension, albeit in a much bulkier frame, the projection of an attraction-repulsion, love-hate at its keenest edge. Unlike Rudy. Rudy was an ersatz Adolf, the brag and bounce, but no will. Freddy is his own man. A fact that has advantages and drawbacks. He is still angry at me for risking his cover by insisting on this hurried rendezvous. He has a primary to fight here. He doesn't want to be asked by some lucky journalist: 'And when did you last see Doctor Gable, Senator Hitler?'

I tell him to calm down. I am setting him no traps. I have data that should be passed directly, no go-betweens. I pledged to be the sole link with his father and that I am carrying out.

'My father – is he dying, then?'

'Your father is a remarkable man. If chance were otherwise he might have left an indelible mark on the world. But now that

83

task is left to others. He has had a relapse, Freddy. Recurring hallucinations, fits of the Fear. The doctor says his heart is still sound. Not Mengele, I have seen to that. An American physician, Browning. A Lutheran.'

'Indestructible Adolf . . . Sleeping while Uncle Joseph faithfully guards the kennel . . .' He motions me for a spot of the brandy I have been modestly sipping. I try to engage his eyes, but he knows my tricks. Speak to me, Frederick, I am the only person alive who can understand your emotions, after Rudy has gone. I am the only one who can comprehend your riven Yankee-Volkisch soul, the hopes that pull you to us, the alienation that urges you to try and escape your destiny. I try nevertheless to flatter him by reminding him how well things are going. What a great job he's doing in the South, buying back our old constituencies with new coins. Telling him to take no notice of the ranting East Coast press.

'The polls show you in the top three, Freddy. Even if the convention goes for Humphrey or Kennedy, the Vice-Presidency should be yours.'

'I wouldn't write off Price yet, and he owes me nothing. And Kennedy's votes come from the niggers and Jews.'

'The Jews will vote Republican. They will kiss establishment ass. The nigger vote is a dog. No, the Democrats need the white South. Dry cleaned of course, the new moderate look.'

The Vice-Presidency, for '69, Freddy. Then the Presidency in '73, even '78. I see him looking at me strangely. At fifty two, he has time. But I? Do I think I'll live for ever? Or will I rule him after my death? I know Freddy cannot overestimate me, but it is not just the Jew Freud's fantasy that youth longs to kill age. What I can offer him is that bloodline endurance, the drive, unslowed, behind the scenes albeit, to build, out of our past defeat, a new power base in a foreign land, to nurse our hate, our love, our determination, to court the very whore Democracy we have to drive into the grave . . . The nag we rode almost to victory in '61 . . . Then, despite the bitter blow, despite the crash, the rising son's death, to start again, to turn to the younger brother . . . Frederick, the would-be defector, the 'house liberal', the one who yearned to flee the coop . . . Allowing him to become addicted on his own to the political opium, and then, bring him gifts . . .

'You've brought the material?' he says gruffly, buckling down to business. I gesture to the briefcase on the bed. 'You'll find it all enlightening, Freddy. Kefauver's commie ties, McGovern's peccadilloes, mounds of stuff on Humphrey, some interesting Kennedy juice. Though I would go easy on that. There are some crosslines. A little knowledge goes a long way.'

'Spare the bon mots, Joseph.' He takes the case, evading my eye. Knowing I've bought just one more piece of him, the addict hating his supplier, but foaming at the mouth for the fix. 'Schuss.' He leaves the room hurriedly. I pour myself another brandy. I am not worrying about Freddy, at this point. He may hate me, but he will play the game. He is a fighter, like the rest of us, and a rebel. In this he reminds me so much of myself. Different times. Different surroundings. But the same battlefield. And the same high, enthralling odds.

The Bible is still open at Psalm 74. Verse number 23: 'Forget not the voice of thine enemies: the tumult of those that rise against thee increaseth continually . . .'

KCSTV Reports
San Francisco, April 15

... the race is wide open now that the early California primary is over. For the Democrats, Price and Humphrey, yesterday's front runners, look like today's has-beens. Joseph Kennedy Junior is out in front with 32 per cent of the vote, and the dark horse of this campaign, Senator Frederick Hitler of Arkansas is in second place with 21 per cent! I asked Senator Hitler the sixty-four thousand dollar question – is this a repeat of 1961 by other means?

HITLER: Not at all, Barbara . . . there have been a lot of smears against me since our campaign waggon started rolling back in February, but my statements stand for themselves. We, the Democrats of the mid-west and south, will not repeat the ghastly errors of 1961 by going for extremist policies. I repudiated my own family then and I repudiate them now. The American Party is dead in the south. I am standing as a Democrat and I am proud to be a Democrat, in the great progressive heritage of our Party.

REPORTER: Your, uh, program is very similar to, in fact, on many issues seems identical to that of your rival Joseph Kennedy Junior. Can you comment on this?

HITLER: I think Joe Kennedy stands for the same ideals as I do, the true ideals on which this country stands, what I would call a Patriotic Democracy. I agree completely with Joe Kennedy that we must bind the wounds of our last two decades of war and civil strife. We need a cure, not the tranquilisers of Nelson Rockefeller. We need a strong dollar, a powerful but not wasteful defence policy and enhanced social programs to solve the problems of poverty and deprivation that still afflict the west and south . . . I think Joe Kennedy would make a fine President, I just think I could do a better job . . .

REPORTER: I next turned to the new front-runner, Joseph P. Kennedy Junior. He is supported here by an absolute phalanx of Kennedies – his brothers John F. Kennedy, Senator for Maine, Robert and Edward, both Congressmen, his distinguished father,

86

Joseph Senior . . . I battled through hordes of admirers to pop the question to him: Would *he* support Senator Hitler if the latter was the Democratic nominee?

KENNEDY: Well, these are early days yet, Barbara, we don't want to start already making promises we might not want to keep . . . [laughter] No, what is important is that the next President of the United States should be a Democrat. Someone who can end this absolutely ruinous succession of Republican incompetents and charlatans who have almost reduced this great country to a political, economic and moral basket case. McCarthy, Nixon, Rockefeller, I say we've had enough. We want every citizen of this nation, be he or she white, black or brown, gentile or Jew, to be able to hold his head high and say I am an American. We want to pull this great nation of ours out of the morass in which we have all been trapped. I stand for that now, I'll stand for that at the Convention, and I'll stand for that as President in the White House if that's what the people choose . . .

Alex
Milan, April 25

The red curtain rises. A man in Garibaldian (red) shirt, waving blood-red banner, crosses the stage. A large card, dangled by string from the flies, announces ITALIA, 1860.

'The Risorgimento!'

Victor Emmanuel II meets Garibaldi right of stage. They freeze on handshake. Curtain.

Sepulchral voices: '1861. Long Live Victor Emmanuel II, King of Unified Italy. Birth of the Italian Nation!'

Rude cries from the stalls: 'An emasculate conception!' 'A miscarriage!' Shouts of protest and abuse. Luigi Aldini is working hard to translate it all into three pairs of un-Italian ears.

Another dangling card: 1870. 'Occupation of the Papal States! Pope confined to Vatican under protest.'

Audience cheers. Cries of 'hang the bastard!' Loud sound of marching feet, cannon fire. Map of Africa drops with thump to stage level. Voice: 'Prime Minister Crispi sends Expeditionary Force to Abyssinia. Italy bites Imperialist cake.' Boos, raspberries, hoots, rifle fire.

'Abyssinians rally against invaders. First defeat, at Adowa, of a European army.' Cheers, cries of support. 'Power to the people!' from the back rows.

'Giolitti era. Bankruptcy of political liberalism. Chronic economic crisis. The strange tones of D'Annunzio are heard in the land:

"A people who wish to participate in the conquest of the world can do without freedom."'

. . . 1905 . . . marching songs, red flags carried across stage, fiery voices denounce the rich, capitalism, the bourgeoisie, a jail door clangs . . . bugles:

'Benito Mussolini, aged twenty two, imprisoned for the second time for socialist agitation!'

A rendition of Benito's harangue: '. . . the Catholic church, that bloated corpse . . . Christianity, humanity's immortal stigma of

opprobium . . .' 1914 . . . cannon fire, coloured smoke. 1915!
'Benito breaks with socialist anti-war colleagues, supports Italy's
entry into War!'

Benito, in mud spattered uniform, enters stage right. An
explosion. He crumples, crying: 'I am proud to have reddened
the road to Trieste with my blood!' Stretcher bearers bear him
off, not before he throws the audience a broad wink. Boos, hoots,
gobs of spit not quite reaching stage.

1918! 'Though on the winning side Italy ends the War bankrupt
and shattered. Liberalism is discredited . . . the only alternatives:
Socialism, or the new, provocative tunes . . .'

Sepulchral voice: 'Politics should not be seen as something
calculated and cold but as boldness, adventure, as a dissatisfaction
with reality, a celebration of the rites of Action!'

Giovinezza! Giovinezza! a short medley of marching songs.
Clump of boots, Benito's voice:

'"The credo of the bourgeoisie is egotism, the credo of
Fascismo is heroism!"'

1920! 'New working class demands . . .' The voice of Gramsci
(applause, cheers, whistles), '. . . factory occupations in Turin
and Milan . . . peasants grab land . . . faced with the "communist
threat" in the wake of the Russian Revolution, the bourgeoisie
capitulate to the fascists . . . Mussolini's March on Rome . . .'

The music stops, darkness descends. A single candle wavers
tentatively on stage. The sepulchral voice:

'DUCE, YOU ARE ALL OF US. MUSSOLINI IS AL-
WAYS RIGHT. OBEY, BELIEVE, FIGHT. For forty-seven
years, the only play in town. Not even the Revolution in Germany
can shake the iron grip. The people are freed from liberty, and liberated from freedom. Everything in the State, nothing against the
State, nothing outside the State. All problems are solved by stating
that no problems exist. For some, relief: circuses, displays, wars . . .
1936, wiping out the shame of Adowa with poison gas . . . 1939,
Albania . . . 1941, the Greeks, such fools, decline the friendly fascist tomb . . . the tomb which is our cradle, our school, our totality:
Obey because you must, because grandfather Duce knows what's
best for you . . . sleep, my children, sleep out the age . . .'

The lights go on. There is a coffin on stage. A long-drawn-out
fart like bugle blast.

1968! 'Grandaddy dies! We wake from the dream to find what? The unsolved problems exist! The country is still bankrupt! Half the populace still illiterate! Our soldiers dying like flies killing people who are just as poor and destitute as ourselves! And so, with hopes, with longings, with new dreams we announce the opening of a new play . . .'

Coloured lights, flashes, bugle blasts, red banners carried on stage. The largest card: THE ITALIAN REVOLUTION!

'*Avanti o popolo, a la riscossa* . . .' A circus compère in worker's overall and battered top hat rushes on, crying: 'Roll up, roll up for the greatest show on earth!' Men and women rush on stage, in overalls, office suits, open-necked shirts, shawls, jeans and khaki, soldiers with carnations in the barrels of their guns.

Liberation April! Mussolini once said of the Italians: 'They are good for nothing except singing and making ice cream.' And now singing and making ice cream have come into their own, along with all the other offences now relegated to the museum of fascist prohibitions: The Sounding of Motor Horns in City Limits, the Wearing of Lewd and Immoral Attire, Dancing in the Streets Not on Recognised State Holidays, Spreading Malicious Rumours, Criticism of State and Party Officials and the Clergy, Defacing Walls, Billboards, Trees and Private and Public Property, Adultery, Seduction, Soliciting and Illicit Sexual Acts . . .

The circus runs free in the streets: workers and students march to the Duomo, women carry banners calling for legalised divorce and abortion, groups of homosexuals emerge who knows from where calling for freedom of sex between consenting adults, Prostitutes For the Revolution, End Puritan Repression, the great thaw, in the Italian spring . . .

We were immediately plunged into the thick of it all. On our very first, groggy day, a plenary meeting of the PdPO (Party of Workers' Power) Executive in the cramped quarters of Luigi's flat at 37 Via Malpighi, Luigi and his comrades: Pietro, thin and intense, Dino, round and bearded, Rafaella, robust and red-haired, appled-faced Margherita, earth mother Elena, blonde Rossana, the twins Giorgio and Mario, Tonino and Alfredo the Fiat machinists, and Natalia . . . ah! We could see Michael falling, plunging into her black eyes, her raven hair, her intensities . . . For him, indeed, a new age . . .

Rachel

Have I been here before? The bright sparks of youth, the passionate involvement, the sense of worlds to remake: the Anti-Fascist League of Upper Manhattan, Marvin Blumenfeld and Sarah Nichols, long nights high on Theory, tempers tamed only by the imposition of the Correct Line, the clash of personalities subsumed in strictly 'political' discord. But here, of course, the game is not all claustrophobic, its surreal, open-ended improbabilities have, by the twists of chance, a real impact in the world outside . . . Alex and Christos are in their element here, but Michael sits apart. He has been smit, obviously by the dark Princess, Natalia, manoeuvering round the room's pouffe cushions to catch her eye, but she is deep in denunciations:

'. . . what Dino is advocating is pure anarchism . . . action for action's sake . . . that is a squadrista tactic even . . .' Protests. Luigi: 'Hey, let's not start calling each other fascists . . . there are twenty parties doing that on the streets . . . the main thing is not to lose sight of reality . . . all about us there are mass strikes, occupations . . . but we can't tell the workers what they should do . . . we are not just an imitation PCI, another authoritarian alternative to bourgeois rule . . .'

He is tearing off great gobs of bread, stuffing them into his mouth at the same time. Arms wave, fingers dig into nostrils and ears, beards are tugged, heads are lowered and clutched in despair. Small tidbits of anchovies, cheese, olives, sliced tomatoes, on paper plates on the floor, disappear. Questions of revolutionary strategy: should the Party join the call for a broad-left coalition or should it pursue its own programme, regardless of accusations of divisiveness, and agitate separately in the streets, shops, factories . . . Defining the state of the nation: what is the true class nature of the Liberation Junta, does it represent merely the old petit-bougeoisie in a new guise or is it the beginning of a 'Commune', a gate through which the Armed People can burst, shattering the base of bourgeois power?

Disputation, well into the small hours . . . words become an addiction, silence brings on savage withdrawal symptoms. The Revolution has conjured, out of the long dead quiet, a hundred thousand larynxes of steel . . . Everyone will have their say, no one will pass go . . . Italy, Golden April! The train conductors are on strike, leaving notices saying, 'Free Holidays Now – Ferragosto in April.' La Scala is closed, as a small tide of Pekinesed stars with their jewellery in hidden suitcase compartments ebbs north to Switzerland and Fascist Austria. Cinemas are packed as censorship vanishes, a sudden flush of Czech or Yugoslav pap and porn, the long banned Soviet epics of Pabst, Ophuls, Eisenstein, and, most welcomed, the works of the returning exiled film directors – from France, Damiani, Bolognini, Olmi, Pontecorvo; from Brazil, Visconti and De Santis; from the U.S., Fellini, Rosselini, Antonioni; and from whatever hiding place in his jungle or deserts, Pier Paolo Pasolini . . . Old hands who stayed to fight the lost cause at home, blinking out of jail cells – Rosi, Brass and the younger generation, fanning out now with their movie cameras into the city slums and the *mezzogiorno*, creating a new, instant, 'neo-realist' art . . . while the film makers who compromised with the régime remain in their villas (De Sica, Lattuada, De Laurentis) . . . Similar homecomings are taking place in the theatre, painting, sculpture, literature, and, most conspicuous of all, in television, taken over by the radical, ultra-left splinters, amid howls of complaint by the 'respectable' mass parties, the Socialists, the Popolari (Christian Democrats), the Communists. Talents subdued and repressed for so long, a spontaneous combustion . . . Art spilling out in the streets, with the mad graffiti of the Urban Saracens, anonymous court jesters of the Revolution (so named in a lampoon of the Duce's self-appointment as 'Sword of Islam'), marking every available bare wall: 'Shortage of Food? Eat the Police!' 'Togliatti for Pope!' 'Zombies of all Nations Unite!' In Florence they have declared an 'Arsenic Republic', taking over the town hall and proclaiming the return of the Medicis.

Talk-Ins at the Universities, Occupations at Fiat in Turin, a Slum-dwellers Council taking over Naples, peasants grabbing land all over Emilia-Romana, and supporters, hangers-on, excitement-chasers, journalists, revolutionaries and film-makers of all nations converging on the great cavalcade . . . courted guests at a vast wedding reception that seems to go around the clock, day after day, timelessly, for ever and ever, or, until the food and drink runs out . . .

And, in the midst of this: Michael and Natalia. The soap opera romance in our midst. Here we thought we had just another unfulfilled wet dream when, bingo, the incompatibles came together, one night, after a particularly fierce Party session at Natalia's flat in Via Moscova. We all left with the comrades, but Michael, somehow, stayed behind, rejoining us at Via Malpighi, the next morning, looking as if he had been plugged into the mains. In the afternoon they were entwined together. Love! Who could not shed a tear? They fought like cats over their battlefield. Arguing incessantly, in the bedroom, in the street, at party meetings, in the parks, in numerous pizzerias and trattorias, on buses and streetcars, in taxicabs, at demonstrations and marches of the unemployed, at the marathon factory meetings we began covering all over Milan. They became a familiar, almost famous couple, the pale, thin, dark, neurotic 'Englishman' and '*la passionaria di Milano*' who yelled back at him in heavily accented English mixed with dialect oaths. The Fiat workers left them a separate table at their cafeteria, egging them on from nearby tables to ever greater heights of acrimony, convinced they were already married: 'Ah! They are made for each other . . .'

The whole Italian Revolution shrunk into a backdrop, it seemed, for Michael in his violent Milan *affaire* . . . heaven knows what really drew her to him, perhaps the very fact of his sullen dissent from the passion/fashion of the day . . . He was trying to convert her to cynicism, maybe seeing in her commitment and faith a mirror image of his hated native Zionism . . . He tried to convince her she was the victim of an Apostate Catholic backlash. Flashes on the road to Damascus. A grain of truth there. Women, in Particular, under Fascism, had the worst of three worlds: the hammers of the State, the Church and personal male machismo, the triple patriarchal blows. It was not surprising they became the most zealous, the most uncompromising enemies of the *ancien régime*. The PdPO meetings' fiercest debates were almost always stalemated over women's issues. Divorce, abortion, custody. 'We can't fly before we can walk . . .' say Dino, Pietro, Mario . . . 'We'll never fly if we just keep on crawling . . .' say Rafaella,

Elena, Natalia. Natalia, most of all, wants to soar. She wants no trace, no echo of trammels, but the iron logic of the Revolution – Nothing Is Impossible. Perhaps she is the most romantic of them all, the most extreme, the most utopian, the most ready to be armed to fight for tenderness, to die for the right to live . . .

Michael

Madness, insanity. It permeates the air, flows from the sun. More! More! More! It definitely is catching. The girl is insatiable. She needs rhetoric, like other people need food. At the root of it all, I think, she is terrified. She tells me dreams, in which it all returns: her father, a black-shirted militiaman, clawing his way from the grave. Can't you have dreams which are a bit more obscure, I ask her? But everything is out on the surface. The hidden, repressed, primal forces, fear, desire, the hunger for attention, the existential urge, all out there on the broad avenues and squares of Milan.

The night I stayed. By some strange click of synchronicity, some unexplained, mutual spark. The politbureau were hardly out the door, clattering down their Odessa steps, and there we were scrabbling on the mattress strewn with applecores, peachstones and leaflets calling for the proletariat to rise! Who would believe it? Dreams come true. But it was a dreamworld not quite mine that I found myself being drawn further and further into. My own fantasy image the blonde, buxom dame, like Gene Tierney with Humphrey Bogart in *The Little Sister*, the real love affair born in the studio . . . But this was Alex or Christos's world, the Winds of the Revolution, the burning light of the True Faith, as Christos sits in the factory cafeterias, sharing the workers' bread and wine, rolling cigarettes with them, stained fingers engrimed, leather-tanned faces with twenty-five o'clock shadow, while Alex, with the Party faithful, discusses Gramsci, Lukacs, Feuerbach, Trotsky, fixed in a rhetorical paradise. Rachel bemused and a way aloof from all this, observing, maybe collecting material for another journal of a Terror still to come . . .

The counter-terror, perhaps, of our fiery nights, as Natalia and I fight for each other's souls, metaphysical claws bared . . . Afraid we would maim each other in the cramped flat, we walked the cobbled streets, shouting at each other, dodging old boots and pails of slops hurled from windows. We had absolutely nothing in common. She believed, God, how she believed! In History as a real thing, a sort of ectoplasmatic force which stretched out its tentacles and shook empires, kingdoms, republics. She believed in the inevitability of a new world in which Capital was banished. She believed in the dignity of Labour. She believed in something called Praxis and something else, called clitoral orgasm, which may or may not have been the same. She would not suck a man's penis for anything under the sun. Not to speak of anal intercourse, which I was not going to speak of anyway. She believed I was the sheerest example she had ever met of petit-bourgeois opportunism. I declared my undying love, which only enraged her further, until the comrades banging on the adjoining wall reduced her to a sullen calm.

So April passed, an astonishing whirlwind of sit-ins, occupations, fantasies. Armbanded student Committees of Public Safety & Hygiene roamed the streets, admonishing litter louts. In Venice the gondoliers went on strike, marooning people behind their canals. In Rome Vatican Guards opened fire on students who tried to storm Saint Peter with red flags. The first blood of the Revolution to be shed since the Army Officers under Major Calvinetti had to fire on Cunt Ciano's guards. I was too busy, with the Victor Blimped Camera by day and Natalia by night, to work out which way was up or down.

Then we were suddenly whipped off, by a Party minibus, down into the heart of the Italian boot, to small villages outside Modena and Bologna, budding with a thousand and one slogans and signs. Rip Van Winkle woken out of some age old slumber, alive with street meetings and disputations which would have been unimaginable two months before. Small churches lying empty, the priests fled, or changed into something more comfortable, the men voluble, the women even more so, with little knots of older women clad in black sitting out this latest craze on small benches, waiting for normality to be restored. Then a tour that Alex and Christos have insisted on, up a high hill dominating the countryside, to the picture-postcard castle of Rocca della Caminate, Mussolini's fortress retreat.

The ogre was gone from the enchanted tower, and two nonchalant armed men waved us through an open gate under the red flag. A makeshift placard over the ornate signpost proclaimed, 'People's Museum of Ancient Relics.' A few families of as yet unhoused peasants were camped out in the baroque rooms, stacked with the gifts the Duce gathered in his forty odd years of residence, statues, paintings, silks, rugs, African masks, the world's largest collection of ancient and modern weapons, including a flamethrower showily mounted on a glass-topped table. Little signs thoughtfully guiding the visitor lost in this opulence 'To the Cinema', 'To the Study', 'To the Zoo' – a garden in the back, where Musso's geriatric keeper, one G. di Steppani, we're told, still croons over the deer, gazelles, giraffes, tigers and pumas and the great Congo apes the nature-loving Duce loved to gape at and admire. The fortress had been bequeathed to 'the public' in Duce's will, but Cunt Ciano's brief tenure in office had not quite sufficed to get the show on the road. Nevertheless, the study, vulgarly furnished like a white telephone film set, was plastered on every wall with framed photographs of the Duce in every one of his thousand and ninety roles as The Italian Everyman – the fencing master posing with his blade, the boxer stripped to show his hairy chest, the riding gentleman on his domain, the proud family man, with his large Italian family, daddy bouncing grandchild on knee, daddy, chin jutting, looking out over his brood, daddy the soldier, in a variety of uniforms, daddy the pilot, in the cockpit of his plane, daddy the politician, with creepy old Engelbert Dolfuss of Austria pinning a medal on to his tit, with British Prime Minister Mosley gazing cow-eyed at him, with Emperor Hirohito of Japan, with Presidents Hoover, Wallace, McCarthy, Nixon, with European leaders Mosley, Koč and Laval, at the London Conference of 1951, and back to wider roles, the hunter standing over a slain Abyssinian lion, the Big White Chief surrounded by puzzled black faces, the young Duce, the demagogue regaling the crowds, Duce the fiery newspaper editor, Duce as college student, Duce as teenager, Duce as piccolo bambino.

Suddenly Rachel gives out a strange choked-off cry, motioning us to a shaded corner of the room, where, on a small nest of tables, a small, framed eight by ten stands alone, forgotten. She picks it up, shaking her head. 'The Rosetta Stone!' she says, incomprehensibly. It looks no different from the rest. The photograph is dated 1957. Duce here was seventy-four years old. Bald as a coot, his face dropping in those massive jowls, apparently prevented from reaching the floor only by the tight thick collar.

His eyes look piggy and tired, as if he's not enjoying at all the company he's in: three prim-looking elderly gentlemen and a tall, stocky young man. Him I recognise, from Rachel's files of her journal: Rudolph Hitler, would-be U.S. President who was gunned down at the peak of his American Party campaign in 1961. Of the older men, one is tall, fat and flabby as the Duce, with a pockmarked face like a warthog in pain. The other two are Duce's height (he was in fact quite small, barely five foot six): the one on the right stands ramrod straight, his short hair a pure white slicked to one side, his face pinched and waxy, his mouth a slit under a clipped snow-white moustache, his eyes unpleasantly agleam. The man on the left is slightly bent, one shoulder higher than the other, grey white hair neatly combed back, the cheeks cavernous, the mouth tilted in a kind of knowing sneer.

'The man on the right is Adolf Hitler, the Senator, Rudy's dad,' Rachel explains, 'the American Party's guru, who couldn't run for President as he wasn't born in the States. The man on the left is Joseph Gable, the Party's brains, the man I met in the Holiday Inn in Miami before the Convention of that year. There were always rumours of an Italian connection, but this meeting was one they always denied . . .'

Vultures of a feather stick together. We retreated through the bizarre galleria, the Duce watching us with his two thousand eyes. Dead deeds, dead plots, dead aspirations. The dustbin of history. And good riddance . . . I yearn, I pine, for my dark-haired princess . . . But we are summoned, instead, further south, to Rome, to witness a new act in the Revolutionary Theatre – a slambam Conference On Africa, set to sign away Independence for the Colonies – Abyssinia, Somaliland and Libya. A political extravaganza, to be attended by a whole host of legendary figures: from North Africa, Nasser and Ben Bella, from West Africa, Nkrumah, from Abyssinia, Walda Sion, and, rumour has it, the most evasive of all, the international troublemaker and Scarlet Pimpernel, Ernesto 'Che' Guevara . . .

Chmielnicki, Ignacy
Las Vegas, Nevada, April 30

Shellshocked, at the wheel of a hired Tucker, I enter the city at 23:30 hours. The glittering neon displays, rising like a delirium tremens out of the desert blackness: 2LB PRIME BEEFER; FREE SLOTS!; JOHN WAYNE LIVE – FLAMINGO SHERATON; WORLDS LARGEST TACOS – 49c! I am lost, reduced to the status of some peasant boy from the sticks seeing the Big City for the first time, as I manoeuvre through the delirium tremens towards the Desert Inn. Europe hides its decadence, behind walls of perfidy and hypocrisy. This place proclaims it with ebullient pride. I have led a strangely sheltered life . . .

An orange-uniformed page takes my bags, leading me into a lobby which looks like a Polish cocaine addict's dream of an Austro-Hungarian brothel. There are slot machines everywhere, being manhandled by large, flabby-armed matrons, their faces intense, sweat congealing in the air-conditioned chill. I give the required name at the Reception:

'Prokosch. Mr Grant reserved a suite for me.'

They are obsequious in that strange American way, dripping with genuine sincerity. 'Have you had a pleasant trip, sir?' I have no interest in indulging their familiarity. No wish to foster their delusion of the lack of hierarchy and order. A bellboy with the muscular look of a trained guard takes me silently up the lift to my rooms. I tip him five dollars for his silence. Behind the façade, I can already sense, nevertheless, the first traces of organisation.

A vulgarly ostentatious suite, wood panelled in a mock stockade style, with desert plants in vast pots. The ubiquitous slot machines, one by the bed, one in the toilet, so that one might try one's luck even in the most debased posture. I leave the local god alone. One hour later, dead on time, a knock at the door, and Joseph Gable stands before me. Immaculately dressed as ever, the grey suit, black tie, stiff white collar, the face a smooth tribute to the cosmetician's art, the hair dyed black, allowing the distinguished grey white at the temples.

'Welcome to Vegas,' he says, giving his version of a smile. 'How do you like our circus of dreams?'

Joseph

'This is a town,' I told him, 'that thrives on folly and greed. A Mahagonny that the Communist playwright Brecht might have conjured up. There is no man so poor here that he is not welcome to become poorer, enticed by the American Dream. A city of makebelieve, a perfect nullity in which to plan. In this celebration of the ersatz, even the greatest apparent threat cannot be grasped, no new arrival is out of place, no accent foreign, no stranger scrutinised, except, of course, by us.'

I assured him of the perfect security of the rooms, as he looked anxiously around. I told him all the 'bugs' in the hotel were mine. Control of the Hughes Operation and the State of Nevada was a sound insurance policy from McCarthy days, which has paid off. I got him a little schnapps from the wall cabinet and we got down to business. I praised the way he had kept Camp Auschwitz under control, the smoothness of his disposal of Skorzeny. The training accident was most convincing. Some people never learn their place. These adventurers always hoist themselves with their own petard, they overreach themselves, and become vulnerable. We discussed the Polish situation. He delivered his usual incisive briefing. The whole thing teeters nicely on the edge. A few bombs in the Kresy, some mutinies in Galicia, and the government lulled in Warsaw. Everything seemed ready. If I could trust this man. Can I? Do I delude myself that I can read past that thick Silesian skull? Loyalty is easy to come by among second-raters, who need to be led and know it. But when one has to rely on a first-order will, it is a tightrope with no safety net. This was what Adolf was like in the early days, though this man has no political ambitions. Or has he? Have I come to doubt my own judgments? And the tigers prowl below . . .

Perhaps the schnapps made me a little maudlin. 'It is just the two of us now,' I told him. 'The others, we can just forget. Amman, Esser, Neubauer, Ley, old age has raddled them completely. Adolf is totally gaga. It is only a matter of time. What is made of The Plan now is up to us, you and I, our combined will. You have to realise this.'

'And Freddy?'

'Freddy will do what he's told. Not for love or loyalty, but ambition. Freddy is fundamentally weak, and weak ambitious men make the best tools. Freddy is clay in the potter's hands.'

I talked to him about America, feeling a strange ability, for the first time in years, to speak frankly. Chmielnitski, buried deep in the Duce's guardhouse, chained to his master's side the only previous time he had been in this country, twelve years ago. America, this strange power, moving inexorably towards hegemony in the twilight of the European Empires, but filled with a people vain, childish, unpredictable, and mongrelised. Slav sentimentality, Jewish venality, Nigger barbarisation. I was aware of this from the first, from that terrible year we first arrived here, a dozen drops in the ocean of the world's wanderers, refugees even, mingling with the Jews, the Poles, the starved illiterate Russkis, the Latin American half-castes. Adolf, one must admit, kept us alive, with the power of his ur-emotion, the very narrowness of his vision. In Germany those visions might have become all-powerful. But in America they were misaligned. It fell to me then to guide him, to mould him and ourselves into a political force here. No easy job. So many organisations about that seemed to serve our purpose, but riddled with delusions, wishful thinking, and above all, corruption, sexual and financial. The Klan, the White Leagues, the Knights of this and that. Religion was their main curse. Protestant fundamentalism. A sort of smudged romanticism. We could not duplicate the NSDAP here, though Adolf tried, and drove us to disaster. What he called his 'cavalry charge to power' . . . Nevertheless, were it not for the bloated, drunken Dixiecrats . . . So Adolf lost his place in History. But I, on the other hand . . .

I outlined the general strategy to Ignacy Chmielnitski, showing him my cards, for the first time, in the vulgarity of the Desert Inn suite. He sat there, entranced by my words. I knew the boldness of the conception grabbed him. He could not resist this lure, this thread of opportunity which only I could play out to its end.

'How much time?' he asked.

'Eighteen months,' I told him. 'Double pregnancy. An apt period.' This time, I promise myself, I will not be deflected by the random dice of another will's illusions, mirages, ghosts of might have beens . . .

Alex
Revolutionary Notes, Milan, May 2

. . . marvellous May Day march yesterday to the Piazza Duomo.
Tens of thousands gathered under the Cathedral spires, the bells
ringing from the church, an air of unity and solidarity. Of course,
the usual number of clashes, mainly the PCI attacking other left
groups, tearing up MSP banners . . .

. . . at least the PCI, for all its authoritarianism, has mass
organisation. The far left's endemic fragmentation is a real barrier
to an effective role. Christos and I came back here, while Rachel
and Michael moved on to Rome, to find the PdPO splitting over
the 'broad left' versus 'particularist' strategy. Lifelong friendships
which stood the test of dictatorship sunder as people denounced
one another as 'petit-bourgeois infantilists'. Natalia is one of the
most rigid sectarians. I don't think Michael would fare so well
with her now, she has joined the group opposed to Luigi . . .
Now they're almost coming to blows over control of the Party's
rusty printing press . . . Christos and I try to keep out of all this,
but it's not easy. We are in effect marooned in Milan, due to
these internal squabbles. But it would be wasteful of us to join
the others in Rome, which would deplete our meagre budget .
. . Luigi suggests we test the ground in Turin, where the Fiat
Workers' Council is challenging the management, and full-scale
occupations might begin any day . . . the struggle at its most
intense, the iron at its hottest . . . Meanwhile, Rachel and Michael
are hobnobbing with the famous, in the Eternal City . . .

Ernesto
Rome, Diaries

May 5: First day of the Africa Conference proper, at the old Hotel Imperiale, now renamed Hotel Ethiopia. Kenyatta, elder statesman of the Liberation Movements, delivers the keynote speech. The grand old man has lost none of his strength. His cry for Freedom cannot fail to move the heart of any decent human being. Nkrumah speaks, briefly, his illness slowing his usually brilliant delivery. Nasser, Jalloud and Ben Bella make an impassioned plea for the struggling Arab masses. Jalloud pledges free Libya as a base for Liberation Movements against all foreign rule. The youthful Lumumba from the 'Belgian' Congo transfixes the Conference with his enthusiasm. The atmosphere becomes truly electric. One feels that the death-knell of Colonialism is finally being sounded here. Britain, France, Belgium and Portugal *must* face the truth they have so long ignored, the truth of the millions crying out to control their own destinies, their own lives. Their absolute rejection of the 'commonwealth' and 'dominion' concepts which seek to perpetuate Imperialism.

General Fraia, in the chair as Minister of Overseas Affairs, seems most unhappy about all this. He is constantly darting his eyes at the crowd of Western journalists who are avidly taking down every word. He knows the Liberation Junta will come under immense pressure now from France and Britain, and the U.S.A., to change its course before it's too late. It's one thing to have students and workers marching in the streets, quite another to be the crucial first crack in the Colonial structure. Major Calvinetti, at his side as Minister for Internal Security, looks impassive. How far are he and the left really prepared to go? Will they allow 'parliamentary' politics to be the wedge with which the Great Powers split the brittle Revolution? Does the cloud stamped 'counter-coup' already gather, wisp by wisp, in the heady air of this Convention Hall?

May 7: Working breakfast with Calvinetti, who confirms my fears, revealing that several Junta members think this open conference is a blunder, that East African and Libyan Independence should have been decided behind the scenes, without the provocation to the West that this gathering of Pan-African champions implies. C., as I know from our first meeting in the Ethiopian mountains, is a decent but limited man trying to do what his conscience tells him is his duty to his people and mankind. Of the true nature of revolutionary politics he knows nothing. The March coup has catapulted him and his colleagues far beyond their capacity to handle the events. He is nonplussed, he admits, by the sheer range and fragmentation of the political forces unleashed by the removal of the fascist lid. Ideologically he is a 'social-democrat', but he is only beginning to understand what that means in practice: the complete readiness to capitulate to the bourgeoisie at home and to Imperialism abroad. We discuss the present breakdown of the 37 Junta members: twelve centrists (socialists, social democrats, Christian socialists), six rightists (liberals, Christian democrats), six Marxist-Leninists inclined towards the ultra-left (MLSP, MOP, PdPO), seven hardline PCI Trotskyites, two Luxemburgists, three anarcho-syndicalists, one suspected neo-Fascist. In a crisis the PCI members would join the centre and the right, leaving the left outgunned, with the anarchists against everybody else. A typical petit-bourgeois configuration, I told Calvinetti, which does not augur well. He sighed over his *briosce*. 'I did not expect such a rat's nest,' he said. 'Then open your eyes,' I told him, 'look around and you'll see where your real friends are – in the fields and factories and colleges, not the barrack rooms.'

In the afternoon addressed students at Rome University. They were packed in like sardines. I was impressed by their enthusiasm, but I warned them against it. They too are captivated by the romance of Coup as Revolution served out from the tin marked Junta. I analysed Fascism's bankruptcy, read them a little Lenin and Trotsky, talked of the process that has to be followed. In many respects Italy is non-European. The massive disenfranchised peasantry whose participation is vital. The slogans should be: Arm the Peasantry, Arm the Proletariat, Only a People Armed Can be Free. A long face on my Junta minder here, Colonel Spinetti, who does not like this at all.

At the end of this session, approached by a rather dishevelled American girl who, together with a Jewish Palestinian cameraman, has travelled from London to film the events in Italy. They want to film an interview. I have already had a bellyful for six months with Pasolini, so I decline gently. I ask the Palestinian if he thinks the Jewish Freedom Forces will overcome their innate nationalistic tendencies and cooperate with the Arab Guerrillas under Husseini. He looks at me as if I had suggested that a fish should mate with a chicken. Even in the heat of events like this, people carry their prejudices with them like so many old men of the sea . . .

May 9: Under a cloud of a dark and sinister incident: the attempted assassination of Pope Pius XIII en route from Castelgandolpho to the Vatican City. A sniper opened fire on his car. Pope unscathed but a Cardinal at his side, Montini, was shot through the head. Scandal and suspicion: the right blames the ultra-left. A strong smell of provocation. The Junta overreacts, proclaims martial law in Rome. Troops manning roadblocks. Of course the horse has already bolted . . . Meanwhile the Conference proper begins in closed session, in the Palazzo war room. The polite truce of the opening week has ended. The Junta and the Dergue confront each other over the Ethiopian issue. Abiye Gebre denounces the Junta for inviting Haile Selassie. Walda Sion strangely silent, his blind eyes staring into a space only he can see. Finally he calms the ruffled feathers: Let us not press our Italian comrades too far to the wall. We control the country, let the old Emperor strut on his empty stage. It's clear to me the old warhorse doesn't share the revolutionary euphoria, he is weighing all factors carefully, he will not miss a trick. He reminds me of Fidel's lesson: trust no one, never assume victory is close. Under the guise of moderation, the blind man is reserving his cards, loth to give the Italians any excuse for a delay. Three of the comrades, however, are more impatient. Gebre, Tessema and Mengistu storm out. Four of us remain with the old man. No longer a united front . . .

May 10: Growing turmoil despite, probably because of the curfew. Violent Catholic demonstration burns down PCI offices. Loud calls for a 'Christian' government. The Junta promises to bring forward its general elections, from September to July. A bad sign of insecurity, dithering. At Conference: quick decision on Libyan Independence, with repatriation of settlers. I feel sorry, perversely, for those *colons*, beguiled by Mussolini's insane dreams . . . They will swell the ranks of reaction at home, causing even more problems . . . When Algeria is free the French will face even worse chaos, and there Fascism might actually replace the ailing Sixth Republic . . . Afternoon seminar at the Rocco Bonaldi works. Tremendous support from the workers for world liberation. Revolution does live in Italy, the Junta would do well to mark this . . .

May 11: Counter-demonstration of the left broken up with ferocity by *carabinieri*. Teargas flowed by the open windows of the Palazzo. Shots could be clearly heard. I tried to phone Calvinetti but could not get a line. Rumours of all sorts abound. Tension as we approach the 'nitty gritty' at the Conference, after the Honoured Guests – Nasser, Nkrumah, Jomo – have left. Haile Selassie expected tomorrow. The Dergue still split. Women killed in a slum demonstration in Naples. In Turin Fiat management have pulled out of the factories, a mass workers' occupation has begun. Talk of a 'Turin Commune'. What am I doing in this bearpit of a Palazzo???

May 12: Yet more trouble. Labour Minister Berlinguer (PCI) assassinated. That may well be a genuine ultra-left act, if so, the height of folly. More calls for 'law and order' . . .

May 13: Betrayal, intrigue, deception. My heart has not been as heavy for years. Selassie arrived, a regal but sinister figure in his Imperial braid. He was accepted frostily by the African delegates, but embraced on the podium by Walda Sion, who hailed him as 'brother' and called, out of the blue, for an Ethiopian 'Government of National Unity'. While this amazing *volte face* was occurring, I was called out into the corridor by Abiye Gebre, who informed me that the German politbureau has told the Dergue no more arms will be supplied unless Selassie is brought in as Head of State. His so-called 'army', kicking its heels in Morocco, is to be recognised as a Liberation force, and allowed to occupy named garrisons. I am outraged, but I recognise the hand of Minister Heydrich. Soviet Germany, cut off from its Russian markets by its feuds with Trotsky, turns now decisively to the west. Trotsky warned me about it. He said, 'They are grocers at heart, ledger clerks aching to be invited for tea at Buckingham Palace . . .'

At the end of his speech Walda Sion left the hall and I cornered him in the toilets. I asked him point blank what his game was. His sightless eyes looked at me, and he embraced me, an odd and embarrassing moment in that setting. 'You are a fine man and warrior,' he told me, in his fluent Spanish, 'your commitment will be an inspiration to millions. But I must be a politician for my people. The German betrayal is a clear warning. Our people want peace, reconstruction. They won't forgive us for choosing endless bloodshed and war. This "Emperor" will not live long, and his heirs are nobodies. We will embrace him now only to bury him later. The Ethiopian has waited three thousand years for justice. He can afford another decade while we consolidate and rebuild.'

But ugly scenes with Gebre and Mengistu. Schism, rift, threats of civil strife . . . The Imperialist wedge is forming . . . I can't in conscience join this 'National Government', nor will I align myself against it. At this point I can no longer play a role in the struggle in that battleground, at any rate until this wound is healed . . . Walda Sion understands. Mengistu does not, and accuses me of being a 'German puppet'. A definite sense of failure in the air at the very moment when success should be enjoyed . . .

May 14: I speak again to the workers, at the Rome Fiat factory, sneaking through the curfew. Again the balm of the people's enthusiasm, so unlike the petty discord of their so-called saviours. I chastise the Junta openly for not arming the workers. Calvinetti phones me later: 'Some people here want your head on a plate.' 'I am not yet à la carte,' I tell him. The Italian Revolution is beginning to stink, like a fish, from the head . . .

May 15: It's happened! The Turin Workers Council has declared a Commune! Support has come from the Municipal Council, the *carabinieri* (amazing!) and the Piedmont Third Army Council! A long list of demands issued: nationalisation of banks, insurance companies, utilities, Fiat etc, councils of peasants, workers and soldiers throughout the land to elect a constituent assembly, legitimisation of peasant takeovers, repeal of the Lateran Accords, a comprehensive bill of rights . . . But in Rome, naturally, pandemonium! The word 'commune' is a red rag to the bull – the bourgeoisie's ultimate bogey! The French Commune, 1871, drowned in the workers' blood, the Berlin Commune, which led to the Soviet German Republic of 1923 . . .

I cannot raise Calvinetti or Fraia or anyone on the phone, they are all in marathon session. The hell with them. I am tired of playing 'realpolitik' – the real politics are out there, in the north. The politics of real people rising from their degradation to take matters into their own hands. I no longer have any hesitation. Goodbye, Hotel Imperiale/Ethiopia! I pack my rucksack and leave Rome . . .

Rachel
Turin, May –,

INTERVIEWER (*myself*): Why the Turin Commune?
ETTORE BRASI (*Commune Executive Committee, Fiat Mirafiori shop steward*): You must understand that before March 5, Agnelli's Fiat and Mussolini's Fascismo were like Siamese twins. Fascismo was the guarantee for the profits of Fiat and other Confindustria giants. Working conditions were terrible, wages were kept low while prices went up, strikes were illegal, the so called trade unions were mouthpieces of the twin-bosses. Hours were long without overtime pay, safety regulations were ignored. In short, we were serfs of the company, with Fascismo as our police dog.
MYSELF: But March 5 brought in reforms . . .
BRASI: Oh yes, in theory, many promises: shorter hours, a minimum wage, free trade unions, the right to strike . . . yes. But the writ of the Junta in Rome never reached Torino, certainly not as far as our management. Fiat resisted reforms, it wants to stay in the stone age. Faced with demands for the implementation of the March 5 reforms they threatened to close the plant down. This affects all of Torino, we are a 'company town'. So we have to say simply: If Rome can't challenge Fiat, then Torino will take up the gauntlet. If the workers are not given their rights then they will take them of their own accord.

Turin, Revolution Town: despite the posters, the clamour, the exhortations, the center of the city seemed strangely quiet when we arrived by train from Rome. Luigi, Alex and Christos picking us up at the station and driving us down the wide thoroughfares, past the clattering trams, the sombre façades of the baroque buildings. Tourists even, would you believe it, meandering about the Piazzas, snapping monuments, window shopping in the Via Roma, consuming *tartuffe bianchi* in the cafes. Traffic guards and *carabinieri* ambling vaguely about, only a closer look revealing the red armbands round the blue or green uniform sleeves. Is nothing happening? It might appear so, until we reach the high grey walls

111

of Fiat Mirafiori, with guards in overalls with old carbines slung over their shoulders manning the old iron gates, the legend LIBERTY, EGALITY, SOLIDARITY painted red upon the grey. Ushered through, up to the main office building, festooned with red flags, the ex-director's office walls covered with the now familiar Marx, Lenin, Trotsky, Gramsci, Bakunin, Malatesta, and a large banner proclaiming:

HONOURABLE LABOUR OUR OBJECTIVE:
WE WANT NOT WEALTH BUT FREEDOM

A mass meeting in the toolroom yard. Over a thousand workers pack the enclosed space, men sitting on iron galleries overhead, dangling their feet, some acrobatic crazies hanging on to the rafters, twenty yards above the crowd. Shop stewards and delegates speak one after the other from the platform, punctuated by cheers, jeers, heated comments, questions and harangues from the floor. Alex, with the Marconi recorder, and Michael, with the Victor camera, are scrabbling for space with several other camera teams, Italian TV crews who have joined the rebellion, German Soviet crews with their sleek Arriflexes, a shifty unshaven small Swiss from Paris called Jean Luc and a reticent, somewhat cadaverous Italian whom we only later discover is the famous returning exile, Pier Paolo Pasolini. The eyes and ayes of the world, waiting for the great moment –

It arrives: the star guest ascends the podium. Ernesto 'Che' Guevara, always the man in the right place, that iconic, militant Jesus face and the clarion cry: 'Arm the people! Only a People's Militia can guarantee freedom!' He is as certain, bold, arrogant as he was in Rome, when we made our first attempt to get him on film. Our first sight of him, in the lobby of the Hotel Ethiopia, conspicuous even in that wild melee of wiry black men in camouflage fatigues, dark glasses and berets, Italian army officers, Ethiopian and Italian radical priests, Asian politicians and Arabs in robes and military uniforms, and the world's paparazzi – 'Scusi!' 'Signori!' 'Hey, Che!' 'This way, Signor Nkrumah . . .' 'Will a free Libya join the Comintern?' 'Are we on the brink of a second world war?' We could not get within a mile of him, then, until, at the Rocco Bonaldi Works, that brief exchange with Michael, incomprehension across the chasm. Still,

112

he could be barely real to me, too, who had carried his image next to the murdered Fidel Castro down Madison Avenue, crying out, 'STOP U.S. GENOCIDE IN CUBA!' We didn't know he had survived the fires then. But even in that brief Roman encounter, the sense of someone whose entire personality was subsumed in its image: the Consummate Man of the Cause. I remember a phrase, in one of his essays: 'Victory can only come when the guerrilla accepts that, for the revolutionary, life is not the supreme good . . .'

Would Papa Levy have accepted that, in his passions for the Workers of the World? You are either for Imperialism or against it, *kindarlach*. You have to know where you are going. There is no middle way. Would he have accepted so extreme a sacrifice of the individual to the collective? Can the Jewish experience of survival above all live up to this fearsome logic? Or do its Christian roots not show – man subsumed in the Body of Christ – the many in the one . . . Surely life, no matter how degraded, is simply all we have? Or is that the rationale of the coward? Revolution playing chicken with our conscience . . . That crazy phrase again: to die for a better life . . . We have to accept our human frailties. Guevara, who does not, ultimately terrifies me . . . But not so Alex, Christos, or Natalia, motored down from Milan but ignoring Michael, gazing up from the front row of acolytes at the saint of her fires, addressing the working classes:

'What you have here is an interregnum. A calm before the storm. You have to decide now – is this just more street theatre, or is the game played in earnest? When the March Five Junta decides to tighten the noose, cut off food and materials, stop all trains and vehicles coming in, blockade the city, what then? And if the right wins the power struggle in Rome and moves the Army in, will you have a military option? Will you defend the city?

'What we do now in Turin determines History!'

Ah, yes, that old rigorous maid again . . . Down the Corso Blanqui (née Corso Agnelli), they stride, thousands strong, red and gold banners in the sun, slogans roared out, a forest of clenched fists flung high, a rag doll with a noose round its neck, labelled 'Agnelli', bobbing above the throng, a *carabinieri* brass band in full dress uniform, with red and blue feathers over their cocked hats, rendering *Bandiera Rossa* and the *Internationale*. A group of radical priests, black cassocks flowing, holding a banner proclaiming 'CLERGY WITH THE PEOPLES REVOLU-TION' (though it turns out later they were not clergy at all, but pranksters from the Urban Saracens). At the hideous Monument to the Hero of Abyssinia, which in 1948 replaced the defunct statue of Victor Emmanuel II, the crowd surges, loud cries calling for the atrocity to be pulled down, like the Vendôme Column in the Paris Commune of 1871. Ropes are thrown around the erect soldier ('looking like a broom was being shoved up his arse!'), but the bronze piece is too massive, the militants merely swing back and forth like performing chimpanzees above the multitude. An Austrian Marxist cameraman tries to climb on the statue, but slips and disappears under the marching feet and has to be retrieved by the stewards. Our film crew is crushed against a shop front and loses a light meter but otherwise we survive. The crowd moves on, chanting, 'Italy, arise! The proletariat is here!' past the train station, to the city center . . . For one afternoon, one day, one week, an irresistible force . . .

Joseph
Las Vegas

'Let me tell you,' I told Chmielnicki, 'about decisive, crucial moments of truth. Let me take you back in time, almost fifty years, to Germany, of 1923. A defeated nation, betrayed on all sides, its currency collapsed under the double-pronged assault of the Jews. The half-hearted passive resistance to the French occupation of the Ruhr. The red whore Rosa Luxemburg seizing the initiative in the streets – and to think our Freikorps units almost caught her and the bastard Liebknecht back in 1919! How differently things might have turned out then! My own ambitions in that year were vague, more literary than political. But, by late May, it was clear one could not stand aside. I joined the NSDAP, the northern branch, which was run by the Strasser brothers. Adolf was in Bavaria, and we had not yet met.

'In Berlin it was a summer of fools. Picnickers in the Tiergarten, wild drinking in the taverns, the Devil take beaten Germany. It was soon clear to me the Strassers were not up to the challenge, plotting with Reichswehr Chief Seeckert, who was just using them as tools for his own Junker class. Being a freshman in the Party, my views were ignored. But in July the Strassers reaped their whirlwind. Realising Seeckert's treachery too late they panicked, falling in with a madcap scheme hatched by Buchrucker, idiot head of the so called Black Reichswehr. This was the famous Reichstag Massacre of July 15. Prime Minister Cuno, Streseman and seventeen deputies were killed by grenades in the chamber. Seeckert gunned down on his way to the War office. This historic blunder gave the reds their chance, their pretext to set up their "Workers' and Soldiers' Councils", the so called "Berlin Commune". Their terror squads went into action ruthlessly and efficiently: the Strassers were captured and shot, Party members brought before red firing squads, "protecting the Republic . . ." With the Reichstag and Reichswehr dithering we got what our clever leaders thought was unthinkable, the Socialist-Communist Coalition, with Liebknecht as Minister of the Interior! A complete catastrophe. And the Reichswehr command accepted this "legitimacy", and the Freikorps were disarmed!

'I was in Cologne, holding together a tattered Party branch. Hitler, in Bavaria, was our only hope. I decided to join him immediately, and, evading the red mobs which were everywhere, I caught the last train south . . .

'It was a scene I will not forget. The train was jampacked, a microcosm of the German state: the bourgeoisie on the run, where to or who it betrayed in its flight it didn't care. Businessmen dressed in cast off suits clutched their bulging suitcases in vicelike grips. Jews who mistrusted their own red compatriots took the best seats, oozing the foul sweat of their fear. Soldiers abandoning their responsibilities squeezed through the corridors guiltily. How could I blame them? Two betrayals in one decade! The mind simply refused to grasp it!

'Only my wits stood between me and certain death at red hands. Union mobs and deserters stopped the train several times, and finally it halted for good at Wurzburg. The reds held the town, but I managed to evade them and found a volkisch couple I knew just setting out, like myself for Munich, in a car. It was another nightmare ride, but, benefiting from the anarchy and confusion that had seized the country, we eventually slipped into the city at nightfall, and headed straight for Party headquarters.

'It was my first meeting with Adolf, and I knew instantly this was not a man whose destiny should be squandered. Unfortunately he was surrounded by clods. Röhm was a strong animal, but a pervert in mind and body. Feder would have his uses later as wheeler-dealer but in the heat of Revolution he was a non-event. Eckart was quiet and dour, neither sweet nor sour. Rosenberg was mad. Hess was an arselicker, but useful to fetch and carry. Amman was and is a good Sergeant, nothing more. Goering cut a dash in his airman's uniform, oozing charm that was then just axle grease. Other Munich nonentities hung about, Pohner, Kriebel, Frick, Rossbach, Weber. The figurehead was General Ludendorff, a brave soldier, but a dunce. Adolf played them as a master his violin, but he spent too much energy where responsibility should have been ideally delegated. But to whom? Thinking of Adolf now, sick, pale and wizened in Carpentersville,

you must cast your mind to how he was then: The fire! The
passion! The power! Clay worthy of the potter, given time . . .
Time, that we did not have . . .

'I need not detail the four weeks of our Munich Volkisch
Republic. The misalliance with the conservatives, Kahr, Lossow,
Seisser, who tried to outflank us with some mad monarchist
scheme. They thought the Allies would invade to save us, but so
soon after their Russian fiasco, I knew this was not going to be.
The blue Jews Rothschild and Samuels nobbled the West while
the red Jews Luxemburg and Bronstein gobbled us up. After
foiling the royalist plot and hanging its perpetrators we ruled
alone in Munich for fifteen days. Fifteen days! What a bitter
irony. For two weeks and one day Adolf was Prime Minister and
I in charge of Propaganda and Security in the Bavarian National
Socialist Government! A sad echo of what could have been . . .

'The reds began their assault on us on September 9, supported
by duped Army units. Ludendorff wanted to fight to the last
man, and Adolf was tempted, but by this time I had gained his
confidence, and was able to convince him our task was to stay
alive to fight another day. It was a struggle, there was a part of
him which wished to burn on Germany's funeral pyre, but, as
you know, I had my way.

'At dawn on the 12th we punched south out of Munich in a
convoy of trucks and armoured cars. Fifty-five storm troopers
and the Party core: Adolf, myself, Röhm, Goering, Eckart,
Amman, Feder, Esser. Rosenberg and a prim young zealot named
Himmler were killed by my side. Hess got himself detached
in the turmoil and I have heard he still rots to this day in
a Communist prison somewhere. Ludendorff stayed behind to
achieve his martyrdom. Goering received the shrapnel wound
that led to his addiction. The rest of us were intact. After three
hours we crossed into Austria, and I remember our last glimpse
of Germany – a ridge of forested mountains, on a dark, blustery
day . . .

'Austria, which as you know, betrayed us. Dolfuss, the combless
cock, having hurriedly staged his own coup, wanted no competition. He ruthlessly crushed the NSDAP in Vienna and Linz. As
the purest examples of revolt against the reds we were pariahs
everywhere, as every government prepared the great surrender –

recognition of the usurpers. Warsaw, Budapest, Sofia, all feared us like the plague. Though in Budapest we were sheltered for a while by the Stahlhelms, whose daughter Annchen, on the spur of an insight, I encouraged Adolf to marry. The Stahlhelms' U.S. finances and interests promised a respite from our wanderings. Just a hiatus, we thought, while we prepared our return, until, once here, I began to glimpse that vision of a different road back, a longer, slower, bolder, potentially more decisive path than we had ever dreamt.

'So long a road, so many years. A lost cause? But we are here, masters of more than we thought. The grand opportunity, finally in sight. Finally, Colonel Chmielnicki, it comes down to the Will, and nothing else. Can the superior intellect triumph, over insuperable odds, over History? Shall we make the world in our own image, or shall we just perish in the mass?

'The United States of America, Colonel. That is the only possible power that can roll back the tide. The ripest time. With Italy fallen into anarchy, with Poland poised as powder keg, soon to be controlled by us, between the Bolshevik wolves. And now the fuse, our own Freddy, the long fuse soon to be lit. Oh, we will make a bang, dear Colonel, that will be heard, that will reverberate all around this sorry globe . . . Everything comes to him who waits, to the man who can command his soul . . .'

Michael
Turin, May 30

The ridiculous, the unwanted, the unbelievable. They have set up the Last Chance barricade, at the Piazza Statuto. At least that's what the ex-shop steward Ettore Brasi calls this double line of sandbags running left and right from the base of the Frejus Memorial. The first glimmers of dawn light a scene out of some Mexican Revolution movie: a long line of grim-faced men squatting, sprawling, leaning against the sandbags, their scrapyard ragbag of weapons pointed ahead at the dark maw of the Corso Luxemburg. A silent scene first, then fade up on the metallic clink of an old Lee Enfield barrel, the click of a tested bolt, the rustle of changing positions, then a muffled mumble of sporadic, hushed dialogue.

How did I find myself in this absurd situation? The John Wayne movie, without John Wayne. Instead, the only slightly more real 'Che' Guevara sits, behind the line, slumped in the front seat of a jeep, his ear cocked to the lashing crackle of a radio set emitting static into the morning air. In the back seat of the jeep the enigmatic Pasolini, cradling his camera, chainsmoking his Ras cigarettes. He had passed the pack round to us the previous evening, when we first arrived, exchanging laconic camera information about film stocks, lenses, lights. Christos, Alex and Rachel beside me, with the accessory boxes and sound recorder. Co-respondents of the war zone . . . And Natalia? Glances, whispers, embers, as she turns her eyes on the Hero . . .

Insanity. Or do I deserve this, for not listening to my alarm bell, the one set to ring at the advent of 'It Is Good To Die For Our Country . . .' Memories: A gloomy Jerusalem winter's night for Michael Pinsker, staying late at the office of Jaffa Films, the newsreel company, on call due to the broken leg of cameraman Moishe Landau, my boss. A telephone call from Agency man Katz: We need a dawn birdwatch for the archives (that was the usual code) . . . Dumb Pinsker pledges his appearance, instead of claiming lack of authorisation (even the most cautious succumb to grandiosity, the chance of a scoop, God knows . . .). Turns up for assembly at 0300 in a clump of pine trees adjoining the Jerusalem Biblical Zoo. The zoo night-watchman watches out for British fauna while eight Haganah irregulars don Brit Army uniforms and creep down, with Pinsker and camera, to the Nebi Samuel Road, to be picked up by two jeeps in army khaki. We speed off towards the Arab village of Nebi Samuel, in the Rammalah canton, a ten minute drive away. We never got there. I never found out if the ambush had been for us or whether we'd been mistaken by *their* underground for a real Brit patrol. It was just another of those crazy inter-communal reprisals: they had put a bomb in a dustbin in the Jewish town the day before, killing an old lady walking her dog. What we had in mind for Nebi Samuel I never found out either. Flashes and bangs tore the night and our jeep swerved into a ditch. We lay there, pressed into the cold mud (it was a bad December in more ways than one) shitting in our pants (or was I the only one?) while bullets gouged out shards of rock. I just clutched my camera tightly as if it were mother and swore this was the last time, God save me, that I got involved in the madness of war . . . God must have heard me, sending the wah-wah of British police sirens, which chased both sides off, staggering through the mud, they back to wherever, we back six kilometers to the Biblical Zoo, with our tails between our legs . . .

Speak not to me of Heroism . . . But for Natalia – sheer bliss! At the feet of the living legend, worshipping every toe . . . Whatever spell it was that had held us together in the heady first days of Milan, it had completely evaporated by Turin, even before she had set her gimlet black eyes on Captain Revolution. 'What do you want from me, Michael? The situation is desperate. There are no more personal problems here. Don't you have any proportion?'

The whole world can come to an end as long as I have my cup of tea. Or a caress. Or one good word. Or the sight of you, birthday sheer. The flow of your hair, the curve of a shoulder. The elemental force, amore, reaping those wild oats.

No. 'This is no time for selfishness, Michael. We have to stand and fight. This is my place, you don't have to be here. You can walk through the lines and goodbye. No one will blame you.'

Oh yeah? Wait and watch them line up to point the finger.

Alex and Christos, the mournful Greeks, carrying their own scars and failures, Rachel, drawn towards the political absurd despite appearing to walk away from it, a curious sideways shuffle leading her to be, it seems, in the wrong place at the right time . . . Principal Kinross, who entrusted his Victor NPR to me, cautioning me to stay out of trouble but his eyes saying, Go get 'em boy, let's see what you're made of. My parents, convinced I would fly the coop only to find how dangerous and venal and unJewish the world outside can be . . . My mother, dragged to pioneer Palestine by my dad from her native Stepney Green, used to sing me a baby song, out of her cockney roots:

> It's the same the whole world over,
> Ain't it all a bloody shame,
> It's the rich what lives in clover,
> It's the poor what gets the blame . . .

Turin is already surrounded, the main exit roads cut off soon after midnight by tank columns rolling in from Chivasso, Venaria, Rivoli and Moncalieri. One clash apparently took place, already, in the winding country road from the south, when an advance guard of the Commune ambushed one unit with two mortars and a grenade rifle. Eight bewildered recruits from furthest peasant Calabria died in their tanks, the first guinea pigs in the Italian Civil War . . . North and South, the Po and the Sangone Rivers were a second line of defence, halting the armoured columns across the bridges. But the western column could advance easily straight into the city, rumbling towards the barricades . . .

The marching workers, in their overalls. The proletariat awakened, the women loading their men's guns, some armed themselves behind the barricades, their children running messages from front to front. The Pabst film, Pudovkin's Mother, Dovzhenko's Arsenal, Brecht's Passion of the Lathe Operator . . .

How did it all fall apart? One moment people seizing their destiny, refusing their manipulation by bosses, politicians, Duces. The next they're chaff before the wind. The Turin Commune obviously disturbed the precarious balance of power in Rome. The spectre of city states, a dismembered Italy, secession, schism, catastrophic rupture. Things falling apart, or rather coming

121

together, in rarified political climates far above my ground level
. . . the Junta's feuds, the internal army pressure, big power
intervention, the East-West thaw, leading to Soviet German
isolationism, nuclear deals in the backrooms and parlours . . .

Natalia: 'You understand nothing, Michael. You contribute to
nothing. The archetypal wandering Jew.' Some of my best friends
are anti-semites. It comes free with most cultural baggage. But
there she stands, a figure out of a Pabst freeze-frame, a rifle
in her hand. No way of knowing whether her worship of the
Great Latino spilled over, in these warm Italian nights, from
the abstract to more earthy spheres, the dialectic of theory and
practice, the sexomarxoid synthesis . . . Damn. In the red heat of
Praxis, the human electrons zip about, meeting, producing new,
strange hybrids, anything is possible, especially in those heady,
wolf hours . . . Sweating, compatible bodies, humping to the
sound of Gramsci . . .

Not tonight. At 0502 hours, with the sky a deep hazy blue, the
first tanks rumble into sight . . . They advance, three abreast,
up the Corso Luxemburg (née Corso Mussolini), churning up
the asphalt of the road. Halting, with a screech of treads, fifty
yards from the barricades. From their ranks a loudspeaker calls
(translated for me by Alex):

'This is Colonel Crespi of the Twelfth Armoured Corps
speaking. I am calling on you by the authority of the Government
of National Liberation and in the name of the March 5 Revolution
to lay down your arms and let us pass. I am required by order to
secure the Palazzo di Citta, the Prefecture, the broadcasting and
transport facilities of the town of Turin. We desire no bloodshed.
Should these facilities be surrendered peacefully there need be no
confrontation, no victimisation. The grievances of the workers of
Fiat are on the top of the national agenda and are even now being
discussed in Rome and in Milan.'

A silence. Then big Ettore Brasi, who told us he was an artillery
gunner in Libya in his national service, climbs on the barricade
with a megaphone (Alex translating once more):

'Agenda and discussions! While you bring tanks into an Italian
city! We know your troops have been told that Torino is in
the hands of fascist counter-revolutionaries. Which masters do
you serve, Colonel Crespi? Which new Roman conspirators?

Soldiers! Tank crews! Is it your revolution to bring tanks against the working class, or that of neo-fascists? Stop your engines! Leave your tanks! Turn your cannons away! Join your brothers, as oppressed Italians!'

The tanks sit in the road like growling dragons, trying to make up their minds if they have an appetite or not. Pasolini ambles up, with his camera. The world famous director of *The Rapist, Morti de Fame, Oedipus Sam* and the Mormon epic *Joseph Smith*. A man about whom several books have been written, the man who 'demonstrates the thin line between dream and reality' (*Cahiers du Cinema*). All I can think of to ask him is, 'What exposure would you give for Eastman 7254?'

'Between two point eight and four.'

I focus on the lead tank. A turrent is flung open with a sharp clang, emitting a khakied figure who waved his tank helmet and ear muffs and shouted indistinctly. Heads raised over the sandbags, trying to catch the words. But they were drowned in a sudden thrum of engines. The two flanking tanks wheeled, rocked on their chassis and then, cannons pointing straight ahead, roared straight for the defence line.

Pasolini pulled me down by my belt as the mid tank swung its cannon into position. An ear- and lens-splitting explosion. The People's Armoured Car, behind us, taking a direct hit, burst into flames. I lay flat on the ground, the world-famous director on top of me (bizarre, untimely thoughts of his pederastic reputation!), while, in front of my eyes, I can just glimpse Rachel, curled in a foetal position.

Rifle and machine gun fire up and down the line. The crash of a grenade rifle. One tank, hit or panicked, crashing into an arcade on the Piazza, jammed in a shopfront, festooned with unsold summer frocks.

Brasi, knocked down by the explosion. Guevara, pulling him away. Festooned with ammunition belts and grenades, sub-machine-gun in hand. 'Bazooka men' he calls out, 'bazooka men!' A two man team in Fiat overalls rushes forward, kneels. The left tank ploughs into the sandbags. 'Fidel Cocktail!' cries Che. A man hands him the paraffin bottle, which he stands up and hurls at the turret, followed by a grenade. The turret catches fire. It opens, a figure scrabbles to get out. He is on fire.

Guevara rushes closer, lobs in another grenade. A spew of flame and a strange, rancid smell I do not want to recall. I suddenly remember I have a camera. In time to film the burning tank. But the ones behind open machine-gun fire. We huddle in the dust and sand. Rachel, Alex, Christos, myself, and Luigi from Milan.

And Natalia? Remembering, suddenly, she had been at the command jeep, by The Hero. It takes more than enough heroism just to raise your head half an inch above the sandbags. Nothing but running feet, hands, smoke, the sounds like an exploding armaments factory.

Remember the Biblical Zoo! Nebi Samuel! The futility of feuds! Not my war, man, not my battles! I live to not fight another day . . . Nevertheless, embarrassing to note, but Christos was there to bear witness, he runs with me across the barricade – leaving the camera with Rachel – we rush past shouting riflemen, towards the memorial in the Piazza center, half a titan already blasted away by tank fire. Beside it the command jeep lies blown on its side, burning petrol surrounding it like a wreath.

She lies on the ground, on her stomach, as if hugging the cold ground. Christos pulls her over. I have seen sights like this before. A bomb, in a market stall, leaves its traces of slashed raw meat and brown red stains. Christos calls out, 'Medics! Medics!' I forgot he did his Greek armed service, another unpaid mercenary in a bad cause, but all they seemed to do, he told me, was hang about the Turkish border masturbating to exhaustion. 'Your external enemies are always inside you,' was his dour conclusion.

Guevara appears, out of the fire. Her face, I now see, is smudged with soot, as if boot polish has been applied. Her eyes, unlike the cliché, are closed. She did not want to see the end. The Hero, with no sign that she is anything more to him than another item lost in the revolutionary mail, lifts her, throwing her over his shoulder like the proverbial sack of potatoes. He runs, we run with him. A dead soldier hangs from a burnt turret. There are more bodies on the road. Some crawl, some propel themselves sideways, like crabs.

'The soldiers are coming!' The après-tank trucks, disgorging. Two men with red cross armbands. A stretcher. The rag doll lifted on it. The back of an old Fiat van, with a makeshift white flag. Guevara dumps the corpse beside several still figures already

124

there. Just fulfilling the last function for a comrade? A medic slams the door, the van screams off. Another vehicle, an old furniture van, Alex, Rachel and Luigi gesturing to us from inside, appears. We pile in. A whole range of vehicles, with overalled figures climbing aboard. The Last Chance Barricade, having shot its bolt, is being swiftly dismantled.

The tale, full of sound and fury, told by an idiot, no doubt, but signifying, nevertheless, something? Later the loose ends are tied: they buried her, Natalia's family, whom she had left and whom I never saw, in Pavia, her birthplace. I'm told it's quite a nice cemetery, not too crowded, lots of trees. In the November elections, which were won by nobody, resulting in an all-party coalition, the PdPO (Luigi's branch, pro-broad left), received 0.2% of the vote. The chief rebels of Turin, such as Brasi, received lenient jail sentences, three to five years. The foreign film crews were deported. The Junta purged and reconstructed. The new Council of the Armed Forces arrested Major Giuseppe Calvinetti on the 2nd of June. Ushered into, what else, a small Fiat Mirafiori and driven off to exile on an island which does not seem to have a name. He is proofreading a provincial newspaper. On the next island along the man he arrested four months before, Count Ciano, the last fascist Prime Minister, is busy writing his memoirs.

In the dark of the furniture van, I think I just laid my head in Rachel's lap and pretended I did not exist. Maybe it wasn't a pretence. Amid absurd events, one becomes oneself absurd. While Natalia's dead body was carried in the other van towards the morgue, and her Hero (ex-lover, in my fevered dialectic?) disappeared into the battlefog night, Colonel Crespi's column drove over the remaining sandbags and headed unopposed down the Via Garibaldi, its shopfront façades just waking up to the sunny new morning. Did people crane their heads to watch, from their windows, gates, portals, peepholes, or did they just keep their shutters firmly closed? There are times to neither see, hear nor speak evil. Luigi, in Milan, uttered the epitaph, quoting the phrase coined by Freethinkers faced with the Inquisition in Italy in the sixteenth century: *Foris ut moris, intus ut libet* – the façade conforms with the reality of the day, the interior to one's choice.

Part IV

Over the Top

January–April 1970

Extract from *Terror Campaign 1961*, by Rachel Levy

Marion, Alabama, November 5: Walter Cronkite's face on the TV set is an ebb and flow of grey lines. His eyes popping out like pingpong balls. For the first time in two decades he seems tonguetied:

'. . . uh, well, as you can see, uh, by the, uh, board, we have a truly sensational situation, a situation, yes, that will be, uh, deeply disturbing to both major parties . . . the north-south split . . . as predicted, the American Party has taken the entire Deep South but it has also gained the electoral votes, on the winner-take-all principle, of Florida, California, Texas, Illinois, New Mexico, Nevada, Arkansas and Utah . . . this is a constitutional crisis, the like we have not faced since the Civil War . . . an unprecedented challenge to the two-party system . . . our exit poll, conducted at the polling stations, gives the American Party 178 electoral votes, with the Republicans taking 182 electoral votes and the, uh, Democrats trailing with 164. This means no party will have a clear majority, and the election of the President of the United States will go to the House of Representatives . . .'

I am home. The nightmare is supposed to be over. New York rasps and blasts all about me. But the terror now blares into my sanctuary, courtesy of FBC News. The Walter Cronkite Hour, as the pundit interprets the world for the boobs, rubes and squares. The experts drivel. Congressmen and Senators are said to be tearing their hair on 'the floor'. One little professor dares to say this may just be the storm before the calm, the constitutional system will cope. He is cut off. There seems to be a panting desire to see America go down the plughole. The political deathwish to match the Pacific War Holocaust. An ingenious compromise is dredged up – Nixon as President, with Rudy Hitler as his Veep. Are we soon going to be crying out, 'Come back, Tail-Gunner Joe, all is forgiven'?

The South still shudders on my retinas. The burning bush of the Reverend King's gutted home, the plumes of black smoke disfiguring the blue, blue southern sky, the truckfuls of drunk young men with shotguns and ropes. No longer are the deeds of death done in hidden corners, in shadows, by the light of the burning cross. The fires of prejudice and fear burn bright in the daylight, in sunny Alabama, charring the dreams, bursting the strange fruit on the trees . . .

In the eye of the cyclone, I sit watching the Terror unfolding on the screen in the anonymity of graphs and numbers. The latest from the House: the ballot will confirm Nixon, but there are fears of a Hitler backlash, secession, a new Confederacy, ghosts of civil war, potential holocausts just waiting for the spark. Rudy, having booked a victory rally in Florida, is going to call for a March on Washington: the Klan's real apotheosis, a lurid echo of Mussolini's March on Rome . . .

I feel sick and turn the television off, walking out into my familiar streets. Broadway, Upper West Side, tingling with the human concoction of all colours, shapes, sizes. My cocktail, my melting pot, despite the November chill. A sudden burst of rain sends all of us huddling in shop entrances, under awnings. The young blacks popping out from nowhere with armfuls of umbrellas for sale. The noisy complaints of bona fide Noo Yawkers about the bitchiness of the weather. The balm of ordinariness and the everyday.

But in Ed's Diner the miasma crawls also. 'The South! Let 'em split off, the bastards. Who needs it? Put a wall up between us and dem. I'm sorry for the *schwartses*, but we went to war once for dem. Sometimes you have to cut off an arm to save your body.'

The burning carcase of Martin Luther King. The flashing eyes of the young disciples, Jackson, Young, melting away into underground resistance . . . we will see them back, one day, with other weapons than charity and kindness . . . another legacy – if they survive . . .

But a man comes rushing into the diner. I have seen him before here, now and again, hunched over a cup of coffee and brooding. Now he waves his arms and the words stumble over each other out of his mouth: 'Have you heard? They shot that bastard Hitler! News just came over on the T.V. Rudolph Hitler – a sniper got him at a big meeting in Florida! Right between the eyes. Dead on arrival! How do you like them apples?'

A bitter sweetness. Stunned silence. Well, waddayaknow,

waddayaknow? For a moment it just doesn't register. Another act of violence in the South. Is that not what it was made for? Isn't that the American way? If Lincoln, why not Rudy Hitler? Finally, an eye for an eye?

Back to my cell. Cronkite in uproar. The Klan is loose and on the rampage. Now the madness is turned inwards, to fractricide. The assassin, thank God (?!), is a white man. And the rest is history, which you all know. Or do you? How many tips of icebergs have *you* scaled?

Joseph
Washington, January 20, 1970

The air of anticipation of the inevitable, as the crowd falls silent. Chief Justice Fortas pronounces the words:

'Raise your right hand and repeat after me: I, Joseph Patrick Kennedy do solemnly swear . . .'

'I, Joseph Patrick Kennedy do solemnly swear . . .'

'That I will faithfully execute the office of the President of the United States . . .'

'That I will faithfully execute the office of the President of the United States . . .'

'And will, to the best of my ability, preserve, protect and defend the constitution of the United States . . . So help me God.'

So help him. A moment of more significance than he can tell . . . In the midst of the crowd, I look up at the podium. My Vice-President elect, Frederick Hitler, leads the tumultuous applause . . .

RBC One News
London, January 23

With the deepest grief and sorrow, we regret to announce the death of His Majesty the King, Edward VIII, Rex Imperatur, who passed away peacefully at 4:45 this morning, at Buckingham Palace. The funeral will take place on Thursday, January 26th, at Westminster Abbey. God Save the King.

The *Times*, Tuesday January 24, 1970:
STATE OF A MOURNING NATION
Today and during the coming week people of all colours, white, black, yellow and brown, of nations at all corners of the globe, will be mourning the death of a man and a monarch, revered and loved throughout the world for his humanity, generosity of spirit and gentle charm. Thirty-four years are a long time for a man who led not by fear or tyranny or political inertia but by spiritual guidance and personal example, to maintain a place in our troubled and cynical times. The Britain that Edward VIII took leave of yesterday morning had grown immeasurably better for his presence at the constitutional helm. Innumerable political storms were calmed by his advice, always offered quietly and humbly, with a deep understanding of the monarch's position in the hearts of his subjects and the affairs of the realm. The reign that began with the famous clash between personal preference and the obligations of office, so decisively decided on the side of service, spanned momentous periods in our modern history, and five great Prime Ministers – Baldwin, Halifax, Morrison, Mosley and Gaitskell – have testified to the immense help rendered by this honest broker in the nation's sore debates . . .

The Prince of Wales now comes into his inheritance and his burden. Every loyal subject will join in our sincerest best wishes for the successful reign of King Richard IV. The new monarch, succeeding at the age of 52, ascends the throne at a time of great crisis for the nation and the Free World. Italy has only just escaped engulfment by the forces of collectivist extremism. Abyssinia is in a state of civil war. Britain's resolve is being tested on a dozen battlefields. The government of Reginald Maudling must face the stark choice of surrender or stand firm in the face of communist subversion throughout Asia and Africa. The vacillations of the luckless George Brown handed the Soviet powers a 'thaw' in Europe combined with a free hand to kill and maim British and Commonwealth troops. The 'logic' of appeasement has lengthened wars that could have and should have been won in the early sixties (one thinks especially of Kenya and the Gold Coast). The new monarch could do much to unite the nation round a patriotic policy of steadfastness and support for our European Allies. Poland, wracked by 'secessionist' terrorism doubtless engineered by Moscow, must surely take priority. Czechoslovakia, Hungary and the Baltic States should not be Oliver Twists begging plaintively for a second helping because our tame 'liberals' and 'democrats' dislike their 'authoritarian' forms of government. All Britons should extend a warm welcome to the new U.S. President Joseph P. Kennedy who was inaugurated last week. (And as he too has seen fit to bury old grievances and bind old wounds we too should welcome Vice-President Hitler without carping reservations.) King Richard could do worse than make rejuvenated Washington the destination of his first royal tour. With her great ally, and with the new King treading firmly in his father's footsteps, Great Britain can regain her dignity, and face her enemies armed with Christian Faith and iron determination in the cause of Liberty and Freedom.

Great Britain, February, Film Reviews

Manchester Guardian:
The re-issue of Pasolini's only Italian feature, the notorious *The Rapist*, is a welcome chance for reassessment of this unique film-maker. It is interesting to view Pasolini's well-known American films in the light of this uneven first masterpiece, and note how Italian in every sense are his preoccupations. Franco Gabardini as Cico, with his uncanny and obviously deliberate resemblance to the Duce Mussolini, portrays in microcosm the fascism Pasolini feels is inherent in the Italian male, obsessed with virility and terrified of the spectre of impotence. One can imagine the storm the film caused in 1959 when it was passed by mistake for exhibition by a dull-witted censor. The sheer enormity of the provocation still boggles the mind. What still remains today is a powerful vision of a twisted world portrayed with utter realism and yet the true stuff of nightmare, a hell more terrifying for being set firmly here on earth. Maria Vacca, as Cantina, excels as the sultry, castrating female familiar from later Pasolini works . . .

On a double bill with 'The Rapist' at the Paris-Pullman comes *The Scarecrow Has Passed Away*, a rather uncomfortably named documentary on Italy's short-lived Revolution made by three graduates of the London Film Academy. The Scarecrow of the title is of course Mussolini, and the film contains a fascinating newsreel compilation of the Duce's years in power. In its current-day footage the film portrays well the temperamental and chaotic nature of the local insurrections unleashed by the Junta of well-meaning but naive young officers, but the narration's heavy bias towards the extreme left, however, ultimately robs it of coherence. The sequences of the 'Turin Commune' nevertheless are a good sample of *'cinema vero'* and the telephone interview with an extremely crackly Major Calvinetti in his exile on the remote island of Lampedusa has a particular poignance . . .

(Derek Malcolm)

Daily Mail:
After the Duce has gone the vultures caw over the carcase. The Paris-Pullman, owned by the communist dominated Contemporary Films, regales us this week with a double bill of anti-fascist cheerleading. The vastly overrated Pier Paolo Pasolini's first feature, *The Rapist*, is a strident ya-boo-sucks at Mussolini's flamboyantly male image. *The Scarecrow Has Passed Away* is propaganda for the extreme Italian left, comprised of old newsreel footage and interminably boring shouting-matches in Italian factories masquerading as 'workers' democracy'. The only point of interest is a brief interview with the Communist adventurer 'Che' Guevara, who provides the 'International' linkage. The film was made by a Palestinian Jew, an American Jewess and two Greek anarchists who studied at the London Film Academy. How far can British hospitality and tolerance be stretched?

(*A. Hawker*)

Daily Worker:
An unfortunately typical example of ultra-left irresponsibility, *The Scarecrow Has Passed Away* falls into the trap so neatly prepared by the retreating ruling classes. Distorting the true loyalties of the Italian workers, it crudely attacks the PCI (Italian Communist Party) under the veneer of a 'Marxist' analysis. Last month we saw an equally dispiriting example from the French 'situationist' Godard. The Italian Revolution still awaits its true cinematic champion.

(*Hilda Cox*)

Revolutionary Socialist:
The film is a valuable chronicle of two months in the revolutionary process. Its somewhat cynical observation of the Revolutionary Left in its internal conflicts, however, does a disservice to its generally welcome message, and we are left at the end with a disagreeably pessimistic prognosis.

(*J. Hardy*)

Michael

But do we mourn? Not bloody likely. It's too damn cold. The freezing winter of 1970. No sign of the sun since mid-October '69. Night falls at 3:45 p.m. or thereabouts. The damp penetrates an overcoat, two sweaters and a shirt, and thick boots over two pairs of socks. The parks and green spots are stripped, barren and muddy, after a long frost. Two children died on New Year's Eve on Hampstead Heath, trapped under the pond's cracked ice.

What was that England on which I set foot, two years ago? The White Cliffs of the Land of Promise, the crying seagulls, the train ride through cabbage smells past trees and meadows, rows of brown brick houses with tiled roofs and chimney pots, ah, the delight of it all . . . and then the great metropolis! Ahhhhhhh . . .

A far cry from that now, though the quick habits of re-acclimatisation . . . the umbilical cord still tugging, despite everything, to the Old Home Land back East . . . Resuming Monday morning's reflex procurement of the Hebrew Palestinian rag *Ma'ariv* from the International Newsagent in Old Compton Street, choking over the latest mad echoes of the abandoned Cause in the swinging carriages of the Gaitskeloo Line:

FARMER MURDERED IN MEGIDDO BY ARAB
    INFILTRATORS
BRITISH COMMISSIONER'S CAR STONED IN
    RAMAT GAN
DAYAN: THE FEDERATION HAS NO FUTURE
    CALLS FOR JEWISH STATE NOW

GOLDMAN: FEDERATION BEST SOLUTION
    Jews and Arabs must cooperate, says ageing Zionist
    Council head. Chief Rabbi Firon: Goldman is a wolf in
    sheep's clothing.

Out of the freezer into the furnace. No return to that, thank God. If the old geezer had meant us to have roots he'd have made us vegetables, though some of us come quite close . . . Nevertheless, I remain here, with Alex, as both Christos and Rachel have left, to pursue will-o'-the-wisps of their own. Christos pining for his Piraeus beaches, willing to take his risks with the State, Generals or no Generals. Rachel having had her own attack of ethnic squitters several months ago, as we watched, together, in her bedsitting room, the November 5 elections in the U.S. The comfortable win of Joe P. Kennedy, the uncomfortable sight of Frederick Hitler as the new Vice-President. A heartbeat from the Presidency, they used to say, since the attempted shooting of Rockefeller in 1965. Old wounds opening up in her skin, as she wheezed, clucked, tore her hair, bleeding metaphorically from every pore.

Does the Negro change his skin? the leopard his spots? Her own unpublished book returns to haunt her with its visions of the forestalled apocalypse. The accident of fate that brought the sniper Homer Hargis within range of Rudolph Hitler in Tallahassee, Florida, on election night, 1961. The victory rally spotlights in his gunsights. The Union saved by the bell of a lunatic who thought Rudy was soft on the Jews . . .

'America!' she said. 'Love it or hate it!'

I could as yet offer her neither, though she was already proposing: 'Why don't you come over to Noo Yawk, Michael? This country is not the solution.' Too true, with its premature decay, its abysmal plumbing and lethal gas heaters. But someone had to stay on and complete the Italian movie, in the cubbyholes of Patrick Kinross's Academy, bent over the Steenbeck editing table in the small night hours. Fierce bouts of ideological and temperamental passions threatening to tear us apart. Not to speak of the pithy despair of the Greeks, eventually, over the reviews. Christos pulling at his Zapata moustache: 'But I am not Jew!' 'Never mind, one stroke of the scalpel and you too can join the brethren.' 'Is racist incitement! How can you stay in this country?'

I tried pointing out to him the bright side in the day's optimism from the *Daily Mail*: 'I SEE THE LIGHT AT THE END OF THE TUNNEL, says Brigadier "Mad Mike" Weemes, commander of the Kenya Expeditionary Force, describing his latest victory against the Mau-Mau. Nairobi's citizens, black and white,

lined the streets to cheer the returning troops after their successful north-western campaign.' But this only depressed Christos
even further. Only Alex seemed to have found his balance among
the alien British corn. This was mainly due to his having found
True Love with Kathleen, a slim and serious lapsed offspring of
an old colonial family, whom he met at his latest adopted leftist
splinter, the Revolutionary Independent Party, R.I.P. (Well, we
found it difficult to believe too.) Now they spend entire days in
bed together, reading Reich, Marcuse, Dichtman and Lukacs,
alternating with bursts of early rising to sell the Party rag,
Independent Revolutionary, at various Underground stations, or to
march against the endless depredations of the powerful against
whoever fails to turn the other cheek. Christos left in late February
for Greece, taking an advance copy of *The Scarecrow* hidden in
his luggage, the cold having finally so got to his marrow that he
preferred the tender mercies of the Generals at home, in the sun.
Apparently he reached Athens safely, unfouled by the customs,
and began organising screenings in basements.

Rachel left in late December, with another project in mind,
sparked off by the November déjà vu. A documentary film, to
follow on as a sequel to the theme of her unpublished tome. A
tour, with camera, through the landscapes she had not revisited
since the 1961 Terror Campaign. The cavalry charge through the
changed regions of the American South and West. Or are they
changed? Does the Fear still linger? This was what she planned
to inspect. Having gained the experience of our Italian project,
completed with the kind assistance of Alex's kebab moguls and
Film Academy Principal Kinross, whose two-year course we were
in the throes of completing, squeezed between reconstructions
of Berlin's twenties and fifth-generation remakes of Jean Harlow
films (bargain basement starlets clogging the stairways), she
yearned for something of her own. Kinross was unwilling to
let his equipment cross the Atlantic Ocean, but, she said, she
was sure she could find finance and support over there . . .

'I'll write you when I get somewhere,' she said, stuffing her
suitcases with the usual garbage she seemed unable to travel
without. Old political leaflets, ancient *Time* magazines, files of
newspaper cuttings, indefinable mementos. Pausing as she packed
the framed photograph she had nicked on impulse off the walls of

the Duce's mausoleum in Rocca delle Caminate, the sepia portrait of her *bêtes noires*, Joseph Gable and Adolf Hitler, the old foxes of Illinois. Fondling the faded echo of the strange cabal fixing their basilisk glares at us out of the past. 'Somehow, somewhere, I'm going to see that man again . . .'

But who am I to pry? We each have our foibles, defects, blemishes, scars and contaminations. Bad memories, like the bloody farce of Italy. The black-haired girl, buried in Pavian soil. Sacrificed, for what? Or is that merely my blindness? At the end of the day, I never knew the girl. I only lived for a few weeks inside my own fantasy of her convictions/delusions . . . The role she played for me, the role I played for her, the roles we imagined each other to be playing. Opportunities lost? Who knows. Breast-beating, stitching film together, I passed the winter freeze, retreated into my shell, my Kilburn High Road hibernation, beating off offers of more Shabbes afternoon tea at my *lantsmens*, or taking refuge now and again in the capacious bosom of Sarah Stein, still at the North London College and sculpting for the Revolution, bizarre shapes composed of old bedsprings and chairs. Now no longer sculpting heads. 'The human figure, Michael, it's a trap. We have to look inside the gut.' One stop before excretion, honey. But what else can I expect? Wandering, waiting for that Rachel postcard, nevertheless, a way out . . . Manna from heaven or anywhere. Anything but wait for the English spring. Other homelands? No, they don't beckon, yet . . .

Ernesto

Moscow in February: intolerable. I spend most of my time entombed in a poky one-room flat in Novo Khovrino, a stone's throw from the Khimki reservoir, huddled round an ancient heating device while minus 20 holds outside. A privileged privacy I could do without, at least other people give off heat. The previous tenant, I'm told, was a Szechuanese pianist who fled the wrath of Chu Teh to the sanctuary of Trotsky, who always had a soft spot for musicians and other artists, but, due to Party reforms, was able to return home on Christmas, leaving his piano behind. Another resident of the building, the British defector Philby, plays occasional English airs on it, a ludicrous combination with the hard ice outside. And in men's hearts too. Passion seemed to die here with the Old Man. Party Chairman Sklyansky appears wholly tied up with the 'Polish Crisis', such as it is. Billboards looming over Pushkin Square proclaim: DOWN WITH NEO-KOČISM, whatever that may be, and POPIEL – PUPPET OF IMPERIALISM. After Italy and the Ethiopian fiasco it all seems just a cruel deception. The Kremlin bureacrats are stamping on Bronstein's grave, making sure that voice will never blare again, bold and fiery, across the world. Once a week, I enter the Radek Metro at Lavochkin and Kamenev and venture labyrinthwards to meet Minister Mikoyan, the wily Armenian giving out the old oil of platitudes and banal bullshit. 'The late comrade Walda Sion was, as you know, a man for the long view. Impatience is the worst vice for a communist. Of course, his death was a blow for us all.' Indeed, a shock, though it could have been foreseen, precipitating me back into that quagmire with the Dergue's request for my 'good offices' again, as if I had any influence here . . . What Mikoyan means is that Walda Sion having been the only Ethiopian who could maintain both the Revolution and the coalition with Selassie, his death means the Kremlin has to take sides in the resumed guerrilla war. No longer a cut and dried decision, in the era of 'Thaw'. Our discussion always ending with the catechism: 'The budget vote is due in early March. Until then my hands are tied.' It is my hands they are tying, with barbed wire. I can only swallow so much. Free tickets to the Bolshoi and the Bulgakov Theatre are not what I crossed the continents for. Once a melancholy voice announcing itself as one Solzhenitsyn, Secretary of the Writers' Union, called, across the deep crackle of the hall telephone, inviting me to a Trotsky Prize Ceremony honouring the Party hack Pasternak. I passed him on to Philby, who enjoys these redundancies . . .

As ever, the poet foresaw my predicament:

> I do not wish to continue in solitary tunnels
> and overcrowded tombs,
> dreaming of light in cold corners,
> shivering like a child in the rain . . .

And yet Neruda also wrote: '– the light is not only a dream . . .'

The wanderer pulls up the roots, dragging them on, behind him, through the unlit tunnels. I will not be buried in these ice flows. Better the pitiless burning of the sun. I leave my invitations for high culture with the Englishman, who has done his bit, and sits in his hole, polishing his medals. Time to set out, for the next station. My train does not stop at this one any more.

Christos
Athens, March –

The Homecoming. One month now, and still that schizophrenia. One part of me here, the other back there, where the world goes by other rules. Alex, with his Kathleen, marching along the Strand and Trafalgar Square, raising the cries of protest. Here, silence. A disorderly order, in which the buzz of a café stops like a swatted fly when a policeman walks in. The low volume of banned Theodorakis tunes stopping when a neighbour walks by. The face of the General, Spandidakis, beaming twenty foot high on the sides of buildings, looking down on his obedient brood. My father, with his lifelong training for silence, hooked on the Armed Forces Television's inane quiz shows and dubbed Italian white telephone comedies from the Duce's Golden Age.

The time warp. But nevertheless . . . Home is home. A familiar prison, with certain privileges and old joys. The sunkissed streets, the cafés, albeit with lowered soundtrack, the beach, forever the beach, and with the beach, forever, Spiros, the Bakuninist Beach Boy, lying in the sun, or at home, sipping his *kafedaki* on his stool on the patio, while he waits for the girls to start their day's pilgrimage to and from his bunk bed. Generals, censors, dictatorships, make no dent in this timeworn, unrepentant tradition, of which, for sure, Rachel Levy would disapprove. The New Woman, demanding an equal place and an end to male domination. It was an enlightening experience, but it is also good to be home without guilt. To be secure in one's identity. Regrettable, I know, but, I must plead, authentic. Returned to my paradox, freedom in my prison, my prejudices, my fucked-up Mediterranean heritage. I wish Alex luck in his chase after the dream of the brotherhood of westernised intellectuals. His love and his desire to spread his wings in an atmosphere free of patrimonies . . . I wish Michael luck in his search for an exit from his Palestinian rootlessness. And Rachel . . . she will find her way. She has her own, searching desires. But I, like the Italian comrades, I need to breathe the air of my country, poisoned as it may be . . .

'Hey, wanker!' Spiros bellows. 'Stop dreaming and come aboard!'

With a rugged thrust, he guns the engine of his Honda motorcycle, wheeled out from behind the working shed. Slapping aside the clothes flapping from laundry lines, with his latest conquest, Evelina, brown thighs on the pillion, hugging his waist tightly. 'There's enough room, comrade!'

The bright Mediterranean light. The petrol fumes. The roar as we accelerate the wrong way down the one-way street, with a jerk that almost tosses us on our heads. 'Careful, wanker!' 'Forward!' As Spiros hurls us into the clamorous, indifferent, dusty, choking, polluted, grubby, wonderful Athens streets, towards the sea at Piraeus . . .

Ernesto
Berlin, March 12

The belly of the beast. Always the shock, disorientation. This once great capital of an Empire that never quite got off the ground. The great public squares, Rosa Luxemburg Platz, Karl Marx Platz, Paul Levy Platz, the vast Karl Liebknecht Mausoleum, the Leo Jogiches Monument, the Pieck Memorial, the Rosa Luxemburg Opera House and the Berlin Kanzlerei, the hub of Soviet Germany. Recalling my first visit here, a wounded, running soldier, plucked out from Havana's ruin . . . dazed in the vigorous street heartbeat, the multitudes of healthy, well-dressed people – a far cry from the horrors of Latin America, its shanty towns and *desalojos* . . . The vigorous intellectual life, or so it seemed to me, of Professors Herbert Marcuse and Adorno, the firm handclasp of Industry Minister Brandt . . . All gone with the cold blast of the bureacracy's vacuum cleaner: Ulbricht, the snow fox, the Organisation Man compleat, with his faithful Alsatian, Security Minister Heydrich, the wax marionette with the snake's eyes. It is Heydrich they funnel me to now, the balding, tall but now stooped figure slumped behind a massive desk in the heart of the Kanzlerei labyrinth. Rosa had made this old palace a museum, to show the public the wastefulness of rulers. Ulbricht and Heydrich moved in to stay. But I know I will get nowhere with this glove puppeteer, who merely wants order in the ant heap. My pleas for Ethiopia fall on deaf ears. 'Trotsky is dead,' he rasps at me, 'and the era of romantic adventurism is over. We live in a nuclear age. We will soon be sending Weltanauts to the moon and to the planets. Science destroys frontiers. We need fear the Imperialist blockade no longer. We will build space platforms instead of weapons and overtake them where it counts most. Ethiopia needs peace, not further bloodshed. Our own industries need wider markets. It is socialist prosperity which will defeat Capitalism, not the threat of mass destruction.'

Peace. The world burns. Men are killed and crippled and imprisoned round the globe, while these heirs of Rosa and

Liebknecht make deals with the killers. I ask to see Brandt. He is out of the country. Perhaps for ever. In this lair one can't tell. I get bolder and ask to see Marcuse, in Spandau. But visiting privileges have been cancelled. A glance of the cobra eyes suggest I can join the old Professor, for good, in the cells. I take my leave politely. This is not the world which dazzled my youth, which fired my hopes for something different, for a liberation that would flare out, out of Europe. More than ever, I know the Third World must liberate itself, free from the alliance of no longer opposites. No contradictions here. Merely the old betrayal. Time for the airport again . . . On the way, a mass movement of trucks, army vehicles, some kind of mobilisation. The late edition of the Party paper, *Spartakus*, explains brusquely: a coup in Poland, the old enemy, the thorn stuck between the Soviet powers. It makes me smile. Not everything, obviously, can be sorted out by gentlemen's agreement. In Europe, too, the barrel of the gun can speak louder than backroom whispers. I am detached, as I sink back into my seat, on the flight out to Paris, en route for the East . . . Who knows what plans and stratagems are ripening here, or gone awry and haywire . . . No, this is not my place . .

Joseph Gable
Desert Inn, Las Vegas, March 12

If there is any option for a Pole to screw things up, he will grasp it with both hands. Luckily, forewarned is forearmed. Chmielnicki, joining me in the Clean Room, brings me coded messages from Rakosy in Camp Auschwitz. Since 0140 hours our people have been monitoring heavy troop movements in Warsaw. A telephone call has been intercepted between President Popiel and the Radziwill. A coup. Warsawski jumping the gun. I scan the readout. The wily President is asking for Kremlin assistance and soothing Heydrich in Berlin. Warsawski is incommunicado and has moved without a word to our own men. The mutt thinks he can break through on his own. I am not worried. Win or lose, he does our bidding.

Nevertheless, he forces our hand in the crucial matter of timing. 'Is our man ready?' I ask Chmielnicki. The big Pole considers very carefully. I like a man who does not leap to conclusions.

'Operationally, yes. But not his cover.'

'In that case we have to consider Plan Alternate. Our only question is the venue.' The intricate links of the chain ... Bringing the action forward means I have the target's itinerary for April more or less pat. 'We have a choice of five,' I tell Chmielnicki. 'Grand Rapids, Des Moines, Dallas, Oklahoma City and Los Angeles. Dallas is out, there is too strong a presence there of the old American Party, which would immediately fall under suspicion.'

'Yes,' he agrees, 'Dallas would be too crazy.'

We open the Rand McNally and consider the options. But one venue stands out in its pertinence. I look at the Coast, that clean mapline, the jagged scar in reality. The prospective date of the visit. April 21st. Adolf's birthday. What could be more appropriate?

I look at Chmielnicki. He looks at me. We are in each other's hands. A bad moment. Have I made that crucial error of judgment I have feared so long? But all that is banished, with the true thrill of closing in for the kill, after so long. An inexorable process, ushered in by Poland's demise . . .

Warsaw, March 13

SHOCK TROOP FOR THE SALVATION
OF THE NATION:
Proclamation Number One:

In the Name of the Resurrected Republic and Her Martyrs!
Poles!

In 1830, 1863 and 1918 the precious blood of our sons
fertilised the heroic soil of our beloved Motherland and brought
forth the seed of our National Independence. In 1921 and again
in 1926 we spilled our blood to protect our birthright from the
onslaught of International Communism, under the leadership of
Poland's greatest son, Marshal Jozef Pilsudski . . .

Today once again we face the brutality and perfidy of our
Eternal Enemy: While proclaiming the brazen lie of 'Thaw' and
'Coexistence' the Commissariat of the USSR and of the GSR
continue to arm the instruments of world domination with the
talons of naked aggression, fomenting subversion and sabotage
throughout the Republic in a futile attempt to incite Poland's
loyal minorities against her. And while this furtive gnawing at the
Nation's roots goes on our own 'elected government' connives
with the Enemy and engages in acts of corruption and personal
intrigue which shame the Nation, sully the hallowed principle of
Freedom and stab the Polish people in the back at the hour of
their need.

Citizens of Free Poland!

We, the Armed Forces of the Nation, Guardians of the Destiny
and Conscience of Poland since she re-emerged with fire and
sword from the Deluge of the Great War, have once again been
forced to come to her rescue from a New Deluge, catastrophe
and possible dismemberment. We have temporarily taken the
Nation's affairs in hand, placing ourselves at the helm until such
time as the intense storm which now wracks the Ship of State
shall pass . . .

Lithuanians! White Russians! Ukrainians! Galicians! The Polish Nation has drawn her greatness from all her loyal champions!

Heed not the Serpent's Hiss from Moscow, the lying promises from Berlin! In the Brotherhood of Christ we are as One against the Atheist Usurper!

In accordance with this determination to place the Nation's Unity above all sectarian squabbling and party politics we hereby decree the immediate proscription of the following organisations, membership of which will be deemed a criminal offence from 00:01 hours March 15:

The Communist Party of Poland.
The Communist Party of Poland – Spartacist.
The Polish Socialist Union.
The New Liberation Peasant Party – Baginskist.
The Ukrainian Social-Democracy.
The Ukrainian National Labour Union.
The White Russian National Socialist Union.
The Pan-German Rights Alliance.
The Agudas Yisroel Party.
The Poale Sion Party (Zionist).
The Hebrew Freedom Party (Herut-Zionist).
The Jewish Workers' Union (Bund).
The Jewish Anti-Zionist Action Group.

In the Name of the Martyrs!
W. Warsawski, Brigadier-General,
Armed Forces of the Polish Nation.]

Rachel
New York, March –

However immune we may think we are from the twentieth century's terrors, the reality leaves us shaken and trembling, directionless, nerve ends on fire. I never again want to feel that moment of dislocation, that sight of Natalia bloodied and broken under the Frejus Memorial, any more than that other terror of my own, fleeing the Klan's wild fury . . . How do you keep your emotions balanced, your outrage against injustice intact and at the same time not be overwhelmed and forced to retreat, to join the legions of the apathetic clustered in front of the T.V.? Or on the other hand not to be pushed into fighting fire with fire, callousness with callousness, violence with violence . . . Can this tightrope be walked, or is the choice always evil or evil?

'They want to paralyse you with your own mortality,' Papa Levy used to warn, 'the bastards always take advantage of our scruples, our ideals, our reluctance to crack heads and spill blood. That was always the motor of social control, of the rule of the schmucks over people.'

I tried to explain the twist and turns of my confusion to Michael as I walked him through the cultureshock of Manhattan's gulleys. He had arrived, using the ticket I sent him, which he admitted he was glad to receive. The whiff of Turin, inevitably, in his trail, though by tacit agreement we shunned that subject. A late snowstorm had almost drowned the city in a sea of knee-deep slush, a fitting metaphor for my state of mind. We had talked about all these issues before, in London, but back in America I could articulate better the particular shades of the syndrome . . . Try and explain the drive which led me to sell Papa's old East Side apartment which he had bought two years before his death, and plough the bulk of the money into financing the film sequel to the unpublished '61 book. Rachel's Folly, a return ticket on Pan American Airways for Michael in London, and cash in hand to rent a proper Bell & Howell self-silenced movie camera. Literally on the house.

151

The almost biological urge of rediscovery . . . I tried to delve into its roots, taking refuge, with Michael, in Ed's Diner, over a bagel with cream cheese . . . Self-analysis, the political background: The seedbed – the Los Angeles Bomb. A jaded trauma, but all-powerful just the same. I was ten years old at the time. I remember my father shut himself in his room for three days, mourning not so much the hundred thousand dead of L.A. but the shattered sanity of Mankind. I understood only that the devilish Japs had killed Clark Gable, on whom I'd developed a crush. So, when three days later, our own revenge bomb struck Tokyo, I ran home from school to cheer, only to meet a terrible look in Pa's eyes that lingered on a long time . . . And then growing up, in the McCarthy age . . . Schoolkids denouncing their parents to their teachers, boys playing 'lynch the Reds' in the streets, the FBI 'Moonlighters' grabbing suspected Jap spies and Commies in the dead of night. The knock on the door . . . And nevertheless, we survived all that, and began through it all to think for ourselves, and talk, and protest, and organise, in the dead, gloomy years of Nixon, thinking that the night was passing for sure. And then – Rudy Hitler arrived . . .

Rereading my old fallow book: the hallucinatory trip into the twilight of the American Nightmare. White robes and burning crosses, evangelists with visions of blood dripping from the crucified, killer judges, murderous policemen, drooling lynch mobs for real, not kids' streetplay, hysteria and confrontation at the Miami Holiday Inn, the fishy stare of Gable né Goebbels and the All-Americanness of Good Old Rudy . . .

Violence and the American Grand Guignol: the irony of Homer Hargis, who gunned Rudy down in Tallahassee, being neither Jew, Negro nor liberal, but a member of a rival sect – the White Knights of Miami, which had denounced the Hitler family as, no less, agents of the International Jewish Conspiracy. Madness begetting madness in the closed circle of traditional American Bigotry – Know-Nothings, Coughlinites, Birchites et al, a very native dance of death . . . And now? All passed and buried? With Vice-President Frederick Hitler, the white sheep of the family, the inevitable press surge of interest. But, despite Republican muckraking, nothing in the shape of hard evidence. Papa Adolf, senile and bedridden in Illinois. Goering dead and buried. Joseph Gable, it appears, is just a retired hotel owner in Las Vegas. Presshounds answered with a polite shaking of the head and a suave rejoinder: 'I am just an old investor living on his investments. I have no political ambitions.' The past is the past. It is all over. History is for the academics.

Is that a fact? I am not satisfied. My nose, my Jewish nose, if you will, bothers me, and I'm damned if I'm going to get it straightened, fall in line with the liberal establishment's desire not to rock the Joe'n'Freddy showboat. After fourteen years of non-stop Republican Presidencies, this one is going to be nurtured, not sniped at. Freddy Hitler has brought the South back to the Democrats. Hallelujah! Tepid water made into wine. Even the Jewish Lobby, the Black Caucus, everyone joins in the lullaby. Let bygones be bygones. Let's look ahead, not behind . . .

A bona fide *kvetcher*, like my poor dead mother, I mistrust optimism. Tempting Michael with the ecstasy of hands on lens and bakelite, I rent a robust Tucker station wagon and pile him in the passenger seat. Locking our safety belts, heading out across the McCarthy Bridge to New Jersey and the hinterland of my exorbitant country, crying boldly:

'Let's go rattle some skeletons in closets!'

Let's just hope they will not be ours.

Joseph Gable
Las Vegas, April 2

Looking out over this city from the terrace of my suite. This garish funfair for dolts gashed across the desert exemplifies everything I have come to hold in contempt in this profligate republic: money to make more money, greed to produce more greed, and all to no ultimate purpose. The imbecility of those for whom this is an end in itself! But one still has to use this, to crack smiles at the dinner tables of affluent oafs, grand moguls of the greenback. Power in the accumulation of material objects is a game of overgrown children. At best just a veil to conceal the real thing: power over men's thoughts and desires, power to shape innermost dreams. Dreams and desires which mould real futures, which determine human history. In the end it does not matter whether one's name reverberates down the ages as a force for good or evil. As long as it reverberates, clearly, as the essence of one's will . . . This is the only soul that survives, one's ghost, bitter or sweet on the lips of coming generations . . .

The inane *Los Angeles Times* lies on the table before me: POL-ISH CRACKDOWN, RUSSIAN TROOPS ON BORDER. ROUMANIA REFUSES JEWISH REFUGEES, TOUGH LINE OF MARSHAL IOUNESCOU. KENNEDY PLEADS FOR JUNTA MODERATION: 'In his coming tour of the Mid-West and West this month, the President's keynote will be Foreign Affairs. The balance of power in Eastern Europe is crucial to the Free World, President Kennedy declared . . . the President's tour will climax in Los Angeles on April 21, the White House announced . . .'

The climax, no doubt! I am ready . . . Turning my back on that tinsel. Sinking back to reprise my files. Some people read cheap novels for relaxation, I like to go through my files. The power in knowledge that is mine alone (and at most one or two subordinates, in this case Chmielnicki), not the passive consumption of some inferior fantasist's ego. For the hundredth time, going over the Alternate, making sure I have not missed a weak link somewhere. I am glad I chose an older, more experienced man, rather than some young braggart. E. M., born Salzburg, Austria. Young Heimatblock Marksman of the Year, thrice running. Son of Commander of Vogelsang Military Academy, an outstanding cadet, chafing under the moribundity of Wienerschnitzeldom and senile Dolfuss. The human glockenspiel piece, hanging in there, through the late 1950s. 'In rigor mortis', the wags used to declare the State motto. Our man has no wish to play toy soldier in this pillbox, so off to Italy he goes, to the colonies, becoming the army's senior sniper. Then scooped up, spotted by Chmielnicki's eagle eye, taken under our wing, nurtured, serving us in Poland and South America. Nine flawless hits. The only drawback, insufficient cover in America. No matter, as the Third Man follows in his footsteps, instantaneously to close the gap . . .

Ernesto
Peking, April –

Chairman Chu Teh received me in the Palace of Heavenly Peace, at two in the afternoon, exactly. A soldier served us little rice cakes and delicate cups of delicately flavoured tea. The Chairman appeared all of his 84 years, looking like one of those deceptively fragile dolls that right themselves when they are pushed over. I could not fail to be awed. For here was the man who had led the Chinese Revolution since its previous chief, the famous Mao Ze Dong, died in a skirmish in 1942. The man who had buried the fascist Chiang Kai-Shek, in the decisive battle of Tsinan. He spoke firmly, in a high-pitched voice, with a vivacious Eurasian girl translating for me in fluent Spanish:

'Comrade Chu Teh is very grateful you have brought to his attention the present phase of the Ethiopian People's struggle against Feudalism and Imperialism, a struggle so familiar to the Chinese People. Comrade Chu Teh is aware of the contribution you, Comrade Guevara, and many other Internationalists have made to the Long March to World Socialism. Comrade Chu Teh wishes to assure you the People's Republic of China will aid the Ethiopian People and will supply their Liberation Forces with sufficient arms to defeat the Puppet Lackey Haile Selassie. Comrade Chu Teh is aware of the adventurist and opportunist policies of the so-called socialist regimes of Revisionist Germany and Russia and their betrayal of the Oppressed Peoples of Africa and America still groaning under the Colonialist Yoke, and wishes through you to extend the hand of friendship to all peoples struggling for Self Determination and Dignity.'

The Chairman bent forward off his dais and extended his small wiry hand. His grip was unexpectedly strong. A twinkle in the old man's eye belied his frail posture. The audience was at an end. I marched out, stifling the atavistic urge to walk backwards as out of a monarch's throneroom . . . A strange, irrepressible feeling of defeat. The knowledge that I am back in business again, yes. But at what price? What is the game played now, way above my head, in the hidden chambers and locked laboratories of naked state power?

Christos
Karpenisi, Northern Greece, April 5

Waiting with Spiros at the open-air café in the town's main square, for the messenger to turn up and tell us the venue of the screening of *The Scarecrow*. An act of suicide, Elena told me in Athens, to bring the film to this mountain province where no one can sneeze without the police and army collecting each germ in a satchel. But one cannot stay on the beach for ever. Plainclothes policemen have already sat in openly on two of our Athens showings, and yet they never made a move. The café tables stand on a raised paving in the centre of the square, round which the meagre town traffic swirls: a motor tricycle cart, a local notable's old Mercedes, a braying laden donkey shitting on the road. At the other cafés and shopfronts flanking the square the people of the town sit carefully weighing the empty passing day. At one corner a blue-uniformed cop lounges, hands on his hips. A green-jacketed army officer stands outside the main store, glaring at his fiefdom from behind his dark glasses. A white bearded priest walks by on a cane. Another priest, beside us, lazily eyes the day's *Eleftheros Kosmos*. At another table an old man with a face like the surrounding trees clicks his worry beads like a metronome. Two black-suited men whisper together, eyes straying now and then towards us.

It is a trap, set by our past. The waiter brings us Fix beer and two grimy glasses, flicking the bottlecaps off with a twist of his metal opener. He too, is eyeing us with a suspicion that may be meaningful or simply tradition. This is how it has been for several hundred years, perhaps thousands. Perhaps those ancient Greeks too, who are always quoted at us, sat like this, looking for the informer. Certainly through Turks and British, Greek 'democrats' or Generals, it has remained the same. The internal colony. The policeman watches over the profane, the priest the spiritual order. No one escapes. History might vary, Kings or Queens rise or fall, Generals interchange with each other, alternate paths twist and turn in the world outside, but here, in this town, the men will sit clicking worry beads and

158

keeping an eye on each other, until . . . But that is unthinkable
here . . . or is it?

We finish the beers and order two more. The long silence
draws through the endless spring day. Of the messenger, as yet,
no sign . . .

Alex
London, April 19

A postcard from Rachel and Michael, dated April 12, from somewhere called Van Horn, Texas. It shows a sweating man in the desert, with scattered cattle bones and a leering vulture, and a sign saying: 'Where The Heck Am I? Van Horn, Texas, Hottest Place On Earth, 150 Fahrenheit.' A long way from our own damp, grey regards. On an overcast, drizzly Sunday we marched, Kathleen and I and a few hundred others, from Hyde Park down Oxford Street to Westminster, protesting, again, as we have had to so often, against British Colonial policy and the massacre, by British Expeditionary troops, of two hundred villagers near Yendi, in the northern Gold Coast. Carrying the by-now faded posters of a dead African child, the placards saying:

FREE WORLD OR BUTCHERY?
AFRICA FOR AFRICANS!
BRING THE TROOPS HOME!

'Reggie Maudling, Hey hey hey, how many kids have you killed today?'

The police cordoned off Trafalgar Square and baton charged the march. Heads were broken, ribs cracked, teargas clouds blew towards the National Gallery, scattering art-loving tourists. Kathleen and I managed to escape into Whitcomb Street and took a number 88 bus up past the bustling shopping crowds of Regent Street back north to Bayswater and safety. On Monday the National Union of Students voted a one-day student strike next week to protest police brutality, and sent a message of support to all bona fide National Liberation Movements. Perhaps things are moving again. The ebb and flow of student skirmishes . . . On the other hand, steelworkers in Sheffield, the Tory press announces proudly, voted to donate a day's wages to the Aldershot War Wounded Fund. It's not going to be a short struggle.

No news of Christos, who seems to have vanished, let's hope just into Mediterranean laziness. I want to write to Michael and

160

Rachel, as they took a copy of the *The Scarecrow* to New York, and I wonder if they found a venue to show it. But I have no address, to follow their wanderings. America. A complete enigma to me, though my employer at the Cypriana Tavern in Camden Town, Mike Dukakis, waxes lyrical about the life he might have made there had his father been allowed an entry visa. Where other restaurateurs have pictures of their Greek home towns on the walls, he has New York, Chicago, San Francisco. He is a great admirer of Joseph P. Kennedy, a true immigrant's grandson, he says, shaking his head. But Joe Kennedy, according to the T.V. news, is touring the western states now. Iowa, Oklahoma, Texas, exotic climes . . . Perhaps he and my wandering colleagues might meet somewhere along the way . . .

Michael
Cross-Continent, U.S., April

Rachel drove first, with one motel stopover, to Chicago, mainly, she said, to dispel the image that name conjured in my brain: Al Capone, gunfights in the streets, gangs of berserk Hitlerites screaming Kill! Kill! Kill! at every street corner. 'It wasn't like that at all,' she said, 'Senator Adolf was the darling of the aspiring middle classes who felt threatened by upward moving blacks. He wooed them at dinner parties and barbecues and even Rotary Club meetings – when it came to votes, Freemasons, even Jews sometimes, were kosher. Not that death by violence was completely unknown. There was Daley, his rival for the Democratic Party machine, even you might have heard of his mysterious car crash in 1956 . . .' I learn something new every day. 'But generally, Illinois was the respectable face of Hitlerism.'

I was certainly glad to hear that. Belting up north from the booming city centre to Evanston, a suburb of lush condominiums, low slate-roof houses with huge lawns and long driveways, garage for two cars, rocking chairs on the porch, paradise, Amerikan nirvana. Off Euclid on aptly named McCarthy Avenue (a blight of these everywhere), she points out the old Gable pied à terre, sold off, it appears, when the good Doctor toddled off west to retire. Down the road, number 95, used to belong to another henchman, Robert Ley, ploughed under in 1965. *Sic transit non gloria.* And on to Carpentersville, on the River Fox. On a rise within sight of the river Rachel stops the car below the sombre hulk of the Hitler Père mansion, a shambling grey thing surrounded by a high brick wall with a massive, closed, iron gate.

'The House of Dracula,' said Rachel. 'Wanna take a shot?'

We get out of the car, under an overcast sky. Pointing the camera towards the brooding mass. No sign of life. Even the windows are opaque peepholes to a world I do not really want to know. But I am just an engineer here. I take the shot. Rachel shivers against the wind and speculates.

'Dead or alive? Or embalmed? Or half dead? Remember that

162

film with Bela Lugosi? White Zombie . . . slithering down the driveway to get us . . . Can you imagine spending your childhood in that house, with Adolf for Daddy? And they say Freddy Hitler is normal!'

No comment. We drive back south, into the city, where Rachel knows some old movement friends. People who marched and demonstrated here ten years ago. No joke in this town. Now they had a home, babies, a dog, no cat yet. They had voted for Joe P. Kennedy and consort, under the motto 'Better a tame Hitler than a wild one. Vice-Presidents have no power anyway.'

Who knows, who knows . . . Next day, loading up again, ripping down the busy Richard Daley Expressway, south, to Kankakee, Champaign, Paducah, Nashville, motels of legend and bad television, and then, further south, with her hands tight on the wheel, towards Atlanta, La Grange, nosing into Alabama . . .

Rachel

Dothan again, and Rosie and Dick Smith, still in the same house, as I'd been amazed to find out by mail, older and greyer as expected, but still straight-backed and exuding that confidence which kept them going in the 'bad times', as they now called them.

'The South has mellowed, but underneath, all the old problems: racism, poverty, ignorance . . . Desegregation hasn't yet got teeth, we can only hope Kennedy makes good his promises . . . We saw Freddy Hitler speak at Mobile, nothing exceptional, nothing demonic. He didn't duck any questions. He seemed to ring true. As Christians, we do believe in forgiveness, and as non-racists we don't believe in tainted blood. So the proof will be in the eating. If you don't mind my saying so, you're on a wild-goose chase here. People want to forget and build for tomorrow. Joseph Gable . . . he must be a bitter old man. At his age, what harm can he do now? Maybe you've been away too long. Things have definitely changed for the better . . .

How I would like to believe that. Polite talk, listen to the night crickets. The old fear, it's true, is difficult to recall here. No burning crosses in the fields . . . Shall we just let bygones be bygones?

Motoring about the countryside. The scattered white mansions. The displaced idyll of black farmers' houses, porches and rocking chairs. Passing through Montgomery, hoping Michael would not notice my sweating hands. Drawn by unexorcised fear to the Greyhound Station. Parked buses, a languid ticket office, the usual black and white flotsam in the waiting lounge. No drama, no banners of Aryan America, just a small blue notice saying 'New Orleans Excursions Now Available Only From Window Two' and some postcards showing the Montgomery State House and a yellowhammer bird with the legend 'Alabama – Cotton State – We Dare To Fight For Our Rights.'

'We're chasing ghosts,' said Michael. You're telling me. We shoot a few street scenes. Not much to hold on to. A small park, with a few drunk black men slumped on benches, named for the Reverend King. The past is all present here but also forgotten. No revolution. No lethal fight for equal rights. Or is it still there, just beneath the surface, waiting to break out again? I can't connect. My friends seem to have been exhausted by the upheaval of nine years ago. I can't blame them. They live here, while I came, was traumatised, and left. Below the surface of their politeness I feel an irrational anxiety in their view of me as a carrier of ill winds. Perhaps the world has moved on, and I've stayed the same. A cavewoman in the new world . . .

'Yallah,' Michael says, 'let's go to Las Vegas. Let's go chase up your bogey man before he dies of old age.'

Off again, down the great curve of the South-South-West. South to New Orleans, then along the Louisiana coast towards Houston. Motel-land America lives. At each stop, I insist on separate rooms, with Michael's sullen and peeved agreement. I know there is really no desire here, maybe a certain need, which I can do without. A little guiltily, I can always raise the ghost of Natalia between us if the going gets a bit hairy. I have to have a strictly professional relationship on this trip, or I know I'll go mad. One Mediterranean male was enough for the decade. (And where is he, the vulnerable Christos, the soft spots below the hardened crust?) Enough of that. Concentrate on the Enemy. The Prince of Darkness. The suave mask of the Miami Holiday Inn. The sepia photograph from the Duce's eyrie, a perverse echo of what might have been . . . Hugging the road through the dull, terrible flatland of Texas, Houston to San Antonio . . . Memories of a Klan Rodeo I saw on T.V. here, with swastika spurs on the cowboys and a shooting gallery with Democrats and prominent Jews on the targets. This desert has always had a lurking menace for me. Even the Lee Oswald Motel takes on a threatening air as a weasel-faced youngish man takes our registration with the shifty look of an old Party stalwart. Jest keep movin', pardner . . .

San Antone to El Paso, Las Cruces, Lordsburg, Tucson, Phoenix and finally across the Nevada state line, a great white notice looming over the border of the Black Canyon State:

WELCOME TO NEVADA CLEAN LIVERS. POSSES-SION OF NARCOTICS – 20 YEARS. TRAFFICKING – 30 TO LIFE!

'Is this journey really necessary?' Michael asks.

165

One might well wonder. A few more miles, and the outskirts of the mirage city shimmer in the blazing ochre haze. Desert scrub giving way to neat bungalows, motels and roadside diners. The bizarre revolving lights of Fun City, full on in broad daylight: Golden Nugget, Paradise, Frontier frolics, Elvis Live, Slots, Slots, Slots! The great hotel-casinos, the Royal, the Riviera, the Circus-Circus, Stardust, the Silver Slipper, and the three curved annexes of the Desert Inn & Country Club. The reverse Oz at the end of my yellow brick road, lair of my personal Beelzebub and also, rumour has it, the legendary hermit, Howard Hughes, Lord of Vegas and alleged bankroller of the American Party from its 1940s inception . . . But what will we really find, in the enchanted castle – a real ogre, or just a tired old man, a pathetic has-been counting his gambling percentages in the boiling desert sun?

Michael
Las Vegas, April –

So here we are, in the Happy Hunter Motel. Finally living in our fata morgana. Coupons! Discounts! Cheapest Wienies In Town! Slots! Slots! Slots!

Pardon my redundancy. This might have seemed a good idea on the road, but having got here, an acute deflation. Where do we go from here? How do we find the Open Sesame to the forty thieves' cave? Rachel does her best, after one day's prowling, to go for the whole pot. Trying her roving reporter air with the assistant-manager of the Desert Inn: Good morning, my name's Hilda Ruckenback from KQBT Boston (a small Nixonite station), I've been asked, to counter the liberal smears against Dr Gable that have surfaced lately, to give him a chance to set the record straight . . . hello? hello? No result at all. The management will not even acknowledge the Doctor stays in the hotel. The reception, too, knows no Doctor Gable. The furthest we eventually get is a hotel press agent, one Lisa Tattleback, who informs us, in the broadest southern twang, that the Doctor is out of town and never gives interviews. An absolute stone wall.

Well, well, well. Reduced to staking out the Desert Inn, hanging about on public benches under the palm trees with camera and sound and a hundred-millimeter lens. Taking on Rachel's obsession, as I had taken on Natalia's. Perhaps for want of an exemplar of my own? But no dice. Just a steady stream of the expected patrons, grey-haired men in brightly coloured shirts, women in bathing gear, lissom starlets draped over muscular arms or thousand-dollar suits, high rollers rolling with Lady Luck. The Vegas rainbow, the gold pot somewhere at its end. Once Jerry Lewis (one of Hollywood's few survivors) bounced out of a Rolls Royce, but his security guards stopped us filming. We were beginning to be conspicuous. Men in dark glasses ambled out of the hotel and looked at us. This could not go on for long.

Drying out, in this parched ambience, the maddening unavail-ability of the manna dripping from every tree. Our rapidly depreciating budget only allowing me feed a few forlorn quarters at a time into the ubiquitous machines in our motel room, in the gas stations, toilets, diners. To gorge on the World's Cheapest Hamburger in lieu of Nevada Bob Quails Veronique at fifteen bucks a throw in the Monte Carlo Room. At night the endless pap of television, the Bing Crosby lookalike competition, the John Wayne show, President Joe Kennedy's motorcade through Dallas, the cheering crowds, the all-American razzamatazz . . . Tomorrow, apparently, another Presidential parade, in Bomb City, Los Angeles. Well, at least they know how to put on a show . . .

Rachel out, alone, at her request, on the town, I decide the time has come to call it all off. End the farce and suggest an alternate project, for example: Faces of the Desert. An impressionistic montage of the mid-west. Which is all I have been shooting so far. The New World: Hope and Entropy. But at the eleventh hour, Rachel returns with a genuine forty-carat deus ex machina: chatting up a lady croupier in the Desert Inn Casino she has come up with the paydirt: a boyfriend with access to the internal hotel registry. (Why don't I get to hobnob with these cowgirls?) In the morning, without fail, we'll have Doctor Gable's room number. So how d'you like them apples, pardner? I tell her I'm no Daniel. In the fiery furnace I burn like any mortal. Never mind. She'll get her way. I am a sucker for Nebi Samuels. Let's hope it's not another Torino. I can't bury too many friends, comrades. It makes my hands shake too strongly . . .

Joseph Gable
Desert Inn, Las Vegas, April 20

Tomorrow: the Day of Judgment. Nothing to do now but wait, through the spring night, contemplating this apotheosis. All around me this brazen city rustles, whirs, jerks itself in its nocturnal paroxysms. I am the calm in the storm, the eye of the cyclone. The machine that I set in motion ticks over, relentlessly bringing the tool and the target towards their critical proximity.

I empty my mind, even of thoughts of the past. Nevertheless, they creep in, contradicting me. Frustrations I had long forgotten, memories of childhood pain. The boy, contemptibly dragging his foot, paralysed, shrunk, doomed by all accounts, by infantile paralysis. My father's sadness. My mother's prayers and endless pleas to Heavenly Father. But I wielded my own powers, with no help from outside. The Army doctors who laughed at me, when I presented my meagre frame for conscription. 1914. A weak body cannot serve its country. No one cares about the mind. The humiliating turn to the priests for assistance to continue studies. But the Catholic Faith! Spare us. As the first Catholic President of the United States floats towards his nemesis . . . Curious thoughts, echoes that I had believed lost for ever. The literary life, that seemed so important to me then – the novel, yes, rejected by the Jewish publishers – *Michael*, 'the diary of a hero'. First fruits, pretty unripe, true . . . The Jews were right then. Inadvertently, they sealed their own fate, closing one avenue and turning me down the path that will lead to their destruction . . . What happened to that manuscript? Lost, in the German Upheaval . . . the mad rush of defeat, the lost battles, the thorns of exile . . .

Enough! By my bootstraps, I've won . . .

I can switch off the lights now, and insert my earplugs to shut out the last echoes of Babylon. Speed the destruction of all this vulgarity. Midnight. In ten and one half hours, the Presidential motorcade will set out, from the corner of New Sunset and Fox, from the foot of the Clark Gable Memorial, towards its starring role in the drama I have written into being . . .

169

Kennedy, Joseph Patrick, President of the United States: April 21, 06:30

Morning thoughts. Finally, Los Angeles. The official tour. The pomp, the crowds, the ceremony. But every time I come here, to this rebuilt city, my mind goes right back to its primal pain. Holocaust Day. February 4, 1952. The day no American then alive can forget. The shock, and the revelation as the impossible was relayed to us in Washington, in the House. It was as if the blast had shaken the dome of the Capitol. Almost everyone was stunned into silence. Then a strange wave of sound swept across the Senate floor, as the news sunk in. Some wept openly, others leapt up, calling for instant vengeance (and there was no need for us to cry for it, the Generals were already loading the 'Hirohito Special' for Tokyo). Myself, then a freshman Senator, still clinging to my father's coat-tails . . . Despite his loud disapproval, my brother Jack and I chartered a plane as soon as we could, and flew west. At San Francisco we transferred to an army helicopter, which hurled us south towards the stricken zone.

On the outskirts of Santa Barbara, the apocalyptic vision began. A vast army of tents had sprung up already round the town, covering the beach where only three days earlier the winter surfers had gambolled. Southwards the highway was totally blocked by vehicles of every conceivable kind. Old Ford Pickups, Tuckers, battered Caddies, Olds, Mack trucks, Chevvies, vans, buses and station wagons of all sizes, trailers, campers and caravans, Buicks, Dodges, Dukes, de Villes, all the symbols of powerful America jammed, up to twelve abreast across all eight lanes of the 'free'way, stalled bumper to bumper, mile after mile. An endless Leviathan frozen in flight, snaking through the hills and valleys. Along the road on either side tents, awnings, parasols, shelters of bits of sacking and cloth spread like an obscene mass picnic at the end of the world, fenced in by an outer line of army trucks, police cars, ambulances, mobile hospitals. An instant city half a mile wide and almost a hundred miles long. And everywhere, the massed dots of the people, the homeless, the bereft, the scattered survivors, the chaff of war, bunched in their makeshift encampments, in their cars, packed in trucks, casting a perfunctory glance at our machine overhead, just one of dozens they must see, frustratingly free of the prison of the road . . . The young, ashen-faced pilot shouts in my ear, 'It's a jungle down there, Senator! We parachute medicines and food and just pray they get through – we know gangs have already formed to grab and sell the supplies . . .'

We can be great, and we can be terrible. In a couple of hours I shall climb into my car, with Helen and the Governor and my bodyguards, and drive down the epicenter of the Holocaust, New Sunset, in Resurrection City. Crowds of live, well-fed, reasonably happy people, supporters or opponents, will be there, in the sunshine of a spring that eighteen years ago seemed to have been destroyed for ever. Cheers or jeers, I'll be glad of either. The only sound, on that ghastly day, was the chugging of the chopper, hovering over a landscape of unimaginable horror and blight: fallen pylons, burnt-out cars, pulverised homes, roofs torn off as if by the most colossal hurricane, fires still burning everywhere, the gargantuan traffic jam continuing until it burnt out in vast clumps of wrecks bunched round the freeway junctions. The Sepulveda Dam was unbreached, though charred. But East, along Ventura, most of the houses were destroyed or damaged, with firescars cutting out wide swathes like the strokes of a giant's scythe. The sky, which had darkened since our entrance to the San Bernardo Valley, turned a distinctive leaden red. We flew through smoke, making out the burnt-out Van Nuys Sherman Oaks park, now a bivouac for frontline gasmasked troops and tanks ranked along the road. As we roared over Studio City (that rotor roar, which I shall always identify with death), the landscape dramatically worsened. From the Hollywood Freeway turnoff the ground was a reddish brown sore, scouring off the living flesh of the city. No smoke, as there was nothing left to burn. The freeway torn up and twisted like a child's toy. Rubble only marking the site of major buildings. Just a scooped-out hill where Universal Studios had turned out miles of celluloid dreams. A boiling bowl of mud in place of the Hollywood Reservoir, bubbling like a massive witches' cauldron. Further on the freeway was fused to the ground like a matchstick, charred on the face of the scar. Of all the neat, exquisite homes fitted into the rolling canyons and hills, the gardens of our weavers of dreams, down to Beverly Hills, nothing except, on slopes turned away from the blast, a handful of charred stumps.

Out of the Land of the Rising Sun the kamikaze pilot had come to blot out our own firmament. Flight Lieutenant Yukio Mishima, as Tokyo Radio gloated, instant winner of the Emperor's Imperial Medal of Honour, the Emperor who was himself becoming dust and ashes on the very day I flew over his handiwork . . .

And the arguments: we should never have held back our own Bomb. We should have known more about the Japanese nuclear project. We should have bombed them first. We were betrayed. The tide of terror and despair engulfing President Wallace, the baying pack of McCarthy . . .

Perhaps we should not have succumbed. But we were not masters of our own emotions, fears, lusts for revenge. At least we had wits enough to sign the Pacific Ceasefire, before we turned in on ourselves.

A war we should never have fought, we should have not been drawn into. Only now, after eighteen years, we can say this. But not in the face of the pulverised dead, the massed walking dead of mutilations . . . the men without faces or eyes, the breastless women, the armless, the legless, the thousands wandering crazed in the parched Sinais of Glendale and Burbank . . . The rich of Beverly Hills staggering in rags, brought lower than Calcutta beggars . . . Nothing could be rational, even in the clipped tones of the army surgeon whose iron detachment is all that keeps him from madness, telling us of the plagues still to come, the disease which would decimate thousands and tens of thousands who seemed safe, who seemed to have survived, the creeping legacy of radiation . . .

So I will pledge, to myself and to the people, today, that this will never happen again. Not in Los Angeles, not in Tokyo, nor any other spot on the face of this troubled planet. No More War, foreign or 'civil' . . . No more needless pain and massed anguish. No more boiling blood, flaked off limbs, charred flesh, blasted bone tissue. A determination to see the task through . . . A firm deterrence against the Communist powers combined with the hand of peace to sort out our differences. Cool down the Polish crisis, guide Europe back to democracy, help the

New Commonwealth to come into being in reality, not only in propaganda, help our allies divest themselves of wasteful, destabilising empires . . . An Open Door, a Commonwealth of Independent Nations, helped by us towards prosperity. If we can raise the American people's eyes from immediate worries to see the global view . . . With God's help, and a large dollop of luck, and Freddy Hitler to keep the South in line . . .

The soft knock on the door. Politics, calling. A good luck call from Helen in Washington. Best wishes from Jack, Bob and Teddy. Time to get the show on the road . . .

Michael
Las Vegas, April 21

Got up 7:30 in the morning. Showered. Dressed. Checked
equipment boxes. Joined Rachel for breakfast at the High'n'Low
Café just across the road from the motel. Orange juice, coffee,
two eggs over easy and brown toast (hold the grits). Those
little dabs of jelly, oh boy. And all around us, slots, slots,
slots.

Having decided to blow with the wind, I felt calmer. Adjusted,
whatever happens, to this American circus par excellence. The
desert bazaar of financial suicide. And a t-bone steak for $1.95!
What else could a real man want?

Back to the motel, got the camera ready, hefted it for handheld
action. Checked the sungun, prepared the Sennheiser recorder
to drape over Rachel's shoulder, microphone connected and
tested. By the time we had done this it was after half past
ten. So let's get this show on the road. Zooting right down
the fairyland of the Strip, past the Tropicana, the Flamingo,
towards Spencer Tracy Boulevard. The three glass towers of
the Desert Inn soon shimmering ahead in the sun. It looks and
feels like a glorious spring day, ideal for a dip in the pool, a long
suntan, followed by some bizarre local cocktails, an afternoon
snooze and a night at the tables, throwing caution to the winds.
Anything goes. Instead we're heading for who knows what sort
of headbanging session with a deadly old man. As we approach
the Desert Inn, though, a helicopter lifts off the roof of the
main annexe and rattles away west, over the Castaways and
the Sands.

Is that our boy escaping, having heard of our coming? Any
fantasy is possible here. There is certainly a hubbub round
the hotel entrance. People running about, by the ornamen-
tal fountains, the palm trees, the ersatz waterfall. Something
has happened. We stop the car. Someone, a middle-aged lady,
dishevelled and tear-streaked, rushes over to us as if she knows
us.

174

'Did you hear? Did you hear?' There is an air of panic. Doormen have broken ranks, waving their arms. Some people are running out of the hotel, others in. A man is slumped, crying, on the lawn, below the revolving Country Club sign.

'They shot the President! They shot the President in L.A.!'

Something cold creeps in along the spine in the dry heat of the desert spring. Rachel looks at me. I look back. The hot air is suddenly icy as we share, in an instant, the same paralysing suspicion.

We unfreeze. I remember us rushing forward, towards the main entrance of the Desert Inn, dangling cables. Me with the camera, she with the sound recorder and sungun. As we approached, a group of dark-suited, dark-spectacled men, clustered round a large, silver-haired military-looking type in a blue suit, emerged out of the main door, piled into two black sedans and drove off, at high speed, in the direction of Caesar's Palace. I tried to catch a quick shot but they'd gone before I could steady the camera.

On, inside. Rushing past startled receptionists, wavering bell-hops in red and gold braid, milling about like the stewards of a sinking ship. The last moments of the *Titanic*. Past marble pillars and formica walls, potted palm trees, dragging through deep wine-coloured carpets and the air-conditioned reek of affluence, some punters, fanatically, still playing the slot machines. Even Regicide can't stop Las Vegas. The 5 cent Jackpot, the Double Double, Break The Bank, Big Daddy . . . A stream of coins shoots out towards the bosom of a small, dowdy old lady. She screams, as the joybells jangle.

'The lifts!' Rachel pulled me towards them, past two bell-hops who half-heartedly block our way. 'Walter Cronkite! Six o'clock News!' she shouts at them. A small poodle leaps and yaps at our heels. On impulse I do the one thing I know in an emergency: camera to eye, calling 'Lights!' to Rachel and hiding behind the whirr of the Bell & Howell. Rising, in the Desert Inn lift, in mounting hallucination. A bubble in the turmoil and panic. Impossible thoughts racing through the mind. They killed the President! Can one believe it? What horrors were loose in the land? I see in Rachel's eyes the shadows of resurrected demons: A coup d'état, jackboots, prison cells, flaming crosses, Tuskegee burning, strange fruit, the Grand Dragon, another assassin's bullet, finally countered . . . But what has all this got to do with me? As we continue to rise in the cold smooth reverse bathyscape of the Desert Inn lift . . .

Chmielnicki, Ignacy (ex-Colonel)
Las Vegas, April 21

I shall try to record the events precisely as they occurred: At 10:45 a.m. we swept into his room, Frederick Hitler and I, and two FIA agents, unannounced, having dealt with the guards. Gable was sitting, sipping his mid-morning drink, in his armchair, watching the T.V. as if nothing untoward was expected, a retired old man relaxing in front of his favourite program. The live broadcast of the Presidential motorcade, making its slow way up New Sunset, into New Hollywood Boulevard. The cheering crowd, the open limousine with the secret service guards on its bumpers, the President, his wife and Governor Kalmbach waving. The cobra watching his prey. Nevertheless, I was satisfied to see the surprise and stupefaction on his face as we entered, breaking through that cosmetic mask. He offered no resistance as I lifted him bodily from the chair and ran my hands over his dressing-gown. Just his hand, uselessly groping for the alarm bell, which I told him would be no use, as the FIA agents took up positions, hands folded, by the door.

'Everything is disconnected,' I told him. 'This is a closed system. I control what happens in this room.'

Frederick, given the tightrope he was now walking, was remarkably calm in appearance, though I could sense, inside, he was wound up like a spring. 'A very neat plan, Joseph, very neat,' he told Gable calmly, settling down in the opposite armchair, looking away from the screen. 'Uncle Joseph pulls the strings of the world marionette theatre. And dumb little nephew Frederick is just another puppet in the show. It's amazing, you thought I would just play my role, no questions asked, no incrimination, what I don't know in advance won't hurt me, I'm in it up to the neck anyhow. You are a clever man, Joseph. But you don't bargain with other people thinking, coming to their own conclusions. You lost touch with reality, sitting here like some real life Doktor Ivan in the center of your web, weaving fantasies with the world. The Wolf Corps, Camp Auschwitz, Warsawski's Polish coup to spark a war with Germany and Russia – the whole salad, and I, little Freddy, would deliver, so that, in the divine twilight of your life, you'd march victorious into Berlin, carried shoulder-high down the smoking ruins of the Luxemburgstrasse . . .'

The old man had recovered his impassivity, coiled back in his chair, though I could feel the darts of Traitor he was hurling at me from his gut. On the screen, the motorcade was proceeding, the anchorman bleating out.

Frederick was still unloading. 'Jesus Christ, Joseph, you are a dinosaur. You're played out. Your mind is addled. The power of the will, it's all nonsense, man. This is the era of the mass, Joseph. Technology, a complex machine to keep going, a system of brakes and impediments. Even if I wanted to follow the script you wrote for me, do you think a President can just do what he wants? Dissolve Congress, ignore the Constitution, piss on the cabinet, the armed forces, the people? You should have stayed in Germany, Joseph, you'd have been a Godsend to the Soviet government. You and that monster Heydrich would have hit it off perfectly. You can't do that here, now, in 1970, any more than you could in 1961. And my brother had to die then for your delusions . . .'

Goebbels spoke up now, for the first time, turning to me: 'And you too, Colonel, you have also succumbed to an attack of democratic piety?'

'I am a Pole, remember, Doctor? I have to survive, as you did.'

'So the Catholic President is spared, eh, comrades? And good old Freddy stays a harmless Vice President . . .' His eyes were mocking, but a puzzled look followed, as Frederick smiled for the first time. Without answering, he drew up the second armchair, settling beside Goebbels in front of the T.V. The motorcade was approaching the crucial corner of the old Hollywood and Vine, epicenter of Yukio Mishima's Bomb, under the D. W. Griffith Building, with its mock-Babylonian battlements over-looking the passing parade. The stone elephants and statue of Lilian Gish gazing out over the rebuilt city. Banners in the crowd below: WE TRUST YOU, JOE! and WELCOME JOE KENNEDY, HOLLYWOOD'S NEWEST STAR! For the second time Goebbels's mask slipped, as he looked from Frederick to me and back.

178

'We haven't taken your Austrian sniper out, Joseph, nor his backup.' Frederick was calm now, having had his say. 'Everything will proceed according to your plan, Uncle Jo, except, of course, for the aftermath. A President has to be a President, not a tool. I am my father's son, after all, Joseph.'

The shot rang out. A mere crack on the T.V., but reverberating around the world. The screen shuddered, the cameras confused, the crowds rising, the announcer stammering, weaving about with his microphone . . .

'. . . what was that . . .? Something has happened . . . Stuart? Stuart? are you there? What . . .? the motorcade is speeding up . . . the secret service men are rushing out of their car, to the President . . . something has happened . . . they're speeding away . . . people are running . . . oh, my God . . . oh, my God . . . oh, my God . . .'

Frederick nodded to me. I turned to Goebbels. Chaos continued on the screen. The old man saw in my face that I knew the full facts. That I too was expendable in his eyes. That he had prepared a triple lock security – immediate death for his Austrian trigger by mafia contract, and another, made out for myself.

'You forgot,' Frederick told him calmly, 'the Colonel has his own independent contacts. If you hadn't been so clever he might have stuck with you. As it is, he came over and spilled all the beans. But I wanted you to watch and realise that you aren't the bees knees.'

'A Pole remains a Pole,' said Goebbels. I whipped off the cord of his dressing-gown. It was not the most rugged material, but the man was old, and he had never been physically strong.

Michael

At the seventeenth floor Esther pulls me out, we run down the corridor to a velvet-hung vestibule at whose end a thick padded door is half open . . . We step through. No guards, no shrieking alarms . . . Just another vestibule leading into a large plush suite, with hanging curtains, panelled walls, potted plants, a tinkling chandelier. Tinkling because a diminutive old man in a mauve dressing-gown is hanging from it, by a cord . . .

The sungun on, my camera whirring. If I take my eye away I might just float away from my anchor into some other world . . . Panning up the thin frame, no more than five foot two or three, the thin hair mussed on a head shining with arrested globules of sweat. Snot, not quite dry, running from the nostrils past the lips to the chin. The eyes open and popping. The tongue protruding, as the books say. A ghoulish expression of glee round the twisted lips? the rictus of failure? or just the twist of the distorted muscles? Just let the camera whirr.

'It's him.' Rachel's words, in my ear, breaking in. Yes, I recognise the man in the picture frame. The sepia Joseph Gable or Goebbels. Dispatched to his maker. By his own hand? The itchy thought of that military-looking group, rushing out of the hotel just ahead of us . . . By leaps and bounds to conclusions . . . The television set, we now notice, is on at the end of the room, its sound low but anxious, conveying confused street scenes, presumably from Los Angeles, and panic-struck commentators. Microphones thrust in the faces of eyewitnesses who have not witnessed anything.

There is a movement at the room's entrance. Nothing can surprise us now. I lower the camera, suddenly aware of aching arms. Three persons stand in the suite's vestibule. Two are young, muscular, bodyguard mean, with faces of teak and concrete. The third a wispy old man with a long white beard. All dressed in spotless white medical gowns, and the old man with a surgical mask covering his nose and mouth.

This latter apparition points at us and motions us forward. As

180

in a genuine dream, we obey. He whispers huskily and coaxingly through his mask, 'Come on now. You don't want to be here, believe me.'

We believe him, following him, like the White Rabbit, as he scuttles down the corridor to a service door which his guard unlocks, ushering us to a flight of steel steps. 'There is a private lift at the back,' he rasps, 'you can get out through there.'

So this is the real Wizard of Oz. Where are the puffs of white smoke? But the man just punches, with a white-gloved finger, the button of a small liftshaft door. 'Gert will go with you,' he says. 'Take the Studebaker. You'll collect your things at your motel. Your car will be brought there. Just get in it and go. No questions.' There was a twinkle in his eye which knew that was an inhumanly impossible order. 'I'm Howard Hughes,' he said. 'I own Las Vegas. I know everything that happens in town. You don't want to know what happened here. You'll read about it in the papers. I own them, so I know what they'll say. Don't worry too much, things are going to continue more or less the way they've always been.'

Our one chance to asked the Wizard about the meaning of life, and all the true stories behind the false ones, and where do we go from here. But instead the cliché, from Rachel: 'Why are you doing this for us?'

He said, 'I don't want your blood on my hands.' The lift arrives, and he just holds its door as he shoos us in. 'Just remember, I had nothing to do with all this. I'm just an observer of the traffic.'

The door closes. We descend, with Gert, strong and silent, down the concrete beanstalk. Hustled into the Studebaker, purring down the suddenly tentative, anxious, mirage streets to the Happy Hunter Motel. Our bags packed and another impassive creature waiting with Rachel's car in the drive, holding out his hand.

'The film,' he grunts. I hand it over. No chance to switch cans. The Studebaker nudges us all the way down to the State Line, at Boulder City, seeing us across, making sure we vanish into the dust of Arizona. The new gorilla only said two short sentences to us, as he ushered us into our car:

'Don't go west, go east. If you want to grow old, just forget you ever saw Nevada.'

Ernesto
Gulf of Aden, April –

Out of range of the Aden coastguard, the old launch gathers speed. The helmsman, a wiry Arab named Feisal, a renegade orthodox Trotskyist, breaks open the crate of refreshments, which turn out to be Coca Cola. Even here, between the devil and the deep blue sea, the Empire stalks its consumers! Feisal refuses to touch it. 'It leads to harder stuff,' he says, keeping to his water bottle. As time has passed, I've become less rigorous . . . It's a scorching, Arabian day. Apart from Feisal, most of the passengers, my comrades, are none too sure in this element. Indefatigable on dry land, the band of brothers is pretty green at sea. Samir, Francisco, Mumtaz, Carlos, even the islander Archie Brown is looking distinctly green. 'On Fidel's boat, *Granma*,' I reminisce, 'everyone was sick as a dog, including the doctor, who was me . . .' 'Don't worry,' Feisal says, 'we are on schedule. We should hit the Berbera Coast at twenty-two hundred. The British concentrate on the Bab el Mandab patrol, we should be clear in this zone.'

I find myself looking out, towards the invisible land, my strangely constant destination. Why Ethiopia? Why not other mountains to climb, closer to 'home'? The Peruvian Andes, or Ecuador, Colombia, even Bolivia? Odd climes, strange odds on which to stake one's life: this boatload of battle-hardened exiles, carrying Chinese arms and ammunition for an army given up for lost by the world, entering its fourth decade, no, practically its third millenium of struggle?

But in the right camp, no matter its location, the colour, race or creed of its inhabitants, can any commitment be too alien, any outcome unthinkable, any forgotten, vanished death too formidable to face, too tough to look squarely in the eye . . .?

The boat rocks, gently. I snap open a Coca Cola. Addictions, they are so hard to break . . .

Alex
London, April –

So we've come full circle now. In the pale haze of the London spring, just a couple of dabs of blue in a grey sky, just a couple of dozen exiles protesting outside the Greek Embassy in Kensington. Each one of us carrying a placard with the name of a person arrested in the recent Athens swoop. Students, workers, trade unionists, rounded up, all the usual suspects and scapegoats for the failure of the regime. Kathleen by my side, holding up the name of our friend, Christos Vangelopoulos, scooped up, we now know, in Karpenisi and held somewhere in Ciano Square.

The police are edgy, on alert since the attempted storming last week of the Iranian Consulate by anti-Shah students. They haven't granted us a licence to demonstrate outside the house in Embassy Row, but we turned up anyway. A phalanx of plastic-masked, helmeted and shielded 'A-Specials' is drawn up opposite us by the iron fence of Hyde Park. We are not particularly brave or over-defiant. We have agreed among ourselves to disperse at the first sign of the law's flexed muscles. But they have not come here to play games. They have come to teach subversives, particularly foreign subversives, a lesson. They come at us in a rush, batons raised. An unwise hand flails out with a placard. A helmet falls. The Specials move in, nightsticks swinging in broad daylight. Blood spatters the scattered leaflets on the pavement. Black-gloved hands grab hair, arms, legs, dragging us to the vans. Kathleen and I are separated. I see her determination as she kicks a leather boot. A hand closes over her face. Sirens wail. Cries and shrieks of pain and frustration. I look up, to see a plastic, scuffed mask with two opaque eyes wide behind it. The heavy helmet bends towards me, as if considering, then swings back and violently forward, smacking against my forehead and nose. The eyes seem to smash directly into me, gluing themselves to my retinas. Winded, presumably bleeding, I feel detached, as if I

183

am watching someone else, not Alex Panoulis, lifted bodily and thrown into the back of the drawn-up police van . . . England, home and glory. The ringing tones of the Internationale in Greek rise, like the wail of violated ghosts, from the other two Black Marias . . .

Adolf
Carpentersville, April –

Darkness coming, but I shall not falter. The pains and agonies
They afflict me with are by now familiar enemies. My task, above
all else, is to break out of this mesmeric spell in which They try
to tie me down, hack off my limbs, dry up my tongue, inflict on
me the unspeakable horrors of a premature death. They have
even buried Annchen behind their wax handiwork and daubed
wrinkles, to make her appear old, to make me believe I am old,
dying, senile, on my last legs. But I know the Truth! There's life
in the old dog yet! My eternal youth is a certainty – Mengele
knows! But They tore him from me, probably destroyed him,
cast his mangled body into the lime pit . . . It must be nearby,
the odour fills my nostrils . . . But I shall not be moved. I shall
not succumb. Did I not write myself: 'Those who do not want to
fight in this world of eternal struggle do not deserve to live'? I shall
prevail, to fight the chaos which has claimed all those around me,
all those who were once comrades at my side. A mere mockery,
all of Them, planted by the Insiders to give me hope, only to dash
it away. No! No! No! even alone, alone as ever, I shall persist!
The mass of numbers, their dead weight will not stifle me. I will
fight alone, against Chaos, Death, Destruction. Now Goebbels is
dead. Hanged himself in his hotel room, an act he should have
carried out long ago. Never trust a man with a club foot, a man
who undergoes cosmetic surgery. Now he is putrescent in his
grave. There must be Truth! Truth! Truth! Oh God, the smell!
the utter stench of it! They are trying the deepest resources of
my will with their putrid stratagems: They have coated the walls
with vomit, the curtains with dung, the very sheets I lie on are
saturated with the urine of swine . . . They have buried corpses
under the floorboards, carcases slowly decomposing, wriggling
with maggots eating their way up towards me . . . They shall
not pass! My resistance is glorious! Now the Annchen Thing
is here, mumbling about medicines. But I shall be drugged no
more! I hear them all wailing, in their coffins: Albert, Hermann,

185

Rudy, Joseph, Frederick – no, Frederick is still alive, They say triumphant . . . Another deception – I have no doubt They will very soon close in on Their Goal . . . Their ultimate Aim, which I discovered long ago, and revealed, as I then predicted: that, if They win, the planet would, as in aeons past, move lifelessly through the endless ether . . . But I will not surrender! I will fight on to the bitter end! Yes, it was the great German, Clausewitz, who said, 'Even a loss of freedom after a bloody and honourable struggle assures a rebirth, and is the seed of life from which a new tree will strike roots . . .'

'She' is sitting by me, leafing through the pages of the *Readers' Digest*. I shall not be moved. I shall pretend everything is normal. I shall pretend I do not see the guards at the door. I shall pretend the world is as it should be, that History is striding in her groove, confident in her inevitability, inexorable in her process, unalterable except by an act of superior willpower and volition.

For it was I who wrote: 'The culture of humanity is not a product of the mass, but exclusively that of the genius of the exceptional personality.'

When I die, the world dies with me. And if the world persists – I, too, cannot fail to be immortal.

Part V

Scorched Earth

April–August 1970

Extract from *Terror Campaign 1961* by Rachel Levy

With the assassination of Rudy the American Party crumbled. Joseph Gable had built a crusade upon the potent Father–Son icon, an obscene and barely concealed mirror of the Christian myth. Party members were pledged to the Leader, adulation replaced discussion, obedience replaced thought. With the head cut off the body turned against itself, limb tearing limb in an orgy of self-mutilation. The Party committed hara-kiri in a welter of recriminations and denunciations. George Wallace's defection was only the first as the renegade Democrat Dixiecrats and Republicans threw themselves off the burning ship. The bogey Civil War to follow the House ballot for Richard Nixon as President never materialised.

Thus far history. But we are left with this: that eighteen million Americans cast their vote for a political party which openly advocated an elected Dictatorship, the racial resegregation of blacks throughout the Union, the segregation and eventual expulsion of Jews and open discrimination against Catholics, Freemasons, Freethinkers of any kind. Out of what shadowy core of insecurity did this terrible decision emanate? What images of terror and malice caused so many ordinary, grassroots Americans to make that dreadful choice? Columnists have speculated: the Bomb, the awful trauma of the Pacific War. Liberals add the unhinged years of McCarthy, the pathology of mass suspicion, of seeing the Enemy in your neighbour, your rival, a believer in another creed. Some pundits go back to the Civil War itself, to the nation born in trauma and feuds . . .

The *New York Times* says the storm has passed. We have matured, through our squabbles. We have learned to appreciate our Democracy, our system of checks and balances. Maybe. Though people in the streets of New York just say: Thank God for Homer Hargis, the man who finally balanced John Wilkes Booth . . . But are we all sure now, in our newfound apathy, great liberals and democrats that we are, that we have banished all those terrors? Are we sure we're immune ourselves, or are we all open to irrational moves, with unknown consequences? Are the fears that made the crosses, and people, burn in Alabama, Georgia, Florida and Tennessee, and even in California, gone or are they latent in all of us, waiting to be woken when the right circumstances arise, when some new crisis we feel we can't face creeps upon us again?

Report: April 24, 1970
FEDERAL INTELLIGENCE AGENCY
From: Director of Operations
To: Director, FIA
Classification: Red. Dir. only. No executive access
Subject: Polecat

. . . favouring strict neutrality. Constitutional matters should not concern the Agency outside the realm of personal ethics. Our role should be to ensure that national security is not compromised, and that both the Agency and the President remain above suspicion. To all extents and purposes it can be accepted that the Polecat Threat has been averted, with the termination of the Polecat (Gable) and subsequent closure of the following files: Amman, Esser, Neubauer, Sanducci and Welch. The successful outcome of the Camp Auschwitz mission has enhanced our Foreign Operations viability (see attached eyewitness account). The rooting out of terrorist cells in Eastern Europe should have the added dividend of enhancing our stature with the Opposition, and it may be far-sighted to consider suitable reports for Moscow and Berlin on a Buy & Sell basis.

. . . domestically we can expect the continuation of some media resistance to the lone gunman (Biscat) scenario, but strict internal security (see attached memo) should cover us in that regard. Inducements and discreditation capability can be held in reserve for persistent 'Doubting Thomases'.

. . . at Executive level, we shall no doubt benefit from a Chief Executive dependent on our discretion. This should augur well for the Appropriations program. All in all, Dick, a pretty satisfying outcome. We've done the job we're paid to do. Freedom, Democracy and Stability are secure once again.

H. Haldeman

Eyewitness Account, Camp Auschwitz (Lt-Col. B. L.):
April 22, 01:45 hours
The parachute drop within the perimeter fence proceeded with

the maximum element of surprise. The attack force was in Polish Infantry uniform, including our three hundred men and the remaining eighty from the Polish Crisis Response Team, detailed to secure the perimeter. The first line of Camp guards was overcome but the firefight alerted the estimated hundred and sixty ex-Wolf Corps and renegade Polish Army personnel, who were nevertheless taken by surprise. An estimated fifty were caught in their underwear in their wood huts, set alight by flamethrowers, cut down by bazooka shells and grenades. Skirmishes began around the blazing huts. By this time (02:00), the column of trucks, which had entered the town of Oswiecim singly during the night under various innocuous guises, arrived at the Camp gate, after their two-mile dash from the chemical plant. Forty more terrorists died in this second wave of the assault. There remained a hard core, led, we later ascertained from the bodies, by Rakosy and Stulpnagel, which rallied by Barracks Number Three for a counter-attack on our forces. It was at this point that I seized the opportunity to deal with Colonel Chmielnicki. Having been dropped with the second wave of paratroops, he was now advancing, giving directions, towards the Camp Armoury. He was a large, obvious target in the flares, but the confusion in the direction of fire I had caused inadvertently allowed a small group of the defenders to break through the cordon and race towards the German border. As arranged, the German posts were blacked out, maintaining total silence. It was an eerie sight, as the five or six last defenders made their way through the muddy pools and weeds of the Birkenau marshes towards no man's land and the river. As they seemed to have succeeded a sudden searchlight was switched on across the Wisla. The explosion of mines could be heard. Machine-gun fire was directed from the German watchtowers. There could have been no survivors.

By 02:30 it was all over. We spent two hours counting the bodies, checking what remained of the faces against the files, removing dentures and rings for identification. We piled the bodies, 165 in all, in the main Camp yard and rendered them down with the flamethrowers. I used my authority to add Colonel C. to the pyre.

In the morning light we could see the shocked inhabitants of the town, straining against the Polish Army cordons, trying to make out what had transformed their forgotten border town into a sudden charnel house. But this is not a country where questions are asked persistently, and of course there is no press to nose about where it's not wanted. Sooner than one might expect, I'm sure, Oswiecim will resume its uncluttered existence as a neglected backwater, a forgotten no man's land . . .

Christos
Athens, May –

The 'soft' interrogator visits me for the third time. He is a small swarthy man in a neat grey suit with a face slashed in half by a razor-thin moustache. He brings with him a tin of Old Holborn tobacco and a sheaf of King Edward cigarette papers. A gesture which he knows to be 'liberal' – rolling tobacco is forbidden in Greece – and threatening, showing that he knows my old personal habits. Given the opportunity, I roll. At least something to do with my fingers.

'You have been mentioned in the British press,' the man says, shaking his head, 'detention without trial by the Greek Dictators. Dreadful barbarian atrocities. Sorry calumnies against our country.' He looks as if he is about to burst into tears, sitting on my cell bed, hands on his knees. I cross my legs on the wooden chair, stick the rolled cigarette in my mouth, wait for the next gesture. He rises politely with a lighter and lights me up. I nod my thank you. He tries again.

'You know you should be thankful you are here without trial. It means you could walk out any moment. A trial before a military court, on whatever charge, that's a bureaucratic nightmare . . .' He raises his eyes, spreads his hands in mock alarm. 'Military courts are such bastards. They hand out sentences of ten, fifteen years for sedition. In the police force, we think that's ridiculous.'

I know he is going to talk about my father. With the police, there are never surprises. In a way he is right, at least with them you know where you are. In prison. This is not news for me.

'Believe me,' he says, 'we're not really interested in getting from you names of comrades, acquaintances. We have all the names we need. We know this stupid mission of yours was cooked up in that left-wing film school in London. It's very common that far from your country you lose touch with reality. You must know that what we want from you is spiritual, not material. Your father would know what I mean. You know he has petitioned in your favour although as an officer of the Law, and a patriot, he's on the other side of the fence. We understand this. A father should be loyal to his son, and vice versa. Don't you think so?'

He shouldn't have given me the cigarette, because I don't have to use my mouth to babble. He does it for me, as if I am the one who has the authority to give absolution.

'You see us as usurpers of democracy. Class enemies. But we are enemies to no class in Greece. We are a force for unity. We want a new order in which everyone shares. Isn't that the same aim as yours? It's sad to find bitterness and anger where love and concord should flourish. I was a communist myself, when I was your age. You know what they say: "If you have not been a communist before you are twenty-five, you have no heart, and if you're a communist after twenty-five, you have no head."'

He sighs as he sees my indifference. 'Simple phrases, but they can convey profound truths. Communism distorts noble instincts, but if the instincts are there, they should be channelled into the right paths, not destroyed.' He rises, leaving the tobacco tin and the rolling papers behind. 'We want you with us, not against.' He leaves. I stay. In the evening the warders come and confiscate the gifts. I am informed my exercise yard privileges have been suspended for three weeks. So much for the 'soft' interrogator.

Well, at least I got three good smokes out of them.

Marcuse, Herbert
Spandau Prison, Berlin, May –

They have allowed my old friend Willy Brandt to visit me. At least I can show off my luxury cell. My shelf of books, my toilet compartment, my television set, which blanks out now and then, coincidentally usually during the news, though what they could be showing there that might be to my advantage I cannot possibly imagine. Nevertheless, my cell depresses him, and we walk for a while together in the First Division exercise yard. I am usually alone here, though they allow some students, now and then, to come and engage me in a basketball game. Keeping my limbs limber, with these young police informers. Heydrich never gives up.

Willy is embarrassed. As what civilised man would not be, bearing messages from the Beast. The usual offers, it's a New Age out there, the 'Thaw', the slackening of Party rule, some voices allowed to squeak in academic journals which will be read by no one. Mine included.

'I am in the right place in the right time,' I tell him. 'All over the world, students and other young people are being beaten up by policemen, jailed, brutalised, exiled. I should at least share that pain.'

'Help me fight it on the outside, Herbert,' he says to me. 'I won't pretend you are not a potent symbol, in here. People are outraged that you can be held here. Even the British have lodged a protest.'

'That'll add three more years for me. A martyr for Colonialists. Soon we'll have the Americans joining in. They've just shot their own President. Our new partners. They are just doing Heydrich's work for him.'

'It's a different atmosphere, Herbert. You know I can't discuss these things here.'

Poor Willy, ever plotting with his band of honest burghers, the Ex-Ministers For Peace, the Good Men trying to reform the Bad. He does not even mention the paper Heydrich wants me to sign, my disclaimer of political action. I shall retain my chair at Berlin if I stick to Psychology, lulling everyone to sleep with technical flimflam.

'Never mind about me, Willy. I have my books, my typewriter. I can work any hours I want. I can conduct the purest research here. I don't act, and they all tremble. What could be more satisfying for an old man who can no longer live on sandwiches and hiking boots? Tell me just, any news of Guevara?'

'Back in Ethiopia. Hidden away in *anus mundi*. He's another one who never gives up.' Round and round, we pace the prison yard, murmuring, contemplating the ironies of fate, hands clasped behind our backs, while, beyond the wall, I know everyday life continues, the number 25 tram clanks its way east to Haselhorst, Pieckstadt, Charlottenburg, through the Tiergarten, and Jogiches Strasse, Engelsplatz and the Chancellery. The rhythm of the city, Berlin, capital of 'world socialism', pursuing, under the veneer of neo-proletarian propriety, her normal arts of discreet decadence, sly deals, bursts of defiance, rumour mongering and all other aspects of the anxious, careful, dangerous but unavoidable business of survival . . .

Rachel
New York, July –

Basking in the summer sun among the crowd in Washington Square. You'd think all's right with the world. The milling rovers, beatniks, dropouts, dopers, bums, tourists and just plain folk out for the day. Splashes of reds, blues, yellows, everything in between. Wrinkled new-moon-faced old men sit at the chess tables with black and Puerto Rican afficionados, watched eagle-eyed by a stripped youth with a shawl wrapped round his neck and a puffy orthodox Jew who lingers, barely holding back from interfering and moving the pieces the way they really should.

The voice of Papa Levy across the years: 'You think you got him licked? So move. In chess nothing is nailed down.'

They say ten billion different combinations are possible. But I can only live with the one I'm stuck with, the concrete coating of the past. I can't change it, neither can I look inside, at the heart of the machine.

The world turned upside down, and yet the same. People walk the streets, buy candy, bargain with stall-owners, flirt, fall in love, fall out of love, marry, divorce, curse their land-lords, read books, see movies, drag the main streets of their lives.

The deed was done. The President is dead. Long live President Hitler. Was I the only one to expect the worst, the jackboot on the step, the flaming cross on the stoop, the rounding up of Jews and malefactors?

Nix. The Fortas Commission sits, in Washington, sifting through mounds of 'information', eyewitness reports, testimony. Five hundred or so witnesses in the New Hollywood crowd, who, collectively, saw nothing. The one crack of the sniper's bullet, followed by the body, rifle with sniperscope in hand, lying at the foot of the D.W. Griffith Building's emergency stairway, neck broken by the fall. Rifle and bullet from target's head match. The perpetrator, a Polish emigré named Stanley Biscat, had a known grudge owing to unanswered

198

letters to Joseph Kennedy petitioning for the Senator's inter-
ference in a landgrant case in Eastern Poland. An open and
shut case.

Indeed? And how had Biscat, a third-rate indifferent ex-
Corporal in the Polish Armed Forces (circa 1951), got the
skill to put one bullet squarely and fatally into a moving target
at 460 yards? What triggered a cranky but non-violent bachelor,
working as a stage-hand for New Hollywood Studios, to plan so
perfect an assassination, and then, what made him trip, like a sixth
rate klutz, right down the stairs and break his neck? Oh yes, the
press speculated. They went to town. They dug and dug. They
did not spare the main suspect. It was not all gravy for Freddy. He
had to run his gauntlet. *The Los Angeles Times*: THE AMERICAN
PARTY STRIKES BACK? *Time* Magazine: CONSPIRACY
OR COINCIDENCE? and *Newsweek* taking the plunge, boldly:
DID THE PRESIDENT KILL THE PRESIDENT? But their
conclusion? No.

Freddy makes all the right moves. Opens his entire life, his
records, his confidential files, letters, to the Fortas Commission.
He appoints Jack Kennedy, the murdered man's brother, as his
Vice-President (buying off the clan?). He swears to uphold the
martyred President's program of social reforms and international
Thaw. He sets one hundred FIA agents permanently on the case.
He swears not to close the file until every avenue is exhausted.
Etcetera.

The stonewall stands. The liberal press don't want to tear
the Democrats apart. In power for the first time in sixteen
years, they don't want to sink on launch. The party rallies
round Freddy. The Kennedys pledge allegiance. The hounds
are slowly called off. The Commission sifts its mountains of
sludge, stolidly. No jackboots sound, no crosses burn. Panic
subsides, drifts off.

Leaving only Schmuck Levy. Doubting Dorothy Rachel, back
from Oz and marinating in my black-and-white Kansas. The
ersatzness of 'real life', as Michael and I rushed back across
the continent, gobbling the giblets of TV in the most incon-
spicuous motels we could find, raging at opaque newspapers,
stewing in our mounting fears ... It was not till New York
that I could root out the hidden, page 5 item in the *Las Vegas*

Courier of April 23, buried behind mounds of assassination flannel:

PROMINENT CITIZEN DIES:
A permanent resident of the Desert Inn, Mr Joseph Gable, retired businessman and one-time political advisor, was found dead in his suite yesterday. Hotel sources say he suffered a heart attack and died in his sleep. Mr Gable was 73 years of age and his health had been deteriorating for some time. He was a widower with no children and was known in the city as a generous contributor to several Vegas charities, such as the Sunrise Children's Hospital Trust and the Richard M. Nixon Rehabilitation Center.

We sat in Bryant Park, Michael and I, among the shitkickers and the tourists, under the Manhattan glass towers, holding this thing at arm's length. Thinking of the roll of film we had left in the hand of the Wizard of Oz's tin man. The only possible 'evidence' of what might have happened in that hotel suite. Suicide, or murder? Remembering the phalanx of goons rushing from the hotel: the large, military-looking type . . . Later the *Village Voice* gathered its own disturbing catalogue of lethal coincidences: Amman, Esser, Neubauer, three of the surviving 'German' clique of Chicago, all croaked within 48 hours, also of 'natural causes'. The strange violent events in Poland, an apparent raid against a 'nest' of ex-Italian fascists, reportedly planning a counter-coup to oust the Warsaw Junta in some unpronounceable border town. 'The Mussolini Connection'. I sat for hours, gazing at my Rocca delle Caminate portrait, hand poised by the telephone to add my fudged tale to their piece. But there was nothing I could add which could not be dismissed as more paranoid conspiracy drivel . . .

The hanging man. The sepia photograph. The thin thread leading to . . . what?

In chess, nothing is nailed down. The parameters shift, constantly. The players in Washington Square are bent over their black and white squares. A tattered black man, looming over them with the perennial 'gimme twenty cents man' is totally ignored. I am back home now, and I have to deal with that. My city, my country, my self. Michael left, on the first leg of a journey he hoped will not take him back to wartorn Palestine.

We both agreed the 'Gable' film had died in the Desert Inn, with its subject. The Terror Campaign would have no sequel. That, at least, should be a relief.

But did 1961 win out in the end? I can only wait and see. A group of black teenagers, in t-shirts and gaudily coloured scarves round their heads, wheel through the square on roller skates. They twist, turn, leap and somersault. The crowd applauds. The hot dog vendor is at the gates. The Village, nevertheless, is alive. I close my eyes, and feel the heat of the sun. Radios blare. Children scream. Dogs bark. The nasal whine of street prophets continues to resonate, blare and quaver, over the ziggurats of our day, the obelisks and skyscrapers . . .

Michael
On British Overseas Airways

Could it have been otherwise? As I fly back to a country sunk even deeper than before in its fish-faced malaise: Britannia, spearing the lesser breeds of the world on her fork, as the waves slap her feet. The 'communist threat' perhaps played down by Thaw, but subversion and 'terrorism' abroad still sending back the body bags . . . Not to speak of the two-way traffic: poor Alex, reduced to contemplating a return to his own shuttered homeland, and Christos, already pap for food parcels. Petitions signed to governments, embassies . . .

And who am I to complain? Roll up, roll up for the Third Palestine Civil War, as advertised by History. Blood and Fire, Victory or Death, etcetera. The first round I was too young to remember: 1948, the Jerusalem Post Office Siege, the Flight of Begin, the Irgun Guerrilla Campaign . . . But I copped the second: 1956, when the Haganah irregulars fighting the Arabs on the other side of the Wall set up sandbags in our Jerusalem home, and sat there eating falafels and waiting for the British troops until the League of Nations ceasefire . . . The newsreels of those days – the Arab families trekking out of Jaffa with all their belongings on their heads, and the Jewish families packed into the buses evacuating them from Nablus and Hebron . . . Yes, all the human flotsam of brave convictions . . . The stewardess passes down the aisle, handing round yesterday's newspapers:

TEL AVIV IMMIGRATION RIOTS AS POLISH JEWS TURNED BACK FROM JAFFA. DAYAN CALLS FOR JEWISH STATE NOW.

PRESIDENT HITLER AND CHAIRMAN HEYDRICH TO MEET IN BERLIN. PALESTINE CRISIS ON AGENDA.

MASSIVE DEFEAT FOR FRENCH TROOPS IN INDO-CHINA. P.M. MAUDLING PLEDGES AID, ADVISORS.

202

Tit for tat, the whole world over. Will the long awaited 'Second
World War' break out over Poland, Indochina, or Palestine? Who
is the next President to get shot? My friends have infected me with
their obsessions. Now I, too, feel guilty for the state of the world.
Tyranny, oppression, wars, dispossession, the slings and arrows
of, to take arms against, etcetera, and by opposing, end them. But
why shouldn't I rejoin the Club of the Apathetic, and live my life
of small moves, small victories, small failures? Millions don't give
a damn, why should I? Or should I take up that Italian legacy,
that push and tug from dead Natalia, to go out and at least bear
witness, observe and record what is, for a posterity I can't even
glimpse vaguely, for a purpose I couldn't define, except that of
preventing my conscience from being crushed into paralysis, an
accomplice of fraud and deception. Record 'the truth', however
appalling, the seeing dog, the camera I . . .

Could it have been otherwise? I asked Esther, when we sat in
a Bagel Nosh, caking our gobs with cream cheese, trying to make
sense of the senseless. 'History, I mean, the whole mish-mash,
the sorry progress of homo sap, could it have done a better job
of it, or is it all just horse manure?'

'I remember,' she said, 'my father and his sidekick, Heimke
Grossman, used to sit over their chess table and argue, what would
have happened if? Would the world have been different if Karl
Marx had been pushed out by Bakunin in the First International?
If Napoleon hadn't made Sergeant? If Lenin had died as a child? If
someone other than Trotsky had took hold of Russia? They used
to construct elaborate fantasies of all these might have beens:
Suppose Rosa Luxemburg and Karl Liebknecht hadn't managed
to evade the Freikorps officers in Berlin of 1919? If they had been
killed, the German Party might have split, the Revolution of 1923
might not have happened, or failed, Germany might have become
an 'Allied' nation, even gone fascist, like Italy. Our own 'German
clique', Hitler and Goebbels, might have stayed behind, risen to
power, with their racialist and anti-communist platform. There
might have been a World War, between the Imperialist nations,
with Soviet Russia even, succumbing. On and on, they would go,
constructing their nightmares, using their invented world like a
football. It was an endless political chess game they played,
making and unmaking combinations. One day, though, my father

203

told me, I must have been about thirteen, and was challenging his more outrageous assumptions: Remember, tsatske, he said – he thought I was cute at the time – however the pieces move, the game remains the same, the basic choices and elements are unchanged: compassion or malice, generosity or greed, wisdom or stupidity, these are the human options, which are what the human race is about.'

'If it makes no difference,' I asked, 'why bother?'

'What we do,' she said, 'makes a difference to us. At the root, it's an irrational choice. An act of faith.'

So we're back to mumbo jumbo. I have five hours before I land at King Edward Airport, London, capital of the *oysgemotert* empire. Until then, I can stay up in the air . . .

Frederick Hitler
Carpentersville, August –

Finally, the inevitable end. Standing with my arm around my mother's shoulder, poor Annchen, still wrapped in her silence. Father had left precise instructions concerning his funeral, set down in a lucid hiatus, before the incomprehensible scrawls that marked his fading. He had left it with that man he could not abandon, Mengele, who handed it to me, wet-eyed, at the airport, when I arrived as soon as the death was confirmed:

Cremation mandatory. Under no circumstances are my remains to be consigned to the soil of exile. The service is to be austere but in keeping with the Aryan ideal. No minister of any religion to be present. My remains will be placed in a simple unvarnished casket of easily combustible wood. It will be carried into the crematorium by six leaders of the Party Youth Corps, wearing the uniforms and armbands of the Founding Fathers, i.e. of the Sturmabteilung (S.A.) of the National Socialist German Workers' Party. The original standards of the NSDAP to be placed at the four corners of the casket, and the crematorium chapel to be lit solely by the light of twenty-seven torches representing the twenty-seven S.A. commando martyrs who fell protecting our rear in our strategic withdrawal from the usurped Fatherland.

The ranking youth leader will read out the following extracts from the original German manuscript of *My Battle* (Ford-Sentinel Press, 1928): Page 31 last para; page 60 last 4 paras; page 263 para 5; page 307 para 4; page 345 paras 6, 7, 8; page 348 paras 2, 3, 4; page 358 para 3; page 598; page 610 last 4 paragraphs. Following this all present will read in unison page 195, paragraph 2. The casket will then be committed to the flames while those present stand to the Aryan salute.

The urn bearing my ashes will be taken to Richardson Air Force Base at R–, Virginia, and there be loaded upon the next surveillance aircraft of the U1 order due to depart on its mission. When arriving over the soil of Germany, the ashes which are my mortal remains are to be ejected into the air, to scatter over the Fatherland, where alone they may achieve their final and fitting repose.

Well, old man, here we are, and your coffin, simple and unvarnished, trundling on its conveyor belt towards the discreet black curtains hiding the crematorium furnace. So far as ordered, but for the rest, no can do. Yourself, Gable, Amman, Ley, Esser, Goering et al, lived so deep in your world of makebelieve you almost, but not quite, made it real. There was certainly something titanic and marvellous about your awesome vision. That Götterdamerung twilight that you foresaw, dragging the world down with you in a mass auto-da-fé. Your imagined victory over the dark forces of the 'Jewish Satan' and his minions. Instead, Gable died scratching feebly for air and you, old patriarch, passed away in the ironic peace of your coma, your hand held by the wife who faithfully attended your days of dreams and nights of nightmares. How incongruous, to leave this world you so raved and ranted at in such a still propriety . . .

The coffin disappears towards the flames. The curtains pull shut. There is a sombre quiet in the chapel. There could have been no question, father, of mounting the grotesque display you had planned. In that, as in so much else, I have to disregard you. I fulfilled the central aim. I rode your plots to ascendancy. I am the President of the United States. But that is as far as it goes. I am no German exile yearning for a bloody revenge. No mad Klansman, dreaming of fires. I am an American, pledged to my country's prosperity. I will see things grow, over your scorched earth. And anyway, poor Adolf, there are no 'Party Youth' leaders left north of the Mason-Dixon Line. The old emblems and standards of the NSDAP stay under lock and key in your attic, to be disposed of, quietly burned, as soon as possible, in the municipal dump. Only I, our dearest Annchen, her two younger brothers, and my Federal bodyguards are in this chapel, with the stoic crematorium attendants. No one here, old warrior, to stand and salute under torches and recite page 195 para. 2 of Your Battle, *Deine Kampf*:

What we must fight for is to safeguard the existence of our

race and the purity of our blood, to restore the freedom and independence of our nation, so that our people may march forward to the fulfilment of the mission allotted them by the creator of the universe . . .

My mother stiffens under my arm as the sudden hum of the furnace receiving its offering reverberates through the room. Later we will collect the ashes. They will not be scattered by a U1 surveillance aircraft over the soil of Germany, but will lie in an urn in Annchen's bedroom, to be buried with her when her own time comes in a small prepared plot in the Chicago German Cemetery, beside the rest of his comrades. The inscription on the stone will then read:

ANNA STAHLHELM HITLER, 1903 –
ADOLF HITLER 1889–1970.
TOGETHER IN ETERNAL PEACE.

**Ernesto
Summer**

A parched land. A desert which will bear no fruit. The ground a
stony, harsh, white ochre colour. The sky a fierce blue about a
brutal sun. The plain stretches pitilessly towards the blue mirage
peaks shimmering at an unmeasurable distance ahead.

In the patchy shade of a lone zegda tree which has stubbornly
rooted itself in the barren soil, I share the noon ration of water
with the fifteen wiry black men, touching their lips in turn to the
tepid liquid in the group canteen. With any luck no plane will
pass to spot us before nightfall, when the long trek into those
blue peaks will resume. My lips are too chapped to raise a
smile. Two years ago it was the Italian planes we hid from.
Now it's the British Spitfire IIIs, scouting and bombing for their
local landlord, the Lion of Judah Haile Selassie. *Plus ça change.*
Only the passage of time, stretching my skin dry, hardening my
bones, though I was never a match for these tough tribesmen
in their *shammas*, for whom a five hundred kilometre walk is
a minor inconvenience. They tamed this land, long before the
delicate European came along to blast it into shape with dynamite,
railways and napalm. But in every generation, they have to reclaim
it again . . . till when? Maudlin meditations of an ageing soldier,
eroded somewhere within by a desire for peace, a murmuring
rebellion against the endless restlessness . . . Enough. The Poet
knew this strain:

> . . . In the untilled fields of the heart,
> the summer beckons to us
> with the lion's roar . . .

The hours go by. The sun begins its slow descent tow. ⁀ds the
rim of the mountains. Softly, like a low buzz rising from the
earth herself, the Ethiopians begin to hum, a slow, haunting
dirge, which seems to come from the pits of their stomachs, to
emerge out of the pores of their skin, their mouths unmoving,
their eyes fixed ahead with a quiet, wistful awareness. With

the hum they appeared to become one collective body, and a strange hallucination took hold of me, taking shape from their telepathic communion. A church, appearing to shimmer in the air, invisible but real, not a clutch of priests and swinging censers and the childish terror of damnation but one carved out of the unshaken solidarity of souls. They hummed, as the sun sank lower, touching the blue hills, rendering them red, then black. Beyond those shadows the base camp lies, the new army of General Gebre, successor to the dead Walda Sion. And perhaps Gebre too will grow old in the struggle, as the puppet emperor dies and another takes his place, backed by British, French, even North American guns. The battle outliving its protagonists. The humming men perhaps grasp this, with the knowledge rooted in this age old experience, fuelling their chant, a rhythm of timeless determination that we frenetic westerners will never understand. Modern man, whitey, technological man, even I, the stranger-brother from overseas, may well appear to them as merely a transient disaster. We, the Marxists, it occurs to me now, have shared with our Capitalist enemies the same view of these people as malleable figures, as clay for our impatient potteries. In the end, perhaps, the joke is on us all. But perhaps too, in our theories, our 'faith', we did perceive the truth which this ancient people confirms – the collective force endures, the individual, alone, is crushed. What fate then, for Ernesto 'Che' Guevara, the individualist *par excellence* who has embraced the collectivist creed? He has to merge with the mass and be one with them, for only together can men and women progress, the disinherited claim their inheritance . . .

Sometimes, Neruda wrote, it is not possible to win except by falling.

The chant grows, swirls, rises into the scarlet hues of dusk, the sun setting blood-red behind the black jagged mass of the Ethiopian Semien . . .

Epilogue
December 1990

Looking back on all this sound and fury twenty years ago, I find myself in two minds about the whole enterprise. What is the point now, after two decades of all these papers and cuttings growing yellow in my suitcase? Now that like an archaeologist I've retrieved the dry bones and found a way, for better or worse, to organise the fragments into some kind of coherent whole, and given the leakage by Daniel Ellsberg of the FIA's 'Auschwitz Papers', we have at last some chance of understanding the murky events of the Kennedy assassination. Is it all an academic exercise? Wiped clean by Frederick Hitler's two terms as a reforming President, the usual public gratitude in the return of the Republicans in 1980, with President Thurmond – what was this predilection for father-figures? So now we have Little Brother – Jack Kennedy. The Great White Hope. And look where it's led us . . .

I thought I'd try to make history live a little. To make a connection, a fictional junction, between public figures and ordinary people I knew. To try and get into the heads of my various characters, imagining the real, rather than realising the imaginary. To try and make some sense out of those traumatic moments in the Desert Inn in Las Vegas where we touched history briefly and were almost blown away by the blast . . .

Michael is still living in London. He tried to make independent documentary films for a while but gave up and began writing strange novels about the Middle East, the farcical-tragic events surrounding the proclamation of the State of Israel in 1973. The parasitical feuding between the two states, Arab and Jewish, that followed the British withdrawal. The People's Republic of Palestine and its austere founder-President, George Habash. The return of Begin and his ascension to power. The permanent state of almost-but-not-quite war. The balance of fear and suspicion. Each side has what it wanted but is never satisfied. So which will swallow the other? Those annual mock-polite meetings of Habash and Begin on the Jerusalem borderline, the Mamila Gate, the faint grins, limpid handshakes and verbal jockeying, one wonders how much longer before the expected explosion . . .

Still, at least they are (at the moment of writing), still at peace,

which is more than can be said for us . . . And at least Greece
is a democracy, so there's somewhere to run to. Christos and
Alex's advertising business in Athens. Times change, for some
people . . . I never thought I'd become an academic, lecturing
to wide-eyed (if I'm lucky) students; Brooklyn College, and the
temptations of tenure. European history in the thirties and forties,
usually considered a pretty lacklustre period. With a course on
the sixties for good measure . . . How to make a living from
your nostalgia. But it was a critical time, I think, when the great
empires began shaking and shivering, then, led by Italy, fell apart.
Maybe this attempt at a 'novel' rather than dry data can make
people look back at their roots. All the mistakes and blunders
that we came from. The ironies of fate, and what would have
happened if . . . etcetera. Who would have thought the Middle
East would be polarised between a Jewish state supported by
Communist Germany and an Arab state supported by the U.S.?
Jews of East and West divided in their loyalties, torn between
ideology and ethnic identity. Who would have thought the glacial
ghhoul Heydrich would give way to the reformist Helmut Schmidt?
The grey soldier rising from the ranks to bring Willy Brandt out
from the shadows (too late for poor Marcuse, dead in Spandau).
A decaying Soviet Russia feeding on old glories, shooting its
students down in the streets. The echoes of dead revolutions, the
hopes of Angola, Ethiopia . . . The bleached bones of Guevara,
ambushed in an unrecorded skirmish . . . Nothing remaining but
the icons . . .

And ourselves? God save America . . . As I sit rattling and
rolling in the Number 3 subway train on its epic journey to
Flatbush I see the headlines of the *Times* juddering at me in multiple screams: JAPANESE TIGHTEN GRIP ON MANILA.
MARCOS APPEALS FOR AID. PRESIDENT KENNEDY:
WE WILL PAY ANY PRICE. Indeed. The logical outcome of
the Pacific arms race: The Second Japanese–American War at
hand . . . What did we expect, with our endless sabre-rattling, our
grandiose speeches, our racial contempt? Fascism, that decayed
also-ran of Europe, found its seedbed in a vengeful Tokyo. Like
a plague dog circling the globe it took a bite out of us and moved
on. Now task forces rush towards the Philippines, Indonesia.
Australia calls for a nuclear 'umbrella'. At what stage would

'unconventional' warfare begin? And the ultimate irony – support for the United States by the ailing Premier Sakharov in Moscow . . . As a historian, I simply give up. Germany and Japan on one side, ourselves and the Russians on the other. The post-fascist states of Eastern Europe burying their heads in the sand. The British, French and Italians mumbling fearfully, caught between rival partners. Lord Benn condemns empires, East or West. There's nothing like a reformed bandit to lecture everyone else on morality. A long way from the Italian commune . . .

Real life so often confounds logic. Will we pull back from the brink of that Second World War prophesied so often since 1919, or should we all rush in, to save white Australia, menaced by the yellow peril? Not to speak of our East Indies investments. And which way will the Chinese dragon jump? All the old bogeys unpacked . . .

The lights are going out all over America, says William Safire in the *Times*. 'Our isolation and disinterest have made us turn our backs on natural allies, who are repaying us now by dragging their feet.' Colonial Europe has gone soft on imperialism. Frederick Hitler tried to sell a new economic partnership, but the Thurmondites wanted nothing but control. I suppose it was an argument over means, not ends, but we're all spiralling out of control now . . . The dream of 'peace'. Too much rhetoric, no proper attention to real needs. It's a topsy turvy world. Should we oppose war, or appease a Japan we helped to arm ourselves, to keep them off our backs? We are as usual our own worst enemies, conjuring real demons from our fears. Perhaps the League of Nations will succeed in bringing about a Japanese withdrawal, at this late hour, but there doesn't seem much hope.

Nevertheless . . . I'm sending this off to my agent. I asked her: Should I burn it all and have done with it? She said: Why did you keep the stuff all these years? I said, I wanted to show how fragile we all are, in history, blown this way and that in the wind. The only answer we have to all these storms and tumult is that we survive, somehow, with our critical faculties intact. I'm sorry if it's not an earthshaking conclusion.

Well, it's as good as any other, said my agent, I'll try to do what I can.

R.L.